Wanted: Wife for Hire

The Diamond Club Series

By Elizabeth Lennox

Prologue

If his life was so cold and desolate, why was steam rising from the asphalt? The summer thunder storm had passed. The intense passion gone. All that remained was the steam as the rain evaporated, slowly dissipating as the sun warmed the air, adding a sultry humidity to the misery. With the sun's reappearance, the world was a stifling, sticky mess.

And yet, he felt none of it. Instead of the intense heat or the residual passion from the storm, Sebastian felt only the tiresome, irritating cold.

Pulling his eyes away from the drifting steam, Sebastian Hughes stared at the architecturally impressive steel and glass building that housed his bank headquarters. It was a massive building, constructed to look strong and stable, representing everything that he'd achieved in his life.

Sebastian had set out to build the biggest, strongest bank in the world and he'd done it. Leaders of both major and minor countries around the world came to him to finance their programs. International corporate leaders relied upon his bank to finance their expansions. Hughes International had helped countries recover from maniacal despots, financed the building of bridges, towns, cities, and skyscrapers, as well as helping launch small businesses and tiny restaurants. Large and small, Hughes International did it all.

And it meant nothing. Just an obligation. He ruled the international business world and yet...it was simply...normal to him. No longer a challenge.

1

Perhaps that's why the woman in the polka dot rain boots caught his eye. She didn't seem cold. Nor did she seem to notice that the world had turned into a steamy, annoying mess.

She was dancing in the rain.

How ridiculous and unprofessional was that? The silly woman was dancing. In the rain.

Sebastian watched the woman twirling happily as she walked from the bus stop down at the corner of the city block. She was a beautiful woman with dark, mahogany hair, a creamy complexion, and a knock-out figure. Great legs. Lush, rounded hips. He couldn't see the color of her eyes from this distance, but he knew they'd be beautiful.

But it was the expression of complete joy on her lovely features caught and held his attention.

Sebastian knew that his driver didn't understand why he wasn't getting out of the vehicle. But he didn't give a damn. He wanted this moment, this vicarious pleasure of just watching a woman who loved life so much that she was lightly dancing, skipping, and half-twirling as she walked along the busy, still-damp sidewalk. Others were watching too and he wanted to order them away, command them to stop looking at the lovely woman so that he could selfishly absorb all of that lightness and happiness himself.

His eyes narrowed as he realized that the exquisite woman was walking into *his* building. His bank? She was a bank employee? Impossible! How had he missed someone that gorgeous?

Of course, whenever he walked into his building, or anywhere, he focused on work. Nothing else. Extraneous issues, such as a woman's beauty, weren't relevant in the workplace. Getting the job done was his only priority. Sebastian considered calling the head of his human resources department to discover the woman's name. But what the hell was he supposed to say? Get the name of the beautiful woman who liked to dance into work each morning?

He doubted that she danced into the office every morning though. Something exciting must have happened to her this morning. Most likely, she'd received good news that had put her into an excessively good mood.

Sebastian checked his watch. It was well after he'd normally reach his office. His days were so regimented that his assistant might call the police if he didn't get in soon. When he looked up again, the woman was nowhere to be seen. His lips pressed together as he remembered her cheery smile. A smile that...

A smile that nothing! He wasn't one to watch a woman dance. A woman who didn't have the sense to anticipate bad weather and bring an umbrella to work.

"Right," he muttered and opened the limousine door. With his usual purpose, he walked into the building.

Two days later, he stepped into the elevator earlier than normal. Yesterday, he'd timed his morning's arrival so that his driver had pulled up to the front of his building at exactly the same time as the day before, then berated himself all day. How absurd to plan one's day in anticipation of a brief glimpse of a woman?!

Unfortunately, the rest of that day, he'd been in a foul mood, pushing his executive team harder than normal, simply because he hadn't seen the woman again.

So today, he didn't risk a sighting, determined to focus only on work. He carried the responsibility for billions of dollars and hundreds of thousands of jobs on his shoulders. Sebastian didn't have time to think about a woman. Besides, his ex-wife had taught him a brutally painful lesson about the nature of women and now, his five year old daughter, Chloe, was suffering because of his error.

Chloe had been a beautiful, happy child that laughed, danced, and clapped with excitement at the smallest thing. Her exuberance had lightened his heart every time he saw her at the end of the day. His ex, Meredith, was one of the most beautiful woman he'd ever seen. She knew the art of makeup and used it to hide her imperfections and, with his money, she'd regularly gone on shopping sprees to drape her perfect figure in designer clothes.

Sebastian hadn't intended to marry the selfish, narcissistic actress. After only a few months of dating Meredith, Sebastian had grasped her true nature. Meredith Henning might be beautiful and an award-winning actress, but she was spiteful, mercenary, and vicious in her attacks after even the smallest slight. But right before he'd been about to break it off with her, she'd come to him with pretty tears in her eyes, telling him that she thought she was pregnant. Meredith had been so excited and asked him what he wanted to do.

At first, Sebastian hadn't believed that she was pregnant. He knew her well enough and she wasn't the type of woman who would willingly endure the hardship of a pregnancy. Nor did he believe she would ruin her figure. Meredith was obsessive about her weight and would literally starve herself if she gained even a single pound. But she provided proof, and even seemed excited about the prospect of motherhood.

So, he'd married her. That had been the worst mistake of his life!

And the best. The moment Chloe was born, Sebastian had fallen madly in love with his baby girl. She was the light of his life and he doted on her. And because of Chloe, Sebastian had given Meredith anything she asked. He was a wealthy man and didn't mind indulging the selfish woman.

Until he'd caught her having an affair.

Unfortunately, divorcing Meredith had proven more difficult than he'd thought. Even with evidence of her affair, the judge awarded custody of his precious daughter to Meredith, who used their daughter as a tool to get more and more money out of Sebastian. Even help from Oz Cole, who was ex-Delta Forces and a good friend who had some pretty amazing resource and capabilities, hadn't been able to smooth out the issue. Oz had unearthed the fact that Meredith had slept with the judge. When Sebastian tried to eliminate that judge from the decision making process, Meredith simply seduced the other judges.

In the end, even with his power and the influence of his friends, he'd still lost custody of his daughter to the scheming, selfish, obscenely vicious actress. The judge said that a single father wasn't a good influence for a child, which was absolutely ridiculous and an insult to men in general! Thankfully, Sebastian still had partial custody, so he got to see Chloe most weekends.

Unfortunately, it wasn't nearly enough. Besides missing her painfully, Chloe had changed. Living with Meredith had turned his vibrant, vivacious daughter into a quiet, withdrawn, pale version of her former exuberant self. She barely ate, was sick too often, and rarely spoke. She just...sat very still most of the time when she came for her weekends with him. It tore him up, seeing her so withdrawn and sickly, but Sebastian didn't know how to help her. Every visit, the smiles and exuberance that used to be part of Chloe's personality retreated further.

Sebastian hadn't seen Chloe smile since before the divorce. He had no idea what Meredith was doing to Chloe, but he knew that it wasn't good. He had to focus his energy on Chloe and not on a beautiful, mysterious woman who couldn't even walk into a building with decorum.

Stepping into the elevator, Sebastian reached out to press the button for the top floor, reminding himself that he didn't need distractions in his life right....

A flash of bright color appeared between the closing elevator doors. A hand slipped through the doors and they opened. Sebastian smothered an irritated expression, then stepped back to make room for the newcomer.

"Good morning!" the woman in question breathed with a bright smile of greeting as she rushed into the elevator. "Goodness, I love rainy days, don't you?" she asked, her green eyes surprisingly friendly.

Sebastian's eyes narrowed. It was her! The dancing woman! Damn, she was a beauty! Not as classically perfect as Meredith, but this woman had a freshness about her, a beauty that was different, but somehow more alluring. Even with her hair plastered against her head by the rain, the woman was...breathtaking!

The immediate and powerful tightening of his body caused by her cheerful smile irritated him. So instead of a perfunctory nod, his mood sharpened. "No," he snapped, even as his hands curled into fists. "They are wet," he told her, trying to remind himself that the woman was a distraction.

Her laughter sent a bolt of lust down his spine. He was shocked by the power of it, and the instant awareness of her scent. Her smile. The glorious light in those green eyes!

"Yes, they definitely are wet," she replied, then turned to face the doors, watching the numbers as the elevator rose.

Silence.

From his angle, he could see her exquisite profile and Sebastian noticed that the woman's lashes were ridiculously long. And she must have walked from the bus stop to the building again, because her skin was dewy with moisture. He wondered if she had an umbrella, then realized that her hair was wet. Obviously, she didn't have an umbrella. For some reason that bothered him.

He paid his employees extremely well! Why the hell hadn't she bought an umbrella? Twice in one week, this woman had arrived for work looking...wet.

The elevator pinged and the doors slid open.

"Well, have a nice day," the woman said with a sweet, bright smile. A slight, nervous wave and then she stepped off, heading for the finance department.

As the doors closed, Sebastian banished the woman from his mind, going through the issues he needed to deal with today. There were meetings throughout the day and he knew there was some sort of fundraiser tonight. He didn't give a damn about whatever the cause was, but he needed to speak with several people he knew would be there, so he'd go and make idle chit chat until he could finalize several lucrative deals for his bank. Then he'd head home just in time to talk with Chloe on the phone before she went to bed.

Thinking of those video conversations, he muttered another curse. They were getting shorter every day, his adorable daughter shrinking back into herself. A five year old should be silly and laughing, but

Chloe was becoming...still. Yes, that was what bothered him so much. She was still. It was as if she practiced not moving. What was that about? Why couldn't she wiggle and move while she talked to him?

The elevator opened up and he walked down the hallway. His assistant, Margaret, was already at her desk and stood up when he walked into the executive area.

"Good morning, Mr. Hughes," she greeted him efficiently. "I have..." and Margaret listed the first few items on his morning agenda, recited a list of the people who had called this morning, and noted who had requested time with him as Sebastian walked into his office.

When she was done, Margaret stood on the other side of his desk, pen poised over her notebook as she waited for instructions.

For a brief moment, Sebastian shifted the files on his desk, trying to get his thoughts into gear. He had questions from several heads of state, another request from an international corporate leader, and another from the Joint Chiefs of Staff. He had important work that needed his attention! Sebastian opened his mouth, ready to give Margaret instructions on how to shift his meetings today so that he could accommodate the newest inquiries. But instead, he heard himself say, "There's a woman down in the finance office. Dark brown hair and green eyes. Get her an umbrella."

Then he went on to other issues, the tension in his shoulders easing.

Chapter 1

"I'm not sure why you need this information," Ryker Thune said as he walked into Sebastian's home office. "But here you go." He tossed the file onto the center of the table. "Want to tell me more?" he asked, crossing his arms over his massive chest as he stared at his friend.

Sebastian didn't touch the file. "No." No explanation, just a slight shake of his head.

Ryker nodded. "Fine. But this woman you asked me to look into, she's a good person. She has no criminal history, not even a speeding ticket. I verified that because it seemed strange."

"I suspected as much," Sebastian replied, standing up to pour some scotch for Ryker, and handing it to him.

"So, if you didn't think the woman was sketchy, why did you need me to do such a deep background on her?"

"Because I am planning on..."

Before he could continue, someone else knocked on the door. "Are you ready to lose more money?" a big man with dark eyes and dark hair demanded as he entered. Sheik Jabril al Mustar, ruler of Piara didn't wait for Sebastian to pour him a glass of scotch but instead, took the crystal decanter from his friend's hand and poured it himself. "I am feeling lucky today."

Sebastian rolled his eyes, but he bent down to grab another bottle of the forty year old scotch, knowing that his poker buddies would drain the decanter quickly. "Last month, you drained over seven million from my personal account," he said to the powerful ruler. "I am *not* having a repeat."

Jabril grunted, but before he could speak, his brother in law stepped through the doorway. "You!" he growled, shooting a glare at Tarin. "You left my sister when she's six month's pregnant?" Jabril demanded.

7

Tarin bin Linar, Sheik of Catare and husband to Jabril's sister, Zuri al Mustar, shook his head. "My wife and your wife aren't waiting around to have their babies. My wife dragged your wife shopping again. Which is the only reason I'm here."

Sebastian laughed, his shoulders relaxing. "Paris?"

Tarin rolled his eyes. "Milan."

Jabril nodded approvingly. "Good. Ilara needs to get something for the reunification ball next month."

Tarin poured himself a glass of the expensive scotch, then sat down. "Zuri will make sure she gets something appropriate."

The four men chatted easily as they waited for the others to arrive for their monthly poker game. It had grown over the years, and no one ever knew for sure who would show up. But it was a friendship that had strengthened as they'd each dealt with their own crises.

Oz and Jayce, brothers and the other partner in The Solutions Group where Ryker worked, stepped into the room. The three former black ops specialists had started The Solutions Group several years ago. Now they were turning clients away because business was booming. Oz and Jayce both looked to Ryker, silently asking the same question. But Ryker shook his head, silently telling his friends that he hadn't gotten an answer about Sebastian's deep background investigation.

Sebastian noticed all of it, the silent communications, the easy cama- raderie, and took it all in. These were his friends. He should tell them what he was about to do. But they had all tried to help him in the past through legal means. It was time he took control of the situation with his ex-wife, although his next plan was a bit...extraordinary.

Chapter 2

"I need a wife."

Deni blinked at the terrifying man with the icy-cold demeanor sitting behind the massive desk, positive that she'd misheard. "I'm sorry?"

The scary man barely moved, his grey eyes didn't even blink. "I need a wife, Ms. Stenson."

Deni continued to stare, waiting for more information. But when it appeared that the man wasn't going to continue, she shifted in her seat slightly. This man...Sebastian Hughes...her employer, was actually an impressively handsome man. Sharp cheekbones, grey eyes, and dark hair. He was tall, with broad shoulders but beyond that, she had no idea what was underneath the dark, tailored suit and snowy-white shirt. He was one of the few men she knew who could knot a tie so precisely that the white of his dress shirt didn't show above the knot. And he was also the only man of her acquaintance that could look so stonily scary, and so...well, all together frightening! For a man who was so astoundingly handsome that he could trade in his abacus to model for a living, Sebastian Hughes was...terrifying!

Why was he telling her that he needed a wife? Surely, he didn't mean that he wanted to marry her! That was...Deni swallowed a giggle. No, laughing wouldn't be good.

Everything inside of her told her to tell the man to go to hell. Or maybe she should simply laugh at the outrageous comment, stand up and walk out. Everything about him, including this horribly uncomfortable office and the ridiculously tortuous leather chairs, screamed that the man was dangerous. She should get out of here while she still could.

But instead of walking back to her tiny cubicle, she looked at the man, suddenly seeing something besides the cold, icy mask. She saw...Deni might have called it nervousness. Or maybe a flash of vulnerability.

She wasn't sure, but that flash of...something...made her pause. So instead of telling him to go to hell or something equally career destroying, she tilted her head slightly, and then asked, "Why?"

The man barely moved. His eyes might have narrowed slightly, or that could have been her imagination, a ridiculous inclination to give this man some sort of human reaction. "I have my reasons. Suffice it to say, I need a wife, in name only, and you need about five hundred thousand dollars." He opened a file folder and looked down. "Or rather, your father does."

Deni reared back, horrified that he knew about her family's financial situation. "I know that..."

He waved her stammered explanation away. "I don't care why, Ms. Stenson," he snapped, his voice dripped with irritation as he leaned forward, looking down at the file and whatever embarrassing information it contained. "All I care about is that you help me. If you marry me, I'll help you."

Deni frowned at the man, thinking about the rumors she'd heard when she'd first started working here at Hughes International. Unfeeling. Bastard. Brilliant. Unshakable. Sebastian Hughes, owner and CEO of Hughes International, had the face of an angel, but was actually the devil. Because she worked in the finance department, too far below the radar for a man of Mr. Sebastian Hughes' notice, she hadn't concerned herself with the rumors.

Perhaps she should have paid more attention!

"Why me?"

He leaned back in his chair and steepled his fingers, those grey eyes seeming to turn to granite. "Your father approached a loan shark yesterday."

That was news, and not the good kind. Gripping the arms of the ugly leather chair, she wasn't aware of her back stiffening or her mouth falling open with horror. "Why in the world would he do that?!"

"Because he received a foreclosure notice yesterday."

Deni's hand lifted to her forehead. "A loan shark? A foreclosure?!" She shook her head, trying to understand. "This...this isn't like him! He's a responsible person! He's..."

The cold, horrible man shifted a paper on his desk slightly. "He lost his job six months ago. He hasn't been paying his monthly mortgage."

Deni's hand left her forehead, floating in the air beside her for a long moment as she slowly absorbed this latest blow. "He lost his job?" she whispered.

The beautiful bastard behind the desk tilted his head slightly. "Six months ago," he repeated.

This wasn't happening, she told herself. Looking down at the floor, she tried to make sense of it. Her father had been fine last week when she'd had dinner with him. There'd been no indication of problems, financial or otherwise. He'd even laughed, a sound she hadn't heard in such a long time.

The bastard glanced meaningfully at his watch. "Ms. Stenson, I have other meetings. I need an answer."

Deni held up a hand. "Okay, let me get this straight." She paused and took a deep breath. "My father is drowning in medical bills, apparently took out a loan..."

"A second and third mortgage," the devil supplied.

She paused as dread filled her heart, tightening the muscles of her stomach. "Right. A second and third mortgage." She shook her head slightly with that news. "He owes about five hundred thousand dollars. In desperation, he's seeking out a loan shark because your bank sent him a foreclosure notice." Her voice turned angry. "So, in addition to losing his wife of thirty years, he's about to lose his home." She glared at him across the polished expanse of the heavy steel and glass desk. Oddly, the thought occurred to her that the man and the desk had about the same level of compassion.

The man tilted his head to the right, then straightened again, and nodded. "I believe you have summarized the situation clearly."

Bastard! "And now, you're asking me to marry you. To be your wife and in return, you'll pay off my father's debts."

"Yes."

One word. No explanation, no comments, no compassion in those icy grey eyes.

"A wife."

"In name only."

Somehow, those last three words only made this whole situation more surreal. Shaking her head, she looked across the desk at the man, stunned by what he was asking of her. "This kind of thing only happens in movies."

"All evidence to the contrary," he returned.

Under other circumstances, his quick, pithy reply would have impressed Deni. But he was threatening her father, who had just buried his wife, Deni's mother. So no, it wasn't funny or pithy, just insulting.

She continued to glare at him. When he glanced at his watch again, she thought about throwing the ugly, steel paperweight at his head.

"I understand that you are impatient. But perhaps you should have scheduled a longer window for a meeting in which you tell me you are about to ruin my father's life."

11

"Don't be melodramatic, Ms. Stenson," he snapped and leaned forward, closing the file folder with an irritated snap. "I'm offering you a simple solution to the problem. Do we have a deal?"

She frowned. This man owned and ran one of the largest privately owned banks in the world. He had money and power, the likes of which she couldn't even fathom. So, why was he offering her such an absurd deal? Something didn't add up.

"Why?" she asked. The flicker in his eyes told her that she'd just gained a bit of power back. Feigning a relaxing pose, she leaned back in the horrible chair, cleared her features of emotion and stared into his cold, grey eyes.

"Why what?"

She didn't smile or frown, but mimicked his cold, still appearance. Two could play at this game, she thought. "Explain why you need a wife."

She watched as his lips compressed and felt an odd spark of triumph at the small sign of his anger. Deni had seen Sebastian Hughes in the hall-ways, obviously. Working in the accounting office of his bank, there was no way to avoid him.

The silly dreams she'd woven about the man that she'd conjured up over the past eighteen months seemed outrageous now, despite those vicious rumors that warned that the owner of Hughes International was heartless. She'd pictured him as a sweet, caring man who was just mis-understood. Sebastian Hughes was definitely misunderstood. Oh yes! People simply didn't fully grasp what an outright bastard he truly was.

The door to his office burst open and a gust of cloying perfume en-veloped Deni. Turning, she watched as a strikingly beautiful woman stalked into the office, pulling off long, leather gloves. Everything about her screamed money and power. Deni didn't know the exact price of the woman's gorgeous suit and matching silk blouse, but sus-pected it probably cost more than her monthly rent. Besides her outfit, the woman had ostentatious diamonds in her ears, around her neck, and sparkling on several fingers.

The woman looked vaguely familiar, but Deni couldn't place her im-mediately.

"Who are you?" the woman demanded, glaring at Deni. But before Deni could even draw breath to answer, the woman waved dismissively. "Never mind, I don't care." Turning her back on Deni, the offensive woman faced the man behind the desk.

"Your child support payment is late, Sebastian."

"Perhaps we should have this conversation in private, Meredith," he suggested with a tone that caused Deni to swallow nervously. The vicious woman was unaffected.

"I don't give a damn who hears that you're late. I want my money, Sebastian."

The man's eyes moved to Deni, then to Meredith. "The check isn't due until tomorrow."

"Yes, well, I need it now." Those leather gloves flipped through the air. She was very Golden Age Movie-Star-like, Deni thought.

"Why?"

"Because I have expenses."

"Expenses for Chloe?"

"Whatever." She turned on her four inch, spiked heel. "Just transfer the money into my account or you don't get Chloe this weekend."

A moment later, the door slammed shut, leaving only a stunned Deni, a seething Sebastian Hughes, and a cloud of perfume that made Deni want to gag.

There was a stunned, tense silence after the door slammed.

Deni wasn't nearly as terrified as she'd been before that interruption. She saw Sebastian's jaw clench and understood immediately. "You need a wife to go back to court and get your daughter out of the clutches of that mercenary bitch. You're willing to pay off my father's debts in order to buy a wife and I fit the bill."

From the fury in his eyes, Deni suspected that she'd hit the nail on the head.

Standing up, Deni stepped closer to the desk. "You have a deal," she extended her hand.

The man looked at Deni, then at her outstretched hand. "When?"

Deni looked down at her hand, not allowing him to ignore her like this. Start as one meant to go on, she told herself.

When he finally took her hand in his, the intense heat shocked Deni. He had a firm grip, strong fingers and, this close, those grey eyes seemed to simmer with silver fury.

"When?" he demanded. There was definitely emotion in his voice now. Furious, vengeful emotion.

Pulling her hand back, it took all of her self-discipline to stop herself from rubbing the skin on her hand. It felt singed right to the bone.

"Get me a contract and a check. Once my father's debts are paid off and his house secure, then we'll marry. And I will be at your disposal to help you gain custody of your daughter."

With that, she turned and walked out of the office, but with a bit more decorum and more manners than the last woman who had walked out.

Sebastian stared at the empty doorway, contemplating his morning.

13

This last meeting certainly hadn't gone the way he'd planned. Deni Stenson wasn't quite the tame, petite miss that he'd thought she was. Conversely, he hadn't thought she'd be that mercenary either.

She looked to be the perfect candidate for a wife. She was sweet and demure and wore well-tailored clothes. For a woman who was so concerned with her father's financial status, Deni Stenson seemed to spend a great deal of money on clothing.

Opening the file folder, he skimmed through the information. She made a good salary, but she'd drained her savings account last year, most likely to help her father pay off the medical bills from her mother's cancer.

Most people didn't believe he had a heart. That wasn't true. He did, but he'd learned the hard way to hide it. Meredith, his ex-wife, had taught that lesson to him repeatedly.

Speaking of mercenary women, he made several notes in the margins of the file, then dialed his lawyer's office.

"I need you to draw up a contract. Air-tight," he cautioned. "Deni Stenson will become my wife in three days' time. I want a prenuptial agreement with these terms." Twenty minutes later, Sebastian ended the call, satisfied that his lawyer would come up with an agreement that sufficed. Several more calls ensured that Deni's father wouldn't be evicted just yet, and he sent someone to ensure that the man didn't go to a loan shark either. What the man would do if Deni turned down his offer was anyone's business. But Sebastian didn't want any reason for the lovely, if prim and surprisingly assertive, Ms. Stenson to back out of their deal.

By five o'clock, he sent a message, commanding Ms. Stenson to appear in his office at five-thirty. He thought about adding "sharp" but refrained. He needed to know if the woman was prompt. She was pretty enough, he knew. And had a mouth-watering figure. But ignoring her physical assets would be a better option. He wasn't going to fall for the woman. His marriage to Meredith had taught him a valuable lesson. He wasn't going to step into marriage blind again. Never!

Chapter 3

Deni stood outside of the horrible man's office, trembling with trepidation. "Pull it together," she whispered. She'd barely gotten any work done today, her mind too focused on Sebastian Hughes' offer.

"He's ready for you now," the stern assistant informed Deni with a sharp nod.

Fabulous, she thought. She'd met her father during her lunch break and asked him about the debts. And then spent the rest of the hour trying to soothe her father who had broken down in tears as he explained everything.

A week ago, after having dinner with him on Sunday night, Deni had thought that her father had pulled himself back together. He'd been devastated when Deni's mother died from breast cancer. They both were. Deni's mother had fought long and hard, but the aggressive cancer had won in the end.

Now Deni understood that her father was barely hanging on. He had no job, no hobbies, he was about to lose his house to the bank, and he admitted that he'd been desperate enough to approach a loan shark about getting money to pay off his loans. "I just needed a bridge, Deni," he'd explained. "Something to hold off the bank until I could figure out what to do."

Deni had hugged her father tightly. "I'll take care of this, Dad."

A sniffle told Deni how humiliated her father was. "How?"

Pulling back, she looked her father in the eye. "I work for a bank. Not the same bank you got the other mortgages from, but I can work a deal with my employer and get this resolved." She'd pulled back and looked into his sad, defeated eyes. "Just don't do anything, okay?"

"Fine. But...don't..."

Taking his hands, she broached the subject that had been in the back of her mind for several months. She hadn't said anything, but it clearly had to be discussed. "Dad, you need to see a grief counselor as well. Will you do that for me?" She'd fought the tears, but they came anyway. Her father had been such a strong, vital man for her all these years. Unfortunately, the death of his wife had really knocked him down and he couldn't figure out how to get up.

"I will, but..."

"No buts, Dad," she whispered, leaning her head against his shoulder. "We just lost Mom. I don't know what I'd do if something happened to you as well."

His arms curled around her shoulders and they stayed like that for a long moment. Then she'd gone back to work, made some calls, and accepted what she needed to do.

Deni considered calling her friends. Carly Cole would know how to get her father out of this situation. Or Danielle, who was now married to a sheik of some powerful country. Deni could even sit down and talk with Charlotte, a psychologist, who could help her sort everything out. But Charlotte was married to Oz Cole. And that man was dangerous. Not in a figurative way, like Sebastian Hughes. Nope, Oz Cole was dangerous in a literal way. Oz, Jayce, and Ryker, owners of The Solutions Group, were ex-military. The elite kind that had skills that she couldn't even grasp. If she went to her friends, those friends would go to one of the guys. It was entirely possible that one of two things would happen – either Sebastian Hughes would simply disappear, never to be found or heard from again. Or her friends would loan her the money.

Deni couldn't allow either of those solutions to happen. No way! It was embarrassing enough that she and her father were in this kind of a situation. She couldn't further humiliate herself, or her friends, by taking their money. Besides, taking money from friends would completely alter the relationship. And her friendships with those ladies were too precious! Deni wouldn't do anything to jeopardize those friendships.

Nope, this was something she'd have to resolve herself.

Besides, this was for her father, she reminded herself, now standing in front of the doorway to the man's office. She'd get a lawyer to look over the contract, just to make sure this jerk didn't pull anything on her.

With another deep breath, she stepped into the office.

He was standing by the window, on a conference call but he waved her in and motioned for her to sit down in those horrible leather chairs.

Instead, Deni remained standing, her hands clasped in front of her while she listened to him discuss percentages and Libor rates, all things that she knew about from school but, as a lowly accountant, her world was different. She reviewed debits and credits while the financial people were more in tune with the cost of money and exchange rates. It was all very fascinating.

As he spoke, he handed her a sheaf of papers. Deni realized that it was a contract. How in the world had the man created a contract in only a few hours?! She skimmed through the pages, surprised by the terms.

In addition to paying off her father's debt, Sebastian Hughes would give her an allowance of forty thousand dollars a month. Forty thousand? Dollars?! For what? What in the world would she do with that kind of money?

The next clause almost caused her to laugh out loud. She couldn't have sexual relations with men outside of the marriage. Like she was going to have sexual relations with a man inside of the marriage? She glanced at Sebastian Hughes. The man was tall and handsome and, she suspected that there were some pretty nice muscles under that expensive suit. But sex? With him? How did one have sex with an iceberg?

Moving on, she noticed other clauses about presenting a united front to the judge. Gaining custody of Chloe Hughes. A full time nanny took care of Chloe, but Deni couldn't do anything that would cause Chloe to think that their marriage was anything other than a solid relationship. How was Deni supposed to convince a five year old that she was in love with the poor girl's father?

Another glance at the man and Deni was startled to realize that he had finished his call and was watching her. More specifically, he was admiring her legs. Uncrossing them, she stood up and cleared her throat. "I'll take this home and get my lawyer to review it. Give me a week and..."

"I don't have a week," he snapped. He lifted his phone and dialed another number. "Jason, I need you to look over a contract. I'm not the client, a Deni Stenson is. She'll be at your office in," he checked his watch. "Twenty minutes."

And he hung up. Had the other lawyer agreed to the meeting?

"Here's your lawyer's address." He wrote something down, then handed her the slip of paper. "He's expecting you."

She took the paper, frowning down at the address. "This is *your* lawyer."

"No. My lawyer is different. I'll pay this man's fees, but I need this deal finalized tonight. I have Judge Miller prepared to perform the ceremony in a couple of days."

Deni struggled to keep up. It was all happening so fast. "This weekend?"

"Yes. As you read through the contract, you'll notice that I have a court date next week and that you may not discuss this with anyone. My ex-wife doesn't know about our agreement yet, but I'm petitioning the courts for full custody of my child."

"But...why so fast?" Deni asked, trying to choke down her sudden panic.

"Because my daughter is in pain!" he snapped harshly.

Deni had been looking at the paper again, but at the normally staid, controlled man's outburst, she looked at him. In that instant, she saw the flash of pain, the look of panic in his eyes. He quickly controlled it, hiding it away. But that one moment, that small window of emotion, hit her like a ton of bricks.

Too often, her friends had told her that she was too soft. Too emotional. But Deni knew that emotions weren't a bad thing. In this case, they might be, but she couldn't turn her back on anyone in pain. And this man might be playing her, but that pain had been real.

"I'll call you tonight after meeting with my lawyer," she agreed softly and turned around, walking out of his office.

Nineteen minutes later, she sat down in the office of an older but handsome lawyer whose sharp, dark eyes skimmed through the contract.

Every few moments, he'd look up.

"You know that you can't have sex with anyone for the next year, right?"

Deni shifted uncomfortably. "Um...that's not an issue."

"A *year*," he emphasized.

The horror in the man's eyes caused a bubble of laughter to burst from her. "I don't think there's a single recorded instance of a human being dying from sexual frustration," she pointed out.

He mumbled something along the lines of, "They wouldn't record it like that," but went back to the papers. "The allowance is generous. But I can get you more if..."

"I don't need an allowance," she stated firmly. "That clause needs to come out."

The man, Jason something or other, shook his head. "No," he retorted and kept on reading.

"Seriously, I don't..."

Without looking up, he said, "Ms. Stenson, you're about to marry one of the wealthiest men in the country, possibly the world. He can afford forty thousand dollars each month. Take the money and enjoy it." And he kept on reading.

A moment later, he tapped his pen against the document. "There's a morals and indecency clause. If you do anything that Sebastian thinks is indecent or immoral, you will owe him the full five hundred thousand dollars, every monthly allowance he paid you, plus interest and fines, to be determined by the courts." He pulled his glasses off and stared at Deni. "That's a huge amount of money. I think it should be deleted, but I doubt that I can do it. I'm a damn good lawyer, but this entire contract is set up to ensure that Sebastian gets custody of his daughter. I doubt I could get it taken out."

Deni had no idea. "What would constitute a violation of that clause?"

He shrugged. "Having sex with another man. Or woman."

Deni laughed, she couldn't help it. "Um...that's not going to be a problem."

The lawyer sighed, and slipped his glasses back on. "Everything else in this contract is set to benefit you. The only issue is that morals and indecency clause." He turned and tossed the contract onto his desk. "And you'd have to be married to the man for a full twelve month time period after he gains custody of his child. There's also gag language."

"What's that?"

"If you discuss the terms of this contract with anyone besides myself or Sebastian, then you owe all the money back."

"Plus interest."

"Exactly," the lawyer confirmed.

She waved her hand dismissively. "Trust me, I don't want anyone else to know about this contract. I won't be revealing anything to anyone."

He tilted his head. "You must really need the money," he commented.

Deni squirmed. "Yes, well..." What could she say? "Is there anything in that contract, other than the morals and decency clause, that I should object to?"

"Nope. It's shockingly fair. I've always thought of Sebastian as a real bastard, tougher than the toughest negotiator. But this contract gives you a lot and all he gets in return is your fidelity."

"Then I should sign it?"

"Depends."

"On?" she prompted.

He sighed, rubbing the bridge of her nose. "On whether you're willing to marry a man for money."

She thought about it for a long moment. Then the image of her father, beaten down and ashamed, came back to her. "Yes. Yes, I am," she decided and took the contract. "Thank you very much for your time and expertise," she said, extending her hand.

He shook it and, it occurred to her in that moment that this was a scary man. But for some reason, he didn't intimidate her. Also, she didn't feel that same, scary heat when he enveloped her hand in his bigger one. Odd, she thought.

"Good luck, Deni," Jason said as he shook her hand. "If there's any-thing more I can do for you, don't hesitate to call me."

She nodded and smiled. "Thank you."

Looking around on her way out, she noticed that the area was still bustling with people. It was seven o'clock at night and the employees all looked to be ready for another shift.

She tucked the contract into the file folder and then into her purse, thinking that this was a strange world.

Chapter 4

Deni stood in the beautiful white suit, her hand warm and secure in Sebastian Hughes' as the judge asked if she vowed to honor and obey. There was no mention of love, she realized. And obey? Deni had thought that the word had been banished from wedding ceremonies. Apparently not.

"I do," she replied, cringing because she had no plans to obey the man if he told her to do something unethical. She just had to trust that he wouldn't. A scary thought, but she pushed it out of her mind. No way was she doing anything unethical for this man...other than marrying him for his money. But...was that different? Did she have grounds to be righteous?

Not really, she thought, shifting in her kitten heels slightly. She hadn't intended to dress for the wedding. But the beautiful suit had appeared by messenger that morning and...well, if he wanted her to wear a white suit, Deni wasn't going to argue. At least it wasn't a full, huge white gown with tons of tulle. That was her dream wedding dress. And since this wasn't her dream wedding, and Sebastian Hughes was as far from being her dream husband as one could possibly get, she wore the stupid suit.

"And do you, Sebastian Avery Hughes, promise to honor and obey Deni?"

Those grey eyes locked onto hers. Was that a moment of amusement glowing in his eyes? Deni thought she was seeing things. But then she felt his fingers squeeze hers slightly. "I do," he replied in a firm voice.

There were some other comments, but Deni didn't hear them. She was too busy staring up at the man about to become her husband. Why was she here? And why in the world had she dressed in this suit? It was beautiful, more sophisticated than anything she owned, but it was white. This wasn't a real marriage. Why the sham?

Then she remembered the clause that stated no one was to know about the terms of the contract. Apparently, they needed to pretend that this was real in all ways. Very odd, she thought, not for the first time. That seemed to be a recurring theme over the past two days and she suspected that it was only going to get worse.

A cold metal band slipped onto her finger. Looking down, she gasped quietly at the shockingly beautiful diamond band that he'd slid into place. Immediately, Deni wanted to pull it off, nervous about having such expensive jewelry on her finger. He must have understood her reaction, because his hand tightened on hers, silently telling her to hold off on commenting.

The attendant handed her another ring and she looked at it, almost laughing when she saw the simple platinum band. But she dutifully slid the sedate ring onto his finger, then looked up into his eyes once more. She was laughing, but doubted he understood why she was amused.

Regardless of the disparity in their wedding bands, she took a deep breath and turned to face the judge.

"I now pronounce you husband and wife." He beamed as if he'd just accomplished a miracle. Opening his arms wide, he continued, "You may now kiss the bride."

Kiss? Deni turned, panic in her eyes. No kissing, she thought. The contract hadn't stated anything about kissing. Only...

And then he kissed her. Just a soft brush of his lips against hers. But... wow! The tingling that the gentle brush left behind was...disconcerting.

It was all over moments later. She forced her lips into a smile when the judge congratulated her. She smiled when the other attendants, all employees of the court, congratulated her. Deni even smiled as she signed the marriage license.

But the whole time, she was quaking inside. Quaking in reaction to that kiss. It had been so startling. So disconcerting. So...strange!

With the formalities over, Sebastian turned and took her hand. "We have plans," he murmured and tucked her arm onto his elbow.

She let him lead her out of the courthouse and into a waiting limousine. There was a bottle of chilled champagne and Deni thought that it was a sweet gesture, although completely unnecessary.

"My chauffer seems to have a bit of a romantic side to him," Sebastian commented, dismissing the champagne as Deni tried to hide her disappointment. So much for the sweet gesture, she thought in resignation.

A moment later, he made a phone call. "Yes, deposit the money and send her confirmation when it is done."

A moment later, there was an awkward silence as the driver pulled away from the curb and Deni felt...cheap. The transfer was the money to pay off her father's mortgage. She'd just sold herself to a man to help her father from going to a loan shark. Lovely. Her life had just been reduced to a business transaction.

"No reason for regrets already," Sebastian said sharply. "You went into this agreement with your eyes wide open."

Deni knew he was right, but she hadn't realized she'd feel like this. Cheap. Trashy.

"We're dining at my house tonight. With Chloe."

The reminder of the child sparked something deep inside of her. It soothed her. Reminded her that she'd done this for good reasons. Turning her head, she looked at the man. "Can you tell me about her?"

Sebastian couldn't hide the surprise when he looked over at his 'wife'. She wanted to know about Chloe? The idea seemed preposterous, but those green eyes of hers appeared sincere.

Unfortunately, after Meredith's unpleasant tutelage, he'd learned not to trust women. They were vicious, cruel, and heartless. Meredith had dumped Chloe off this morning, saying that she was on her way to Paris. How his ex-wife was going to get to Paris and back by their Tuesday court appearance, he wasn't sure. He'd been to Paris with the woman. Sebastian knew that Meredith lost herself in her shopping sprees. The woman could shop more than anyone else he knew.

Besides, she had a fresh stash of money in the form of Chloe's child support payment, which had been deposited right on time, as usual.

"She's five years old, correct?"

Sebastian nodded. "Yes. She's five and very impressionable. We have a court appearance on Tuesday morning at nine o'clock." His eyes skimmed over the white suit, trying to hide the expression of disapproval. Deni looked exceptionally good in white. Almost innocent, he thought. If he hadn't just deposited half a million dollars into her account for her fifteen minute performance at the courthouse, he might even think that the woman looked beautiful. The terms enticing and alluring popped into his mind, but he quickly dismissed them.

Focusing on his daughter's plight and the court issues, he stared straight ahead. "Chloe has been through hell while living with her mother. The court appearance is to petition for full custody. But my ex-wife loves the child support payments as well as the court ordered requirement that I maintain her household and the staff. So, she'll fight tooth and nail to keep Chloe."

"Does Chloe look more like you or your wife?" Deni asked.

He gritted his teeth against wanting to believe that she genuinely cared. Deni Stenson didn't care. This was all just more of a performance and Sebastian had endured enough performances from his ex-wife.

Even so, Sebastian thought that it might be a good idea to answer a few of Deni's less prying questions. "She looks like me." In fact, he'd had a DNA test done, just to confirm that Chloe was his child. He'd suspected Meredith had been cheating on him long before he'd had actual evidence of her perfidy. He had pictures, but hadn't used them. Not until Chloe was safely in his house.

"She has my eyes and Meredith's hair color." He looked out the window, thinking about his little girl. She was so precious and so scared. "She's...She's been through enough. You will *not* manipulate her affections to get more money from me. Is that understood?"

He watched as the woman shrank back into the leather seat. Good, he thought. He wanted control in this relationship. Meredith had done enough harm to Chloe. He had to get his daughter back, to help her recover. And he had to protect Chloe from anyone else who might harm her. Once he had her safely back in his house, he'd help her grow into a strong, confident child again. But until then, he had to tread lightly.

Chapter 5

Sebastian's house was monstrously huge and located in the center of the city. Three stories of elaborate, intimidating magnificence. Each room had been decorated with elegance in mind, forgoing comfort in many cases.

He'd left her in the foyer with a cryptic, "Have a look around and choose a bedroom. You can have any bedroom to the left of the staircase." And then he was gone.

The housekeeper, a friendly woman by the name of Debbie, showed her around. "Mr. Hughes is probably with his daughter now," she said as they made their way up the grand staircase. "He dotes on that child!" she continued. "Goodness, I've never seen a man more gentle with his daughter than that man," she laughed.

Deni chose one of the smaller rooms towards the end of the hallway. The room obviously hadn't been used in years. The furniture was still covered with the huge, white sheets that kept the dust off. After Debbie had left her, telling Deni that her luggage would be brought to her room, Deni had explored the house. There were twenty bedrooms in the house. Twenty! Most of them were still covered with the dust-sheets. What did the man do with twenty bedrooms?

In addition, there were four formal living rooms, a massive kitchen that seemed bigger than a restaurant could need, a dining room with a table large enough to seat thirty people, a music room, a conservatory filled with so many plants she couldn't even name half of them, a ballroom...literally, a room with a wood parquet floor that looked like an old-fashioned ballroom with no other furniture in it other than the massive fireplace flanked by double, glass doors and chandeliers that would have done Versailles proud. On the lower floors, there was a gym with every conceivable piece of exercise equipment, a sauna, hot tub and, when she turned the corner, she found an indoor pool. A HUGE indoor pool!

When Desi stepped outside, she discovered an elaborate maze made out of boxwood hedges, a formal garden, an outside pool, and a stone patio that ran the length of the house. Everything was on a massive, formal scale and Deni was more intimidated now than when she'd sat in his office.

The house was a veritable palace! Who would have known that such an elaborate residence was hiding behind the trees?

Yet, for all of its pristine elegance, Deni absolutely hated the house. It was cold and impersonal, making her feel like she was in a museum. The grand staircase had a beautiful curved wooden bannister, but the thought of sliding down that staircase was...well, one just wouldn't do something so outrageous. Especially because there was a massive round table at the bottom with a huge bouquet of fresh flowers in the center. Sliding down the bannister might result in crashing into that table. And the crystal vase those flowers were in probably cost more than her annual salary!

So, here she stood in the courtroom, standing next to a man she hadn't seen since he'd left her in that too-formal foyer. (So much for having dinner with Chloe!) She knew that he'd been in the house...some-where...all weekend long. But she hadn't seen him or the mysterious Chloe.

Even now, she wondered if this was all an elaborate joke. There was no Chloe. Meredith was real, but...was Deni somehow trapped in one of those elaborate games the uber-wealthy people of the world created when they were bored with their lives?

Was someone going to jump out from behind the judge's stand and announce, "Just kidding! Get back to work."

"Don't cringe like you've just been beaten," Sebastian hissed at her as another man joined them at the table. "Smile and look like you love me."

The other man, Sebastian's lawyer she presumed, leaned over. "You need to sit behind the bar until the judge asks for you," he directed, pointing to the seats behind the wooden barrier.

"Of course," Deni quickly moved to sit on one of the benches. She didn't want to sit at the table anyway.

As soon as she sat down, the judge in billowing black robes stepped into the courtroom. "All rise!" someone called out and Deni automatically stood up.

The judge sat down and peered over the top of his glasses at the occupants of the courtroom. "Where is Meredith Hughes?" he demanded, looking at the courtroom.

The man sitting at the other table stood up, buttoning his coat. "Ms. Hughes has been detained, Your Honor. She tried to get back in time for the court appearance, but wasn't able to catch a flight."

"A flight from where?" the judge asked, obviously bored from the explanation already as he shifted papers around on his desk.

The other lawyer hesitated, looking uncomfortable. "Paris, Your Honor. She wanted to introduce Chloe to the French culture."

The judge looked up from his papers and frowned at the other man. It didn't take a genius to see that the judge wasn't happy. "I thought that I ordered the child to be kept in the country. Neither parent was allowed to take the child outside of the United States."

The man opposite Sebastian stammered slightly. "Your Honor, Ms. Hughes went by herself, wanting to bring some of the culture back to her daughter, since she couldn't take her with her."

Not a good answer, Deni thought. The judge sighed, shaking his head as he shuffled some papers around on his desk. "So Ms. Hughes isn't here?"

"No, Your Honor."

The judge leaned back in his big, leather chair. "I have a petition for full custody from the father," he said, lifting one of the papers up as he read it. "Are there any objections from the mother?"

"Yes, Your Honor," the other man began. "The mother..."

"The mother isn't here to object," the judge snapped.

The lawyer puffed up importantly. "Yes, but I'm here representing her interests."

The judge looked down his nose at the attorney. "From what I've heard from these affidavits," he said and looked at several papers, "the mother is rarely home with the child. There's a nanny for three different, eight-hour shifts. When I granted custody of the child to the mother, I was informed that Ms. Hughes wanted to be a stay at home mother for her child."

Deni glanced over at Sebastian, startled by that news. Other than his fingers curling into fists, there was no outward reaction to the news that his daughter was being raised by strangers.

Deni hadn't even met the child, but her heart melted for the poor thing. Deni had memories of going fishing with her father, trying to bait a hook with a worm but, when she'd screamed in horror for the poor worm, her dad had used on a piece of bread instead. They hadn't caught anything that day, but had laughed and told each other jokes. She remembered coming home from those trips to find her mother pulling warm cookies out of the oven, her arms already open for a hug while her father unloaded the camping and fishing gear, storing it away in the garage. Deni and her mother had spent the next half hour talking about their day, eating warm cookies, and hiding them from her father because he was a "cookie monster" her mother declared. He always found the cookies though. And Deni's mother would simply smile and shake her head as he scarfed down three of them, then moved over to grab Deni's mother, kissing her neck until she squealed with laughter.

Deni banished the memories, focusing back on the present and the irritated judge. "So the mother has abandoned her daughter to go on a shopping spree in Paris *again*," the judge surmised.

"Your honor," the other lawyer began but the judge lifted a quelling hand.

"Don't bother with your smarmy explanations, Mr. Thomas. Your client isn't here to defend herself and these reports indicate that she spends more time in night clubs than she does with her daughter. In fact," he skimmed down the reports. "It looks like Ms. Hughes doesn't spend *any* time with her daughter." He took off his glasses, staring at the mother's lawyer, waiting for an explanation.

"Your Honor," Sebastian's lawyer stood up, buttoning his jacket just as the other lawyer had done several moments ago. Why do men do that, Deni wondered? "Mr. Hughes has just remarried and is petitioning the courts for full custody of the daughter."

The judge nodded as the lawyer continued. "The reports in front of you from the social worker indicate that the father has been an integral part of the child's time when he is with her. He's also been present for the child's school events, and there are multiple affidavits that indicate that he has a good rapport with the child."

The judge looked down his nose at the lawyer. "And the new wife has indicated a willingness to be a positive influence for Chloe?" Deni shrank back when the judge's gaze locked onto her. "Ms. Hughes," the judge called out.

Deni stood up, fighting back the fear and the desperate sense that she was doing something wrong, since she'd never even met the child. "Yes, Your Honor?" she answered, trying to pretend as if she weren't trembling in her shoes.

"This report says that you married Mr. Hughes on Saturday. Is that correct?"

She breathed a sigh of relief. "Yes, Your Honor," she answered honestly.

"And you're not going to fly off to Paris to," he tilted his head slightly, "bring back French culture?"

Deni laughed. "No, Your Honor. I have no plans to go to Paris, although I'm sure it is a lovely city."

"What do you do for a living?" he asked.

"I'm an accountant."

"And how did you meet Mr. Hughes?"

Deni wasn't sure where this line of questioning was going, but she could honestly answer the questions. "I saw Mr. Hughes almost every day as he walked into the office."

"And what was your impression of him?"

She looked over at Sebastian, a man she suspected cared very deeply for his child. A moment later, she focused all of her attention on the judge, blocking out the smug lawyers and other people in the courtroom. "My initial impression of the man was that he was incredibly handsome." She glanced at the man in question. "The other ladies in the office also looked, but they were wrong."

"Why is that?" he asked.

Deni hadn't looked away from him. "The other employees in the office fantasized that Mr. Hughes was a cold, diabolical playboy, one who had a different woman in his bed every night."

"Is that the case?"

She pulled her eyes away from Sebastian's surprised gaze. "No, Your Honor. As far as I can tell from the gossip around the office, he hasn't approached any woman who works in his building for anything other than business purposes."

"Is that how he approached you?"

Deni smiled, still feeling as if she were on safe ground. "Absolutely, Your Honor. Every conversation we had in the office was absolute business."

"So, your initial impression of him hasn't changed?"

She took a deep breath and slowly let it out. "Your Honor, my initial impression of Sebastian Hughes has changed many times in the short time I've known him," she pulled her eyes away, glancing briefly at Sebastian again. "I thought he was a bastard of the first order. I thought he was cold and heartless." She looked over at him and saw the telltale traces of amusement. "I thought he was the devil, the face of an angel but pure evil inside."

Everyone in the courtroom laughed with her description. "And now?" the judge prompted.

She pulled her eyes away once again and looked directly at the judge. "Now...I'm still not certain that he isn't the devil, but yes, my opinion of him as an unfeeling bastard has changed. Dramatically. He adores his daughter, Your Honor. He loves her more than life. He would do anything for her." She looked over at him. "Literally, anything to protect his daughter."

There was a long silence as electricity shot between herself and Sebastian. She didn't know if he was feeling it as well, but there was something there, at least on her part. She might not like the man, but she respected him. He was a strong businessman who kept hundreds of thousands of people employed in secure positions, and he loved his daughter. If the silly, school-girl fantasies that she'd thought up as she watched the man walk into the office each day were obliterated, that was fine. Every daughter needed a good father. That was enough.

"The petition for full custody of Chloe Hughes to Mr. Sebastian Hughes is granted," the judge announced, as he pounded his gavel. "Ms. Hughes..." the judge looked right at Deni with a smile, "The former, Ms. Hughes, is hereby ordered to give over custody of the child, Chloe Hughes. Mr. Sebastian Hughes is released from his obligation for child support and Ms. Meredith Hughes is hereby ordered to give up residency at the home that was granted to her for child residency."

A moment later, the judge stood up and left the room, ignoring the calls from the other lawyer who apparently vehemently objected to the judge's decision.

Deni watched, shocked at the sudden reversal. She'd expected the judge to order house monitoring by a third party. Or a social worker's visit to determine the appropriateness of each residence or how each parent interacted with the child. For the judge to simply order that Sebastian now had full custody seemed...arbitrary.

But Deni didn't have time to wonder about it. As soon as the judge disappeared, Sebastian was in front of her and he'd pulled her into his arms and kissed her. It wasn't a gentle brush of his lips, like he'd done for their wedding ceremony. This was a full out, open mouthed, tongue tasting, hands exploring, arms lifting kind of kiss that left her head spinning with the power behind it.

When he lifted his mouth and lowered her back down to the ground, she couldn't catch her breath. It was too much and...not enough. Her fingers rested on his shoulders and she knew that she should pull back, but she couldn't move.

"Thank you," he whispered, leaning his forehead against hers. "Thank you! And Chloe thanks you too!"

"Umm...you're welcome?" she breathed, shivering as he laughed softly, the sound vibrating through her body.

His hands were still holding her hips and she wasn't sure what to do. After Saturday and the cold, almost angry attitude he'd had, this was unexpected.

His lawyer put a hand on Sebastian's shoulder. "I'm going to get a copy of the court order. You should be able to pick Chloe up this afternoon."

The other lawyer stepped in, glaring at Deni. "This isn't over, Hughes," he snapped. And then he was gone, but paused just long enough to give her a glare that promised retribution.

"Ignore him," Sebastian said. He squeezed her gently, then stepped away. "I'm going to go get Chloe. Thank you again for what you said. It worked."

Deni watched as he hurried out of the courtroom, stunned and not sure what was going on. But she was glad that the little girl was away from that horrible woman that had stalked into Sebastian's office last week. The bigger question was if Sebastian was worse than the mother.

Chapter 6

The noise woke her up out of a deep sleep. Deni wasn't sure what it was, but the retching sound made her throat tighten convulsively.

Pushing the covers off, she slipped the robe over her shoulders. She'd been living in this mausoleum for the past two weeks and had hated every moment of it. But she'd agreed to remain married to Sebastian for twelve months. She still went to work every day, none of her friends or co-workers realizing that Deni was now married to their ultimate boss. He wasn't saying anything to anyone and Deni kept silent as well. And since she enjoyed her job, appreciated the mental challenges it presented, she arrived at her desk on time every morning. Then again, what else was she supposed to do?

She also visited her father. He'd agreed to see a grief counselor and was looking better. Deni hadn't realized how tired he'd been looking. He'd been exhausted for so long, neither of them had recognized the symptoms.

"I'm good, honey," he'd told her last week. "Sad, but getting better."

She felt better knowing that he was safe and she bought him groceries each week. On Sunday afternoons, they cooked meals together, laughing and talking, just being together as they worked to package the meals into freezable plastic containers so he only had to re-heat the meal. Deni felt guilty for not realizing how depressed he'd become. But thankfully, things were working out.

Thanks to Sebastian, she thought.

She hadn't seen much of him over the past two weeks, but she often thought back to that kiss in the courtroom, wondering what had happened. Such a fluke. But...she'd like to experience that again.

Out of the question though. Right now, it was more imperative that she discover what was causing that horrible retching sound.

Walking down the hallway, she found the source.

The nanny, Jenny, was bent over the toilet in the bathroom across the hall from Deni's room. "Jenny? What's wrong?" she asked. The woman worked from seven o'clock in the morning and brought Chloe to school, then met her after school and stayed with her until Sebastian came home from work in the evenings.

"Don't come close," Jenny gasped and bent back over the toilet as another wave of nausea hit her. "Sick."

"You poor thing!" Deni gasped and wet a washcloth, handing it to Jenny. "What happened?"

"Seafood last night. Went on a date."

"With the new guy? Where?"

"That sushi place over by the bank. Not good!"

"Have you been like this all night?"

She started to shake her head, but froze as the movement caused another round of vomiting. "Just this morning. Felt bad all night."

Deni felt horrible for the nanny that had also become her friend. "Honey, who should I call?"

Jenny rested her forehead in her hand, breathing slowly and deeply. "Mr. Hughes. I've got to get someone to take care of Chloe today."

"Don't worry about Chloe. I'll take care of her."

"It's Sunday. You have your thing with your dad today. Mr. Hughes has meetings this afternoon, but will be back later. He was going to take her..."

"Chloe can come with me."

That was all it took to get Jenny to relax. "Thank you," she sighed, then turned back to the toilet for another round. "But you have to go now! I don't want Mr. Hughes to know that I was sick because of bad fish!"

"I'm not leaving you like this," Deni assured her. "Here," she said, handing the nanny the washcloth. "What was the name of the restaurant?"

For the next half hour, she and Jenny talked until Jenny felt well enough to get back into bed. Deni turned off the lights in the nanny's room, pulling the thick, ornate curtains closed so the morning light didn't seep in. Jenny needed sleep, time for her stomach to heal and recover.

When Jenny was finally asleep, Deni returned to her room, showered and pulled on a pair of jeans and a tee shirt. It was going to be another warm day today, but because of the formality of the house, she didn't feel comfortable wearing shorts. So, I finally get to meet Chloe, she thought, pulling her hair into a ponytail.

Chapter 7

A couple of hours later, Deni sensed the other presence before she saw anyone. She wasn't sure what it was, but a change in the air indicated another human being was present. But when she looked around, Deni couldn't find anyone. Sipping her coffee, she watched carefully, suspecting....

Bingo! There she was.

"Are you Chloe?" she asked of the bush on the side of the stone patio.

The bush wiggled.

"I'm Deni," she said.

The bush wiggled again and, a moment later, a pretty, blond girl with bows in her hair peered nervously through the leaves. "Are you my stepmother?" she whispered, then glanced behind her warily.

Deni stared at the girl for a moment. Stepmother? "Yes, I suppose I am your stepmother."

"Are you mean?" the girl whispered tremulously, her big, grey eyes taking it all in.

Deni considered the question. "I don't know. I suppose I can be mean when I'm hurt or upset about something."

The girl contemplated that response for a moment. Then she looked at Deni curiously. "Are you hurt or upset now?"

Deni laughed. "Not even a little."

The girl stepped around the bush, standing on the stone patio fidgeting with her pretty, pink dress. "I'm Chloe."

"I suspected as much. I'm Deni. Would you like to have breakfast with me?"

Chloe thought about it for a moment, eyeing the empty chair at the table carefully. "Don't you want private time?"

Deni suspected that's what Meredith said to the child. Probably too

34

often. "No. I think I've had a bit too much private time this weekend. I'd love some company." She pushed the bowl of strawberries closer. "Would you like some strawberries?"

The girl eyed the berries with obvious yearning. "I'm not allowed to eat strawberries," she whispered, but there was longing in her voice. "I might get juice on my dress."

Deni looked at the girl's pretty dress, twisting her mouth slightly as if she were trying to figure something out. "Well, I suppose that is a possibility." She picked up one of the berries and bit into it. "But these berries are so good, they might be worth it."

The girl watched in fascination, stepping closer. She really was a beautiful child, if a bit too clean. Children should be exploring and having fun, running around, jumping and getting dirty. At least, that's what Deni had done as a child.

"Why don't you use this napkin to cover your pretty dress while you eat some strawberries?" Deni suggested. "They are very good for you. And your cook has discovered a way to find only the sweet strawberries. I've been eating them with my coffee all morning and I haven't had a sour one yet."

Chloe stepped closer, obviously eager to try the "dangerous" fruit. "But if I get some on my dress..."

Deni smiled gently. "If you get some on your dress, then I will help you change into something else so that no one will know. Would that be okay?"

Obviously, Chloe thought it was a wonderful plan and she stepped closer, carefully sliding onto the chair next to Deni. The girl took one of the napkins, draping it over her chest, just to be extra careful. As soon as the child bit into the ripe berry, her eyes widened in shock.

"It's good, isn't it?" Deni offered.

"Yes." She popped the rest into her mouth, chewing carefully.

"Would you like another?" Deni asked, pushing the bowl of strawberries closer.

"Where's Jenny?" Chloe asked, her eyes darting to the bowl of strawberries, then back to Deni.

"Jenny got really sick last night."

The five year old girl's eyes widened. "The date?" she whispered.

Deni nodded. "Yes. Unfortunately, the sushi Jenny and her date had last night wasn't good. She had a really bad tummy ache this morning."

Chloe's grey eyes shifting from Deni to the bowl of berries, but nothing else about her skinny, tiny body moved. It was as if she were pretending to be a doll or a statue. It was very odd.

"When will my father be home?" she asked softly.

35

Deni's heart ached. She knew that Sebastian spent most of his time with his daughter. He came home from the bank at seven o'clock every night and spent the next hour and a half with her. He'd also spent as much time on the weekends with her. She'd even heard them in the pool, swimming together. Sebastian was giving his daughter swimming lessons and trying to get the beautiful child to laugh. But Chloe never laughed. As far as Deni could tell, the child never even smiled.

"Unfortunately, he had meetings today." When the child's face didn't move in any way, Deni knew she'd have to do something. "And I have to go over to my father's house this morning. But I have an idea, if you're up for an adventure."

Chloe didn't move. There wasn't even any interest in the child's eyes. "What?"

"Would you like to come with me? My father is a very nice man, but he's an absolutely horrible cook. I go over to his house on Sundays to cook him meals for the week and just to visit."

"Why can't he cook?"

Deni laughed. "Because my mother used to do all of the cooking."

The child's grey eyes barely blinked. "Why doesn't she do it now?"

Good question, and something that Deni didn't like to talk about. "Well, my mother died several months ago. I suspect that my father doesn't like to cook because he's sad about her being gone. They used to have a lot of fun in the kitchen when she cooked."

"Fun?" Chloe asked. "I watch my daddy cook sometimes," she admitted. "He mutters a lot." The girl looked far too serious for her age. "Cooking doesn't seem very fun."

Deni laughed, although the sound seemed a bit stiff. "Cooking is loads of fun. I remember sitting at the kitchen table growing up and my mother would be trying to get dinner out of the oven. My dad would come home and he'd take her into his arms, then dance her around the room. She'd laugh and try to get out of his arms, but she was usually laughing too hard to be serious about trying to get back to her cooking."

Chloe's eyes widened. "He danced with her?" she whispered, leaning forward ever so slightly. "In the *kitchen*?" she continued, finishing the word as if it were a gasp.

"Yes!" Deni replied, smiling at the memory. "He loved to dance. When my mom finally got out of his arms, he'd usually come over to me, lift me into his arms, and dance with me. But I was much shorter and he'd have to lift me up into the air. He'd swing me around, left and right, sometimes even upside down and I'd giggle until my stomach hurt."

Chloe didn't smile. She simply stared at Deni, solemnly taking in the story as if memorizing it.

"So that's why I think my dad can't cook for himself. Because of those fun memories." Deni bit her lip, pausing before she continued. "Would you do me a favor?"

Chloe didn't move, didn't respond. She looked at Deni, silently granting permission for Deni to continue.

"Would you come with me today to help me cook for my dad?"

Chloe leaned forward slightly. "But...he's not my father."

Deni tilted her head slightly. "Technically, my father is your step-grandfather. And a step-granddaughter is even more important than a daughter." Chloe leaned forward a bit more. "I promise to have you back home by the time your father finishes with his meetings."

Chloe thought about it for a moment, still and contemplative. Then she nodded. "Okay. As long as your father won't mind a child being in his house," she replied with a politeness that was unheard of in a five year old.

"I think that my father would appreciate your company more than you realize," Deni told the child honestly.

After encouraging Chloe to eat more strawberries, they went up and changed clothes. In the deep recesses of her closet, Deni found a pair of jeans. They still had the tags on them, and Chloe warily pulled them on. Next, they found a pretty sweater and Deni pulled the girl's hair into a pony tail and they were ready!

Sebastian's chauffer drove them over to her father's house, Deni not having a child seat in her car. When they pulled up outside, her father stepped out of the house, forewarned by Deni's texts that Chloe was coming with her.

"Hello!" he called, and Deni almost cried at seeing her father's previously worn out features wreathed in a smile of greeting. He even bent down on his knee in order to greet Chloe. "Hello, pretty girl," he said to Chloe. "It is a pleasure to meet you. I understand that you are a very good cook and you are going to make me cookies today!"

Chloe's worried eyes moved to Deni, confused.

Deni rolled her eyes. "No Dad. We're not making you cookies. We're making you Brussel sprouts," she warned, naming her father's most hated vegetable.

Mark made a face and Chloe's worried eyes glanced at Deni again.

A moment later, they all marched into the house. Deni tried to get the chauffeur to come and join them, but he refused, preferring to stay outside in his formal attire.

For the next several hours, Deni cooked while Mark and Chloe sat at the kitchen table. Mark taught Chloe how to play "Go-Fish" and lost repeatedly to the adorable girl. At one point, she even smiled ever so slightly!

On the drive back to Chloe's house, she stared out the window. It had been a warm and happy afternoon, although Chloe hadn't smiled. Not even once.

"Are you okay, honey?" Deni asked.

Chloe continued to stare out the window, her features doing that expressionless thing that her father had perfected.

"He didn't dance," she whispered.

Deni saw Chloe's lip quiver and Deni's heart ached for the lonely child.

"I suspect that my father didn't want to insult you by dancing with you, honey," she explained.

Chloe simply continued to stare out the window.

Chapter 8

"What are you doing here?"

It was Thursday morning and Deni was at work, still upset that she hadn't gotten Chloe to smile on Sunday. Jenny was back to good health and caring for the child until Sebastian arrived home in the evening, so Deni had no more contact with her.

She was back to lonely meals by herself every morning and night. And because she couldn't talk to her friends about this farce of a marriage, Deni hadn't met with Carly, Charlotte, or Jessa in too long. She was miserable, angry, and more than ready for a fight!

Sebastian happened to step into her office at just the wrong moment.

Deni looked up from her computer, blinking to focus on the tall man standing in her doorway, more than ready to take him on, despite the intimidating scowl on his handsome features. She suspected that caution was probably warranted, even though she had the crazy urge to poke the bear. Probably dangerous, she warned herself sternly. Bears bite. Bears roar.

And yet...

"I'm working," she snapped before she could come up with a sarcastic response that might get her fired. She might be married to the man, living under his roof, but he was still the boss' boss' boss...or whatever.

He stood there for another moment and it took all of her concentration not to fidget uncomfortably under his intense, grey stare.

"Why?" he finally demanded.

She watched, oddly fascinated by the straining fabric when he crossed his arms over his chest. His arms were bigger than she would have thought, considering the man sat in an office for hours on end. Still, he probably wasn't as buff as the stretched material implied.

"Because I have work to do," she told him, her chin lifting slightly.

She told herself it wasn't a defiant gesture, but she was feeling pretty defiant right at the moment. If he was going to fire her, Deni was going to fight that. She'd only agreed to marry the man and live in his ugly, horrible house in return for getting her father out of debt. At no point had he added in a clause that she'd have to stop working.

Although, staring at his arrogant self at the moment, she could picture him demanding that. Because he was a jerk.

A good looking jerk. A jerk that seemed to have a few more muscles than an office-jerk should have.

But still a jerk.

His eyes narrowed at her tone. Or maybe it was because she was glaring right back at him. She didn't care. She was sick of this terror she had for the man. And sick of being jerked around. Her mother had passed away a bit more than six months ago. Her father had lost his job and almost lost his house. Time for action. Even if that action seemed small and petty.

Nope, she didn't give a damn!

"Why do you...?"

A challenging lift of her eyebrows caused him to press his lips together. In a whisper, she leaned closer. "Sir, you realize that I work in a small office and my colleagues that are working late are listening intently to whatever you might ask of me?"

Instantly, Sebastian pulled back and looked around. Sure enough, several of her co-workers quickly pulled their heads back into their own offices, pretending not to have heard anything. But Deni was sure that they were all listening, eager to hear what might happen next. "In my office. Now!" he snapped.

Deni watched him walk down the hallway, suspecting that she should follow him immediately. He probably wanted her to cower. But nope. She wasn't going to do that either. Nor was she going to jump at his snappish tone. She was working, for goodness sake! Deni was doing bank business! There was absolutely no reason he should be so snappish!

So, why did she feel as if she should cower?!

Yeah, he was the boss. The head honcho. The big cahoona. But she wasn't going to cower!

Saving the file she'd been working on before he'd interrupted her, she stood up, smoothed her dress down, and thought about stepping into the restroom for a moment, just to touch up her lipstick, or maybe run a brush through her hair. Then she realized where her mind had gone. Good grief! The man barely even knew that she lived in his house. So, why would she even think about looking nice for him?! Nope, she refused to fluff her hair or touch up her appearance.

Although, delaying might serve to irritate him further. And...she smiled at her next thought...irritating him might make her feel better.

Instead, she walked down the hallway at a leisurely pace.

When she turned the corner, she realized that he was waiting for her at the elevator. Yikes! She hadn't thought about that, Deni realized. A small elevator with just the two of them. She looked behind her, praying that someone else would come around the corner. Someone important enough to need to ride up the several flights in the small, wooden box to the executive floors.

Unfortunately, no one appeared.

Deni turned to look up at the man, surprised that he was staring right back at her.

"Don't say another word," he snapped as she opened her mouth. She wasn't completely sure what she might say, but it was probably something along the lines of an apology for being so snarky moments before.

But at his unjustified tone, she closed her mouth, the apology dissipating.

The elevator doors opened and she warily stepped inside. Once the doors closed again, she was shocked by the instantaneous and intense tension that seemed to increase right along with the elevator as it ascended to the top floor.

She almost sighed with relief when the doors opened. But then he put his hand on the open doorway, pulling back to wait for her to walk through the doors. It was a very gentlemanly thing to do, but Deni didn't want to walk that close to him. She didn't want to smell his aftershave or sense the heat coming off of his body.

Immediately, she remembered kissing him right after the ceremony and then again, in the courtroom. The heat, the need. The shocking sensations that she didn't really understand since she didn't actually *like* the man. They all came right back as she realized she'd have to brush by him in order to step out of the elevator.

"I'm not going to bite," he promised.

Her eyes moved higher, locking onto his and she felt her heart pounding. One beat. Two. They stared and she held her breath.

"Right," she finally said and stepped through the doors.

It was just as bad as she'd thought! Moving close was dangerous and she didn't understand why. She wanted to feign indifference, but the moment her breast accidentally brushed his arm, she felt that same burning sensation heat up her body. She gasped and quickly moved out of his way, then turned slightly, trying to understand.

This kind of reaction seemed so completely out of proportion for what had just happened. She'd brushed by the man. Perhaps a fraction of an inch of her breast had brushed his arm. And yet, through several layers of clothing, she'd felt him. She'd felt that crazy heat hit her so hard that she felt it all the way down to her toes.

Looking up into his eyes, she couldn't figure out if he'd felt that kind of electric zap as well. His eyes were blank, but she saw a vein throbbing on his jaw. Was he angry?

"This way," he said. For some reason, his voice sounded deeper. Huskier. What in the world?!

Then he did something that really made her head swim with crazy feelings. He put his hand to the small of her back, guiding her down the hallway to his office.

"No calls or interruptions," he snapped to his assistant. The older woman looked up, startled by the command. Then her eyes widened when she noticed Deni walking alongside him. The almost instant disapproval hurt. Deni tried to pretend that it didn't, but she couldn't seem to escape the censure in the woman's eyes.

"Okay," the door slammed behind them, "why the hell are you here at the bank?"

Deni blinked, startled by his question. "Where else would I be?"

He tossed the papers onto his desk before turning back to glower at her. "I don't know. At my house. Shopping. Having lunch with your friends?"

She pulled back, confused. This was why he was pissy? Because she was at her desk working? "Why would I be shopping? I have a meeting in," she checked her watch, "twenty minutes. And I really need to prepare for it," she told him.

His eyes narrowed. "A meeting. Really?"

She was angry now. "Yes. I have a meeting to discuss last month's mortgage variances. I know that's not really high on your list today, but I find it fascinating. And I don't appreciate you interrupting my day." She moved closer to him, getting revved up to her argument now. "I don't interrupt your day and demand that you come down to my office in order to ask ridiculous questions. Why are you disrespecting my day by doing so right now?"

"You think I'm disrespecting you?"

She glared up at him. "What would you call it?"

"Trying to understand what the hell you're doing." His voice was ominously low.

She rolled her eyes, throwing her hands up in the air with exasperation. "I told you. I have a meeting. There's no nefarious reason the meeting was scheduled for today. It happens around the same time every month."

He stared at her for a moment, those eyes blinking once. Twice. Then he shook his head. "But I gave you an allowance."

She shook her head. "No, you give your children an allowance. I removed the allowance from the contract."

His hands fisted on his hips. "Your lawyer kept it in."

"Then he's not my lawyer any longer," she snapped and crossed her arms over her stomach, irritated that her request had been dismissed so unceremoniously.

"He was doing the right thing, Deni," he told her, his voice placating now. "He was protecting your interests."

She rubbed her forehead. "Mr..." she stopped, seeing his eyes narrow at the slip. "Sebastian," she corrected, "I don't want your money. You saved my father's home and his dignity. That's all I needed. That's all I agreed to." Her arms dropped back down to her sides. "But I really do have a meeting soon. I enjoy the intellectual challenge of my job and I'm not giving that up. I also earn a very good salary, so I don't need the monthly amount that you stuck into that agreement."

He didn't relent. "Your savings account was depleted several months ago."

How in the world did he...oh, right. As bank owner, the man had access to all of her bank accounts. It would be simple for him to find out how much she had in her accounts. "You're right. I paid off the first round of medical bills for my mother and the funeral expenses." She paused as pain hit her. Pain for the loss of her mother. Pain for how much she missed her every single day. She swallowed back that sadness, just as she'd done every time it had come to her since the day her mother had succumbed to the cancer. "Regardless of my bank account balance, I don't need your money."

He sighed and Deni thought that he looked...tired? No, that wasn't quite the word. But different. Sebastian looked different for a brief moment. "Deni, you married me in order to get money. You can't say you don't need my money."

Good point. "Okay, I don't need *more* of your money. Other than what I earn by doing my job." She stepped closer. "I know that you have all the power in this relationship. You control everything right now. But please, I'm good at my job. I like it and I enjoy the people I work with. Please don't fire me, on top of everything else that I've had to deal with over the past several months." She paused for a moment, trying to tamp down the panic. "I apologize for the way I spoke to you a few minutes ago in my office. That wasn't appropriate and it won't happen again. Please," she looked pleadingly at him, "don't fire me. I really am good at my job."

Sebastian blinked. She *liked* working? Every woman of his acquaintance considered working a job to be beneath them.

No, that wasn't accurate. He had many women on his staff that were outstanding employees. He prided himself on promoting a gender neutral workplace. He'd even gone so far as to bring in a third-party company to evaluate if there was any gender discrimination or pay inequity. They'd found several minor issues and he'd already ordered his personnel department to rectify those and put other policies in place that would go even further.

It was only his ex-wife and her friends who were leaches on society and their husbands. Their career, literally, was hooking the wealthiest man they could find, marrying him, then one-upping each other on their spending sprees.

Deni was so completely different from his ex-wife in every way. She was fresh and alive, vibrant and caring. And yes, there was a chemistry between them that was intense and startling. Of all the things he'd tried to anticipate during this custody battle, being attracted to his 'wife' wasn't one of them.

"You enjoy the job?"

She shrugged and his eyes moved lower, noticing her breasts pressing against the material of her dress. Damn, he shouldn't notice things like that. But...

"I love my job." She laughed softly and the sound made his body react even more intensely than before. "Not all aspects of it. There are times when I am standing in the copy room for too long, trying to get copies for a meeting. Or when I mess up. I don't enjoy that."

"What do you mess up?" he asked, his eyes sharpening.

Another laugh and he gritted his teeth. "I'm not going to tell you what I mess up," she replied, and damn if he didn't like that too. There were too many things about this woman that he liked.

When she glanced at her watch, he wanted to pull her into his arms and kiss her until she forgot about her damn meeting. Which was absolutely absurd. He wasn't that kind of man! He didn't allow his passions to interfere with...anything!

But even as he thought that, he realized that he'd never felt this kind of passion for a woman before. An ironic occurrence, he thought. He had the absolute worst luck with women lately. First he married a woman who was a cold-hearted, mercenary viper right to her core. Then he meets a woman who...well, she seemed to be honest and sweet.

But so had Meredith initially, he thought and pulled back. He

44

wouldn't ever trust another woman. Meredith had driven that message home in the most painful way. And Chloe was suffering for his mistake. She didn't deserve what had happened to her, but at least he now had his daughter in his house, in his care.

Never underestimate the power of a woman, he reminded himself. They were scheming, conniving liars.

"Right. I'll leave you to your meeting then."

Deni smiled and he gripped the arms of his chair, trying not to react to her eager expression. "Thank you!" she gushed. She started to step forward, then obviously caught herself and pulled back. "Right. Gotta go. Variances," she whispered. He suspected that she was surprised by her actions and was trying to get away.

She turned on her heel and Sebastian couldn't stop his eyes from lowering to her butt. The dress she had chosen for the day hugged her bottom perfectly. And damn it, there weren't any panty lines. So she was either wearing one of those tight things that were like a girdle but called something else. Or she was wearing one of those sexy pairs of panties that didn't leave lines.

Hell!

The door closed gently and he was left with an aching erection and more curiosity than he knew how to handle. Women weren't curiosities, he told himself even as he moved over to his desk. Women were nice and had a very specific place in his life.

"Ms. Eldrich," he said, pressing the intercom.

"Yes, Mr. Hughes?"

"What's on my calendar for the next two hours?" he asked, not really sure why he was asking. Ms. Eldrich was incredibly efficient and always warned him when there was a meeting well in advance so he could review the materials.

"You have a lunch appointment in an hour. And you have the quarterly reports from the directors at two, sir," she reported.

He considered for perhaps two seconds. "Find out where the mortgage variance meetings are being held. The next should be in ten minutes."

There was a pause and Sebastian thought his usually unflappable assistant's expression would be amusing.

"Yes, sir," she replied back.

About sixty seconds later, she walked into his office and handed him a piece of paper. "Would you like me to get copies of the reports?"

He took the piece of paper and looked at it, noted the conference room number and nodded with satisfaction. "Excellent. Thank you. And no. I don't want to give anyone advance notice of my attendance."

He stood up and hurried down the hallway, eager to see his 'wife' in action.

Minutes later, he stepped into the conference room filled with people he'd never met before. As soon as the door closed and the occupants recognized him, all conversation halted.

"Please continue," he encouraged. One of the men sitting at the table stood up, offering his chair to Sebastian. But instead, he chose a chair over by the wall, wanting to listen and observe.

He couldn't stop a chuckle from escaping when Deni glared at him. But he only lifted an eyebrow while the others around the table struggled to continue.

The conversation faltered for several minutes, but eventually, the meeting resumed, although it was much more stilted than before.

When it was Deni's turn to speak, Sebastian couldn't help but be impressed. She was articulate and precise. When her manager asked a question, needing more information or clarification, she knew the answers immediately. The others who had spoken had been good, but they'd occasionally replied, "I'll get that information for you." Which implied they weren't completely informed. His directors knew that being unprepared for any meeting with him was a deadly sin.

At the end of the meeting, he slipped out without a word to anyone and headed back to his office. He had to give Deni credit. She'd done an excellent job. He wondered what she would do if he called the human resources department and told them to promote her.

With a chuckle, he instinctively knew that she'd be upset. How he knew that after their few brief conversations, he wasn't sure. But he just...knew.

Chapter 9

Deni walked into the house that night, ready to do battle. It wasn't fair for Sebastian to invade her meetings like he'd done today. Her boss had been confused, worried that she'd done something wrong. In fact, all of the managers had been a bit disconcerted by his presence.

Deni looked around, irritated again that there wasn't a place for her to toss her keys. In her apartment, she'd just toss them onto the counter. But in this mausoleum, everything looked so neat and organized. That's when she saw the little girl. "Chloe? Are you okay, sweetie?" Deni asked, stuffing her keys into her purse and dropping it right by the door before walking over to Chloe, who was sitting on the stairs, looking small and worried.

"Are you my stepmother?" she asked.

Deni tried to hide her surprise, but Chloe always watched so carefully. They'd sort of had this conversation that day on the patio. But neither of them had delved into their relationship too closely at that time. "Yes, I guess I am," Deni said, sitting down next to the small girl on the stairs. "Is that okay with you?"

"Why do you guess?"

Deni wasn't sure how to respond. Honesty was probably best. "Well, it's true that your father and I married a few weeks ago. But we have a different kind of relationship than most married couples," Deni qualified.

The child's grey eyes watched Deni carefully. "Different how?"

Oh boy. Deni should have anticipated that one. "Well, your dad and I are friends."

The child contemplated her answer. "My mom and dad aren't friends. They hate each other."

Yikes! That's a pretty heavy burden for any child to have to carry.

47

"I'm sure they don't hate each other," Deni said with hope.

"My mom says she hates my dad. She says he's a cheap bastard and I should ignore him and stay away from him."

This just kept getting worse, Deni thought. "Well, you've met my dad and I like my father very much. So, I can't imagine avoiding yours."

Chloe looked up at Deni earnestly. "What do you do with your dad? Besides dance in the kitchen. Which he didn't do the last time you were there." Deni smiled but turned away. She'd already mentioned to her father that he'd have to dance with Chloe if he ever saw her again.

"Oh, we talk mostly," Deni explained. "When I have problems, I go to him and he helps me work through the issue. Sometimes, we just sit and talk about memories."

"What kinds of memories?"

Deni swallowed the pain, blinking back the tears. Memories of her mother popped into her head. "Of good times we've had in the past."

"Like what?"

Sheesh, Deni needed to figure out how to talk to kids. They liked details. But Deni thought back to conversations she and her father had had over the past several months. Memories from times when her mother was alive. Before the cancer. "Every year, my mom would go on this church weekend retreat with the other ladies in our church. So it was just me and my dad at home together." Deni smiled. "As soon as she walked out of the house, my father and I would rush to the store and get white chocolate chips, milk chocolate chips, whipped cream – the real stuff that we had to make ourselves with a mixer, and lots of sugar." Deni smiled at the memory and Chloe's eyes sparkled. It was the first real reaction Deni had seen on Chloe's face. "We'd get a bunch of strawberries. Then we'd pack everything up, stuff a blanket into the car, and head out to find the perfect picnic spot. Sometimes we'd find a place up in the mountains. Once we found a waterfall. Another time, we hiked to a big rock. Wherever it was, we'd spread the blanket out, take out the whipped cream and melted chocolate and other stuff. Then we'd eat strawberries dipped in melted chocolate or dunked in the whipped cream until we were sick!"

Chloe giggled, just as Deni had hoped and the sound was pretty amazing!

"What happened next?"

Deni shrugged, leaning back against the stairs as she slipped her heels off, stretching her feet. "Then we'd head back home and watch movies for the rest of the weekend. We knew when my mom would be home so we'd make sure to clean everything up before she arrived back." Deni smiled at the girl. "She never knew about our strawberry festival, but we did it every year."

Chloe leaned her arms on her tucked-up knees. "Do you still do that?"

Deni thought about it. "No," she replied, with quiet surprise. "We haven't done it since I went away to college."

"Why not?"

"Time," Deni explained. "When I got older, I didn't have the time for it. But I should have made the time," she thought wistfully.

Chloe was silent for a moment. Then she said, "I don't think my dad would take me on a picnic like that," she said and there was a bit of sadness in her voice.

Deni nodded. "Yeah. I don't think he would either. But I bet your dad would do other things with you."

She nodded. "He reads with me every night." Her face turned sad. "When I'm with him. My mom doesn't want me with him though."

Deni knew that the evil Meredith didn't want this sweet child to be with her father because that would limit the child support payments. She wondered what was happening with those now that Meredith no longer had full custody.

"What else do you and your dad do together?" Chloe asked.

She thought about it for a moment. "We used to go camping. That was always a lot of fun."

Chloe looked confused. "What's camping?"

Deni laughed. "Well, it's when you go out to the mountains or maybe the beach, set up a tent and sleep in it. We would cook over a campfire. I used to fish with my dad, but then I decided that fishing was boring."

"What did you cook?" she asked, more curiosity in her pretty eyes now.

Deni had to really concentrate to remember what they cooked. "One year, we got one of those heavy metal pots, I think they are called a Dutch oven, but I don't know why, and we made fried chicken and biscuits in that." Deni laughed. "I wouldn't recommend that though."

"Why not?" Chloe asked, obviously fascinated.

"Because it's really hard!" she laughed. "And camping should be fun. The last time we went camping, we brought all of our food so we didn't have to cook. But we still had a camp fire and made s'mores." At the confused look on Chloe's face again, Deni explained. "S'mores are when you roast a marshmallow over the fire until it turns nice and brown and pretty, then put it in between two pieces of chocolate and two graham crackers. The warm marshmallow melts the chocolate and, in theory, the crackers keep the sticky stuff from getting onto your fingers. But as soon as you bite into the s'more, the chocolate and marshmallow ooze out and it's a delicious mess! It's the absolute best part about camping!" Deni smiled. "In fact, just the thought of making s'mores makes me want to go camping again!"

The heavy front door opened and Deni watched as Sebastian stepped inside. Immediately, the housekeeper appeared to take his coat and briefcase, whisking both away. It occurred to Deni that the housekeeper hadn't magically appeared to whisk away Deni's purse and coat. Hmph!

Chloe saw her father and jumped up, running over to him. "Dad! Can we go camping and make s'mores and fried chicken and sleep in a tent?"

Deni cringed when Sebastian looked over at her. "Camping?" he asked. The word came out like a curse.

Deni stood up, grabbing her shoes. "Don't knock it 'till you try it," she said with a forced smile. "I'll leave you two for..."

"But what about dinner?" Chloe asked. She turned to her father. "Dad, Luther's family always eats together as a family," she said with the kind of pleading voice only a five year old could get away with. "Shouldn't Deni eat with us too? She's family."

"I have work to do," Deni said, trying to give a plausible excuse so Sebastian could eat privately with his daughter.

"That's what my mother always says," Chloe pleaded. "I want to hear more about camping. Please?" she begged.

Sebastian turned to face Deni, clearly not amused. "Chloe would enjoy your presence at dinner tonight. Perhaps you could do your bank business later, if we promise to be quiet and not disturb you?"

She could hear the sarcasm in his voice, but wasn't sure how to get out of dinner. Chloe was dancing around them, obviously excited at the idea of them having dinner together as a family. Since this was the first time that Deni had ever seen anything even close to excitement on the small child's features, she didn't want to deny her.

Giving in, Deni pulled her eyes away from Sebastian's and looked at an identical pair in the more inviting child's face. "Let me just go change clothes and I'll be right back down, okay?"

Chloe clapped her hands in delight. "Thank you!" And she turned to beam up at her father. "Deni is going to join us!" She leaned in and gave her father a hug around his leg. "This is going to be much more fun than having dinner in my room at Momma's house!"

Deni had just turned away when she heard that announcement. She looked over her shoulder at Sebastian, who was looking at Chloe. They shared a startled glance. Had this sweet child been relegated to her room while living with her mother?

Deni was starting to realize that anything was possible where Meredith was concerned.

Ten minutes later, Deni walked downstairs. Walking into the kitchen, she found the housekeeper busy putting food on three plates. But Chloe and Sebastian weren't anywhere around. "Do you need help with that?" Deni asked.

The kind housekeeper smiled, shaking her head. "Goodness, no dear. You just go on in and sit down at the table. I'll serve dinner in just a moment."

Since Deni had been grabbing dinner and taking it up to her room for the past few weeks, she had no idea where the dining room might be. There were several doorways, but she wasn't sure which to take. Unfortunately, the first one she tried led to the pantry. The second led to another doorway. When she stepped back and turned to look at the housekeeper, the woman smiled and tilted her head towards the next door.

"Thanks," Deni whispered, embarrassed.

When she stepped through the doorway, Deni found Sebastian and Chloe sitting at a long table. It wasn't the banquet table that she'd stumbled upon during her first tour through the house. But it was just as unbearably formal. The shiny wooden table gleamed under the overhead lights and there were about twelve, stiff-backed chairs around the table.

"You're here!" Chloe smiled, wiggling excitedly in her chair, but as soon as she realized what she was doing, she darted a quick glance at her father, and stilled.

Deni felt as if all of her efforts were worthwhile after that smile and wiggle. Breathing a sigh of relief, she walked towards the table. "I'm here, although it took me a few tries to find this room." But before she could sit, Sebastian was there, pulling out her chair and holding it for her. Deni looked at him, startled and not exactly sure what to do. Men didn't pull chairs out for women anymore. But she thought back to the black and white movies, giving him a brief, awkward smile before moving around to the front of the chair and sitting down.

Immediately after, the housekeeper appeared with three plates, setting one before each of them.

"Thank you, Ms. Hopkins," Deni replied, adding a smile for the woman who looked back at Deni, startled. Ms. Hopkins glanced nervously at Sebastian, then back at Deni. "My pleasure, ma'am," she said before pushing her way through the room to the kitchen.

Uh oh, another error in household protocol, Deni thought as she suppressed a smile. No speaking to the hired help? But then...wasn't she the hired help as well? So, if that were the case, then perhaps it wasn't such a blip on the manner's ledger that she'd spoken to a colleague. The thought caused a bubble of laughter to well up inside of her. Thankfully, she was able to suppress it quickly, but a glance at the man sitting stoically beside her let her know that her amusement hadn't gone unnoticed.

"Right," she muttered under her breath. "What's for dinner?" she asked lightly, trying to ease the tension in the room.

"Nice of you to join us," Sebastian commented darkly.

Deni turned to look at the small girl and noticed that she was eating the exact same meal as she and Sebastian. Salmon? And asparagus? Blech! She didn't like either of those and it didn't help that there was a small drizzle of the lemony-yellow hollandaise sauce on the green sprigs. She hated asparagus and salmon was just...fishy. No, not fishy but...

With a sigh, she pulled her napkin out and spread it over her lap.

"What did you do in school today?" Deni asked, cutting up her asparagus into bite sized pieces.

"I don't go to school," she said, taking a bite of her salmon.

Deni glanced up, then looked over at Sebastian. "Why not?"

"She has tutors," he told her with a voice that warned her not to question the issue.

"Ah," Deni sighed. A tutor. What a lonely world. "Well, that sounds like you have a lot of special attention then. What did you and your tutor work on today?"

"Math. I'm working on multiplication tables," she announced, although she slaughtered the word.

Deni looked up, startled once again. "Wow! Multiplication? I didn't learn how to multiply until I was in third or fourth grade." She took another bite of her salmon, then cut her asparagus up into smaller pieces, shoving most of it underneath the smallish pile of rice pilaf. Oh, for a mountain of rice right about now, Deni thought, only half listening as Sebastian listed Chloe's assignments and studies.

"Do you think your father needs more help cooking this weekend?" Chloe asked, her eyes bright with hope.

Deni quickly glanced at Sebastian, trying to gauge his reaction to his daughter's question. "Well," she replied cautiously, noting the confusion on Sebastian's icily handsome features. Then she realized that this whole exercise was to benefit Chloe, not to pacify the chilly father. So she focused on Chloe. "Yes. My father will need help for a little longer. But even when he doesn't need help, he still loves the company, especially yours."

The small child grinned, but at the dark look in Sebastian's eyes, her grin faded away.

"What's this about dinners?" he asked, the cold note in his voice sending icicles in Deni's direction.

Chloe obviously realized that her father wasn't happy and cringed. Deni hated that haunted look in the girl's eyes and turned to glare at Sebastian. "Jenny was sick last week," she started to explain. "It wasn't her fault that she got sick, so please don't blame her."

"Perhaps this is a conversation that you and I should have in private?" he suggested. When Deni opened her mouth, prepared to argue, one, dark eyebrow lifted, stifling her outburst. Deni could handle an argument but this cold, impenetrable look was her undoing.

"Right. Later," she sighed, then pushed a bit more asparagus under the rice and finished off her salmon, swallowing the vile meat with a gulp.

The sound didn't go unnoticed either and Chloe giggled, her chubby hand coming up to cover her gaffe and the smile completely disappeared when her father's head swiveled in her direction. So instead of being silly, as she should be at her age, she bowed her head and ate more of her dinner, not complaining one bit about the asparagus or the salmon, and completely ignoring the rice.

"Do you not like rice, my dear?" Sebastian asked, and Deni was surprised by his gentle tone.

Her grey eyes, so similar to her fathers, lifted higher, her lip trembling in confusion. "Mother says that rice is a carbo...carbohi-something and I shouldn't eat them because of something about my figure."

Both Deni and Sebastian stared at her for a long moment, her grey eyes looking from each of them, growing more worried as she wondered if she'd just said something wrong.

Deni could see Sebastian wasn't sure how to respond to that. So Deni stepped in, unconcerned with being right or wrong.

"I eat carbs all the time!" Deni announced.

Unfortunately, both of them looked at her plate that still had the pile of rice, that looked bigger now that the asparagus was stuffed underneath.

"But..."

Deni knew exactly where Chloe's mind went and she took up her fork and scooped up a large bite of rice. Unfortunately, because of her hatred of asparagus, she got more of the disgusting vegetable than she did of the delicious rice. Deni refused to give in though. She chewed the rice-asparagus carefully, maintaining a serene expression on her face.

Chloe looked up at her father, needing additional confirmation that carbohydrates weren't the enemy of a female body. When he nodded, Chloe lifted her fork one more time and scooped a small bit onto her fork. When she tasted the rice, she tilted her head to the side. "I think I like the rice more than Deni does," she said, and scooped a bigger bite.

Deni glanced at Sebastian and, darn it! He knew what she'd done. He glanced down at her plate, then back up meaningfully, silently ordering her to finish her dinner.

Deni glared at him. If he hadn't challenged her with that look, she might have just put her fork down and explained that she was full. But Deni refused to give him the satisfaction. She ate the entire pile of rice and asparagus, choking it down with a large glass of water.

At that moment, Deni wasn't sure if she truly hated him, or if she wanted to laugh at her childish hiding of the asparagus and the fact that he'd caught her.

Chapter 10

Sebastian kissed Chloe's forehead, tucked the blankets around her, and slipped quietly from the room. She was wiped out, understandably since she'd been taken from one home to another, trying to learn the rules of each parent as quickly as possible. He was fairly sure that she didn't understand any of it, if tonight's dinner confusion was any indication.

No matter how much he tried to shield the small girl from the trauma of a contested divorce, there was only so much he could do. She was only five years old! Damn Meredith for telling the small, precious child that carbohydrates were bad for her!

Taking her out of his ex-wife's house was the first step in ensuring that the girl might have a normal childhood, he knew. Thankfully, other than a few blips, like tonight's rice issue, the transition seemed to have been an easy one, but only because Meredith was still in Paris. As soon as she returned home, the woman would cause a massive uproar. Hell, she was probably already doing that on the way home from Europe.

Sebastian didn't envy the pilot and crew of whatever flight Meredith was taking to get home.

But regaining custody of Chloe was the right thing to do. The child was hurting. He could see it in the wistful way she looked at Deni and the excited chatter during dinner. Not to mention, the casual comments Chloe made about life with her mother. Eating dinner alone in her room each night was only the tip of the iceberg. Apparently, the child had three nannies. And the nannies had been fired several times over the past several months, meaning that new nannies were brought in, further confusing the issue.

Over the past few days, Sebastian had learned from Chloe's comments that Meredith had thrown lavish, drunken parties and there had been a slew of different men coming through Meredith's life. Sebastian didn't care how many men his ex-wife slept with. She could have sex with whoever she wanted, but when she left Chloe alone in the house, that wasn't okay. Not in any way.

But his ex-wife was a subject for another day. Right now, he needed to find his current "wife" and thank her. Their dinner tonight had been much livelier because of Deni's assistance. Her stories about her own childhood had given Chloe hope. And Deni had made Chloe laugh. For that alone, he owed her a debt of gratitude.

Knocking on her door produced no sound. Obviously, Deni wasn't in her room. After their wedding, he'd encouraged her to tour the house and use the facilities. Thinking now, he remembered mentioning the indoor pool.

He decided to check there first, thinking that a swim right about now would be refreshing. Perhaps he would join her.

Deni pushed harder, needing to feel her muscles burn. She mentally counted strokes, regulating her breathing with as much precision as she could muster. Anything to get the image of Sebastian Hughes carrying his tiny daughter upstairs after dinner. The man might be a bastard in the worst way, but he loved his daughter. The way he'd lifted Chloe gently into his arms, tucking her head against his shoulder...it had been incredibly sweet. But nothing had prepared her heart for that brief moment when she'd seen him close his eyes, as if he were trying to savor the precious moment.

What was a woman to do? How could she protect herself when the jerk stopped being jerk-like? When he had those tender, human moments.

Exercise, Deni told herself. Push him out of her mind with exercise. Don't think about Sebastian Hughes and his beautiful daughter. Focus on bringing her arm up and over with perfect form, breathing in, holding her breath for several more strokes, then breathing out quickly and breathing in. Repeating it until she had the rhythm in her head and nothing else.

When she finally couldn't go another meter, she floated over to the side of the pool and...

He was here?! What was he doing here? She hadn't thought anyone would be here at this time of the night. Not that she would know since the whole house looked to be in pristine condition, she couldn't tell which rooms were used regularly. Not a speck of dust was allowed to float onto any of the priceless antiques in this house. Nothing out of place. Even her black tote bag had vanished from the front hallway. Some mysterious person had probably brought it up to her bedroom and it would magically appear at the front doorway again tomorrow morning when she was ready to walk out the door.

Living in a rich man's house certainly had its perks.

One of which was watching said man as he tossed his tie over one of the pool chairs.

"What are you doing?" she demanded when he began deftly unbuttoning the buttons of his dress shirt.

"I'm going to join you for a swim. It was a brilliant idea, Deni. Glad you thought of it."

One button released. Then another. She stared, willing him to speed up. Wishing he wouldn't continue. If he would just move faster, she could see more of his tanned skin before she got out of the pool. But she couldn't get out of the pool at this particular moment because... well, her body would broadcast exactly how excited she was to watch him unbutton those stupid buttons! Darn it, she wasn't attracted to Sebastian Hughes! He was cold and unfeeling! He was rude and uncompromising, a jerk-extraordinaire!

Another button released and she could see more of his tanned skin. Tanned? The man shouldn't be tan! He worked in an office for twenty-three hours a day! Shouldn't he be white? Deficient in Vitamin D?

Another button released and she held her breath as more tanned skin was revealed to her shockingly hungry eyes.

She crossed her arms over her chest, hiding her body's reaction.

He chuckled, as if he knew exactly what she was doing.

"Are you done swimming laps?" he asked, walking over to the table that held several rolled towels. He grabbed one and started to open it up and she realized that he expected her to step out of the pool and into the towel. She could just imagine those strong arms wrapping around her, enclosing her in his embrace.

But that's not going to happen, she told herself. She was a bank employee that was helping him to regain and retain custody of his child. She was expendable. She wasn't here for any of the hanky panky that her body was clamoring for.

"Deni?"

Huh? He'd asked a question and, she blinked, realizing that he was standing beside the pool, waiting for her to step out and into the towel.

Was she done? Laps. Deni looked behind her at the softly rippling water. The pool was heated and, even on the coldest of nights, the pool would feel luxurious. So, *was* she done?

Not if she had to step out of the warm, sensuous water and into his arms!

"Oh. No, I'm going to keep going," she decided. Then she turned, ignoring the burning in her arms and legs from the previous forty minutes of exercise and pushed off again, heading towards the other end of the pool. Executing a perfect turn, she pushed off at the other end and started back again. But this time around, her heart was pounding from more than just the exercise.

And then something else occurred to her. She stopped in the middle of the pool and looked up, pushing her hair out of her eyes. She'd pulled it up into a band, but the water had pulled several locks free.

"You're not..." she stopped and turned around, frowning at him.

"I'm not what?" he asked, shrugging out of his shirt and tossing it on top of his tie.

She stared at him, unaware of her mouth hanging open. "You're not going to swim *naked*, are you?" she gasped, horrified and fascinated at the possibility.

He blinked, and threw back his head, laughing. When his laughter finally slowed, he walked over to the edge of the pool, his eyes still glowing with laughter. "Would it bother you if I did?" he asked softly, almost gently.

How was she supposed to answer that? "Yes. I think it would bother me a great deal," she said, her voice breathy and deeper than she'd ever heard it before.

When she could no longer maintain the intensity of his eyes, she pushed off again and started swimming, putting all of her effort into the strokes. Faster and harder. She pushed herself, trying to pretend that Sebastian wasn't about to enter the pool in moments. And he wouldn't do it naked! Oh please, please! Don't let him be naked! Deni wasn't sure what he would look like, but magnificent came to mind. Amazing, probably.

And not hers!

The current pushed her and she wasn't expecting the change. She lifted up, but slipped on the bottom of the pool, water filling her mouth and causing her to choke. She floundered for only moments before strong, rock hard arms lifted her up and pulled her against an equally strong and muscular chest.

Deni gasped, water coming into her mouth and lungs, causing her to choke again.

"Easy," Sebastian soothed, pulling her in closer.

She grabbed his neck, but then her fingers jerked away, resting lightly on his biceps, his chest...but those places seemed too intimate. She tried to figure out where to put her hands, then finally just let them rest on his forearms.

"You okay?" he asked when she'd stopped sputtering.

"Yes. Thank you. I'm normally not this clumsy in the water."

"I know."

He knew what?! "I'm sorry?"

"You're a strong swimmer. I just caught you off guard."

"Right," she replied, not sure what to say. Then she realized that he was in the pool and...was he wearing a swimsuit?

"I'm wearing a swimsuit," he assured her, obviously reading her mind. She relaxed and he chuckled. "Would it horrify you if I wasn't?"

"Yes!"

"Why?"

She couldn't answer. Instead, her fingers tightened her around his arms for a brief moment before pushing away from him. Thankfully, he released her, but kept his hands on her waist until she'd regained her foothold.

"Thank you. I was on my swim team in high school, so I'm normally a good swimmer."

"I noticed."

She dipped her gaze lower, verifying that he was truly wearing something and relieved when she saw the blue bathing suit.

He laughed, following her eyes and she glared up at him. "I know it's funny to you, but put yourself in my position. I'm married to you but in name only, living in your house, but an employee. In both your house and your business." She shoved away from him, heading for the side of the pool. Unfortunately, he didn't take the hint and swam next to her, easily keep up with her.

She looked at him...really looked at him this time. "You have muscles!" she exclaimed, shocked by the power in his body. She'd felt it earlier, but looking at him gave her a much better understanding of what was underneath those expensive suits.

"Of course I have muscles," he teased. "Everyone has muscles."

"Yeah, but yours are...a bit more obvious!" Significantly more obvious! How dare he be rock-hard-buff?! That just seemed like he was cheating somehow!

He chuckled, a pleased masculine sound. "Should I take that as a compliment?"

She pulled herself up and out of the pool, ignoring the heat as she felt his eyes on her back and bottom. Quickly, she walked over to the towel he'd dropped onto one of the chairs and hid herself within it.

"You know that you're a gorgeous man, Sebastian. And you've probably heard women compliment you over and over again. There's no need to add me to your fan club."

He laughed, then pushed away, swimming down to the other end of the pool. She watched in fascination as his arms sliced through the water. He made it down to the other end of the pool in a fraction of the time it would have taken her. She might be a good swimmer, but Sebastian Hughes was a *really* good swimmer!

She realized that she was just standing there, watching him swim because he was right back at the other end and lifting himself up to rest his arms on the side of the pool. He grabbed a towel, then walked closer to her. "Thank you for dinner tonight. If I could have figured out how to get you out of it after Chloe asked, I would have. But she enjoyed herself tonight. And for that, I'm grateful."

Deni wasn't sure what to say. The thanks was so unexpected, she was speechless for a long moment. But then she rallied and nodded slightly. "You're welcome. Chloe is a beautiful girl, inside and out. It was a fun dinner for me as well."

He tilted his head slightly. "Really? You...enjoyed her silly comments?"

Deni smiled, relaxing because this man's daughter was a much safer topic than the man himself. "Yes. I thoroughly enjoyed her silly comments."

"They didn't annoy you because they were so childish?"

Deni rolled her eyes. "Sebastian, she *is* a child! Her comments should be childish. And no, they didn't annoy me. Chloe is adorable. I love it when she smiles and it's even more exciting when she giggles."

"I agree. It's just that..." he shrugged and her eyes were drawn to those yummy muscles there.

Pulling her eyes away, she turned her head so that she was looking at the chaise lounge. "She's delightful. She has an intelligence about her that counters her childishness, but when she laughs, she's all girl and all child and that's one of those sounds that the world needs more of."

He wiped his face with the towel, then moved on to other parts of his body. The chair wasn't nearly as interesting and she couldn't stop herself from watching.

"I agree. I love hearing her laugh. Which is one of the reasons I had such a nice time during dinner. She doesn't laugh enough. From what I can tell, whenever she's with Meredith, she's been cooped up with her nannies or her tutors. She doesn't get to socialize with other kids her age enough. I think she's been around adults too much. And even when she's with the adults in Meredith's house, Chloe is only brought out as a sort of show and tell for my ex-wife's friends. Meredith would dress Chloe up, parade her around and, when everyone had said the appropriate comments, Meredith would then send her back up to her room. Meredith only wanted the numerous accolades for producing an exceptionally pretty child. She never cared about Chloe's feelings or what it was like to be alone for so long during the day. She was..."

He stopped, but only because Deni put a hand to his arm. He stopped, his anger dissipating with her touch.

"She's safe. She's with you now and she seems to be happy. I don't think that there will be any lasting damage done by your ex-wife's callous treatment."

There was a tense moment while they stared at each other, then Deni stepped backwards. "I'll just...well, I'd better get to bed." That sounded like an invitation and she stammered out. "I mean, I have an early morning meeting and...I just...I need to sleep," she clarified.

Sebastian tossed his towel onto the chair, his hands fisting on his hips, but there was a hint of a smile to his hard lips now. "Early meeting tomorrow."

She nodded. "Yes," she backed up again, tightening the towel around her chest. "Well, it's one of those hard meetings and I need to get in early to more fully understand the numbers. Some of them are...I didn't quite..." she realized that she was talking to the head of the bank. The big boss. She was admitting that she didn't know something required for an important meeting to the man who could fire her for just about any reason.

She sighed, feeling a bit defeated. "I'm leaving now," she said firmly, adding a nod for emphasis. "Goodnight."

"Goodnight, Deni."

She walked out, wondering why his words felt almost like a caress. And as she turned the corner, heading towards the staircase, she looked behind her and realized that he was still watching her. Since the towel was still wrapped tightly around her body, there wasn't much for him to see. Her butt probably looked like it was encased in a burlap sack.

Still, she hurried out the door, praying that he couldn't see the blush that formed on her cheeks from the look in his eyes. Or maybe it was caused by the ideas flashing behind her eyes and had nothing at all to do with whatever he was thinking.

Or maybe it was because Deni knew what she was thinking, and possibly hoping that he was thinking the same thing?

Deni slammed the door to her bedroom, wondering what in the world she was doing! Boy, her mind had wandered into dangerous territory! She couldn't have sex, or even sexual thoughts, about a man like Sebastian! If he wasn't being driven by a chauffeured limousine, Sebastian drove a top of the line Mercedes! She drove a ten year old SUV that needed new tires! He wore suits that were specifically tailored for him. She sometimes made her own clothes! Her bank account was currently at zero. Possibly even less than zero if the bank noticed and applied the low-balance fees. His bank account was...well, she couldn't even imagine what his bank balance looked like.

Just comparing the places where they lived told her that they lived in two different worlds. Literally! Her entire apartment would fit into this bedroom with room to spare! The man didn't just have a staff at his office. He had a *household* staff. Not just a housekeeper or a team of cleaning people who came in every other week, which is what the rest of the world might be able to afford if they were lucky. The man had an entire staff of people dedicated to making his life run more smoothly.

In fact, Deni was part of the man's household AND business staff! She might have a wedding ring on her finger, but there was no mistaking her position in this household. She was a member of his staff and she'd be smart to remember that!

After showering and changing into a soft, well-worn tee shirt, she slipped between the sheets of the enormous bed. Every time she slipped into this bed, she was surprised by the unparalleled softness of the sheets. Plus, the mattress was amazingly comfy. But even though she was exhausted after a tense weekend and a long day of meetings, she couldn't get to sleep. She kept picturing Sebastian as he came out of the pool, the water dripping down those muscles that were much more pronounced than she ever would have guessed.

The man looked so cold and...benign in a suit. But all of that power was hidden and she thought the difference was...tantalizing.

Chapter 11

"We're going camping!"

Deni had just stepped into the foyer after a long, exhausting day and an almost sleepless night. So she wasn't prepared for the energy of a five year old. He swallowed a chuckle when Deni practically jerked backwards as the exuberance of Chloe's announcement and energy hit her full force.

"Chloe!" he admonished. A moment later, Sebastian stepped into the foyer. "I said we'd consider it. This isn't a done deal." He bent down and picked her up, trying to contain her energy so that Deni could come inside and take a breath. He knew that she'd had a hard day. The meeting she'd referenced last night hadn't gone well and he wondered why.

He watched Deni's features soften and something inside of him softened as well. Stiffening, he reminded himself to keep his distance. Women were not to be trusted when it came to marriage. Deni was his wife in name only and even a pretty, if exhausted, face shouldn't affect him. Chloe was his priority now. He'd never make the mistake of trusting a woman again. The contract with the lovely Deni was still in place and he wouldn't do anything to violate the terms, nor would he allow Deni to renege on her end of their bargain. It was imperative that Chloe be protected!

He hastily swallowed his chuckle at the icy glare in Chloe's grey eyes. It was a look that he'd perfected over the years. She was a fast learner. "Daddy, you said that we could go camping, just like Deni did when she was little."

He chuckled, shaking his head. "I told you that we *might* go camping. I made no promises, honey."

"But...!"

63

"And I never said Deni would be coming."

Chloe's jaw dropped and she stared beseechingly at Deni. Deni looked just as confused and stunned as he felt. Because Deni looked so tired, his first thought was to go to her and wrap his arm around her, kiss her forehead, and ask her what had gone so wrong. His second thought was to pour her a glass of wine, take her hand, and ask her what had gone so wrong.

Chloe was oblivious to his distraction.

"But she *has* to come!" his daughter pleaded. "She's the only one who knows how to make s'mores! You even said you've never even heard of them before."

Deni smiled and he rolled his eyes in her direction. "Chloe, I said we'd talk about it later."

"At dinner?" she asked. "Dinner is later." She turned to Deni. "You're eating dinner with us tonight, right? You're not going to..."

Sebastian saw her chin wobble slightly and he couldn't help it. "Of course Deni is joining us for dinner. Why wouldn't she?"

Chloe dropped her head onto Sebastian's shoulder and he felt his heart ache. Even Sebastian realized that he was completely wrapped around her tiny finger. Controlling her manipulations when she got older was going to be a challenge, he thought.

Turning to Deni, he was just about to say something to her, willing to offer her more money if she'd agree to dine with them. But Deni was already there, stepping in and laying a hand on Chloe's back. "Of course I want to eat dinner with you! Where else would I eat?" Her nose squinched up and even Sebastian wanted to laugh. "And I would be delighted to go camping with you!" She leaned forward slightly, looking into Chloe's grey eyes. "Could you imagine your daddy trying to make s'mores alone?" In a conspiratorial whisper, she continued, "I doubt he even knows how to make a camp fire."

The girl giggled, lifting her head back up, and Deni smiled. Sebastian relaxed, then Deni stepped back. For the first time today, he saw her. Really saw her. She was wearing a pencil skirt that hugged her hips and legs, with high heels that caused his mind to go blank for several moments. The sweater was loose, but in his mind, he was picturing her stepping out of the pool and his mind wandered back to the too-brief glimpse of her lush, full breasts.

His mouth watered. Abruptly he remembered that Chloe was there, watching them and he quickly hid his lust behind a bland expression.

"I believe that dinner is ready," he announced. Turning to Deni, he said, "We'll wait until you're ready, of course."

She beamed and his mind blanked again. From a smile? Hell, he was getting damn irritated by his pathetic lack of self-discipline. A woman's smile should not be enough to turn him on, he told himself resolutely.

"I'm starving so, if dinner is ready, then let's head on into the dining room."

She moved ahead of them and it took Sebastian several moments to remember to walk. The only reason he'd forgotten was because Deni walked towards the dining room and he got a good look at her backside in that tight skirt. It was incredible! He'd seen her butt last night and it had been wet and beautiful. But he'd convinced himself last night that he'd exaggerated its beauty.

Obviously, he was lying to himself.

Her butt wasn't just nice, it was magnificent!

"Daddy?" Chloe prompted.

He ripped his eyes away from Deni's rear. "Right," he replied with self-deprecating humor. "Dinner."

Sebastian carried Chloe into the family dining room where his house-keeper had set one end of the table. Deni waited until Chloe was settled before sitting down in her chair.

She watched the father and daughter together, noticing that Chloe had a bit more sparkle in her eyes today. Personally, Deni had spent her day trying to catch up. Her lack of sleep last night had prevented her from being on top of her game during the day and she'd messed up on several questions asked of her during her meeting.

But Chloe looked as if she'd had a wonderful day and Deni wondered how much of that was because her dad had taken the afternoon off to be with her. Had they spent the afternoon playing? Swimming? What had they done? She wanted to ask, but felt it wasn't her place. She felt more like a guest here at this house, despite...or maybe because of... her interlude at the pool last night with the fabulously aloof, irritatingly confusing, and shockingly muscular man sitting at the head of the stupidly large dining room table.

Deciding that a change of topic was needed, she straightened her shoulders, pasted on a smile, and asked, "So what's this about a camping trip?"

The housekeeper appeared, setting a plate down in front of each of them. Chloe looked down at her plate and frowned. "I don't like this," she announced.

Sebastian already had a knife and fork in his hand. "What don't you like?"

She sighed. "None of it."

"Sounds like we can't go camping then," he announced with a shake of his head. Chloe looked up from her plate, her mouth hanging open in horror. "Why?" she whispered, dismay in her pretty, grey eyes.

He sliced some of the chicken with a rich, creamy sauce on his own plate. "If you think this is gross, then you're really not going to like s'mores."

"I'm not?"

Deni wondered where he was going with this. Not like s'mores? Was he nuts? Everyone liked s'mores! And even if they didn't like parts of the delicious camping dessert, they were still fun to make.

He shook his head slowly. "I looked them up online today. They look disgusting."

Chloe pulled her gaze away from her father and looked at Deni, silently asking for confirmation. Deni suddenly understood where Sebastian was going and played along.

"He's right," she said, stabbing a crisp green bean. "S'mores look pretty gross. But they are good. It takes a strong person to try something that looks so...gooey."

Her eyes widened with horror. "I thought they were made from marshmallows and chocolate."

"They are. And graham crackers. But when you smoosh them all together and the marshmallow comes out the sides, melting the chocolate, it gets all ooey and gooey," she sighed and shook her head. "Well, it doesn't look appealing. It looks horrible and you probably wouldn't like it." Deni bowed her head, trying not to laugh at the devastated look in Chloe's eyes. "It takes a very brave person to try things that may not initially look like they would taste good." And to emphasize her point, Deni took a bite of the creamy chicken. It really was amazingly good. Deni suspected that the dark flakes of cracked pepper were what Chloe thought she might not like. Although, the sweet child ate the salmon and asparagus last night. Was it a good or a bad thing that she was asserting herself and her preferences today?

"I will! I promise!"

Sebastian picked up the conversation from there. "If you're going to be adventurous, then you're going to have to learn to eat lots of things that you might not think you like."

Deni stepped in again. "I remember making pancakes over an open fire too. And biscuits. The outsides were black because some of the fire's ashes got into the pan. But once we tasted them, they were the best biscuits we'd ever made! We put real butter and lots of honey on them and forgot to make the eggs because the biscuits were so good."

Deni could practically see the gears turning as Chloe thought about it. Then she looked down at her plate. She picked up her fork and took a bite of the uncovered chicken, her meal already cut up into child-sized bites. The next bite, she dipped into the peppery, cream sauce. There was a tentative taste, then a bigger one. Finally, Chloe chewed and swallowed. By the way her shoulders pulled back and her spine straightened, Deni could tell Chloe was proud of herself. A moment later, Chloe nodded seriously. "Okay, I'll eat it."

Sebastian looked over at Deni and they shared a conspiratorial smile. She felt a small flare of...something hit her with that connection, but she dismissed it. She wasn't going to have another sleepless night. No way!

The rest of the meal was just as delightful as the previous one and Deni struggled to keep her eyes away from Sebastian. The more he interacted with his daughter, the more intense the longing became. This was crazy! She refused to be attracted to the man.

When the housekeeper removed the last of the dinner plates, Chloe pushed up onto her knees, eagerly looking to her father. "So can we go this weekend?"

Deni thought that was a great idea. Being out in the fresh air, away from computers and phones, roughing it in the outdoors, away from makeup and razors and anything that might make Sebastian look good, she'd get over this fascination with the man.

"I'm up for it," Deni announced, shocking even herself.

Sebastian sighed, resigned to his fate by the dual attack. "I'll clear my schedule."

Chapter 12

Deni stepped out of her old SUV, staring at the doorway of Sebastian's house where a stream of servants were packing camping gear in the shiny, new SUV in the circular driveway.

With dread, she realized what was happening, even though she'd hoped all week that Chloe would forget. "What's going on?" she asked, shifting the heavy tote filled with work she needed to finish over the weekend.

Sebastian returned her stare, but his grey eyes looked...resigned? Irritated? Deni wasn't exactly sure. She was only just starting to understand his various, subtle looks. She could imagine a lifetime of trying to interpret his expressions...then stopped that thought it in its tracks. Sebastian needed a temporary wife. Nothing more. She'd be gone as soon as he had full custody of Chloe permanently.

"Camping? Remember our conversation over dinner the other night?"

Deni gulped. "Um...no?" Even though she'd been hoping Chloe would have forgotten. She remembered clearly, but since the topic hadn't come up again, Deni had sort of pushed it out of her mind.

Sebastian moved closer. "Well, Chloe woke up this morning, excited about the weekend, demanding that I look up the weather report. She then declared that this weekend was the perfect time to delve into the world of camping and s'mores."

She heard the derision in his voice and covered her mouth, trying to smother a burst of laughter.

"I see," she finally replied, afraid to look up at him for fear that he would know that she was trying not to laugh. At him? Yeah, a bit. But also with him. Chloe might be only five, but she was a force of nature. A bit like her father, Deni thought.

Straightening her shoulders, she lowered her hand, and smiled at Sebastian. "I think that a camping trip is an excellent idea! When do you two leave?"

He moved even closer and Deni thought she should be intimidated by his height and the muscles she knew were underneath that expensive outdoor shirt.

"Oh no, my dear wife. This is not a trip for only Chloe and me. This is a *family* trip."

Deni knew where this was going and her mouth fell open. "She wants...!"

He nodded, his grey eyes sparkling with...anger? Mischief? "You're coming with us."

Okay, now Deni was intimidated. Camping was...well, it was intimate! Gone was her plan to see him looking rough so that she could get over her fascination with the man!

It was one thing for Deni to pretend that she was Sebastian's wife when they were alone in a monstrously huge house with servants, guest wings, and separate bedrooms. It was a whole different ball game to sleep in a tent with one's 'husband'. There wasn't a great deal of room in a tent. No matter how big of a tent, it was still a tent and Deni doubted that there would be walls that could separate her from Sebastian in a tent. Sure, some of the fancy tents had those fabric "walls", but...her eyes skimmed over his broad shoulders, his flat stomach and... then back up to his mouth. Fabric walls wouldn't be enough. He'd hear her at night! She dreamed about this man every night, about him making love to her, showing her what she'd been missing all these years!

"Um...I don't think that's a good idea, Sebastian," she sighed even as she thought about other problems with camping. Showers? Bathrooms? Cooking? No, surely cooking wouldn't be a problem. They'd go out to eat. Deni couldn't imagine Sebastian cooking a meal over a camp fire. The idea seemed so ludicrous, she almost started laughing again.

Sebastian lowered his head. "I agree with you," he murmured almost menacingly. "But *you* told Chloe about all the fun you had camping with your parents when you were a kid. Now she wants that too. Sleeping in a tent, ghost stories and...she ate the chicken the other night. Now she feels she deserves s'mores. I taunted her with the s'mores, but honestly, I'm not entirely sure what they are. I've heard other people talk about them, but...we are apparently having s'mores."

Deni backed up slightly. "S'mores are roasted marshmallows in a chocolate and graham cracker sandwich."

She fought down a smile when he rolled his eyes. Deni suspected that Sebastian wasn't in a humorous mood. He looked almost angry, although she couldn't figure out why.

"I'm sorry, but you're about to spend a wonderful weekend with an adorable little girl having new experiences. Why are you so angry?"

She watched in fascination as his jaw clenched. "Because I have work to do. I don't want to spend the weekend out in the dirt. And I don't want my daughter to get filthy either!"

Deni cringed. "But...kids are *supposed* to get dirty, Sebastian," she pointed out, trying to soothe his temper.

No eye rolling this time. He looked at her with those pale, grey eyes and her heart thudded in a crazy manner. "No. They're not!"

Huh? He thought kids should be clean? All the time? Oh, he was going to hate camping! "Of course they are! That's how they learn! They get out into the woods and explore, their minds open up and they see things in a different way."

He leaned even closer. "That's what I pay tutors to do, Deni."

She gulped, not sure what to say. "So...why are you going camping?"

He shook his head slightly. "You don't understand, Deni. *We* are going camping. *You and I* are taking Chloe camping this weekend. *We* are going to show her that this isn't a good idea so that *we* won't ever have to do it again."

If he hadn't been so close and she wasn't able to smell his aftershave or his masculine scent or whatever it was that made him smell so delicious, Deni might have laughed. His horror at the idea of camping, not to mention, his assertion that Chloe would learn better through a tutor, was hilarious and ridiculous. Also, she was aware that he'd bought a slew of new equipment in order to take his daughter on a trip that he didn't want to do. Despite his fury, his actions were painfully sweet, she thought.

"I can't go camping this weekend, Sebastian," she told him firmly.

"You're going," he told her, but thankfully, he pulled back.

Stubbornly, she resisted. "I have work to do."

He chuckled. "Deni, as owner of the bank at which you work, I can safely guarantee that you don't need to work this weekend."

"I do!" she argued. "I have to get the data reports done for my boss. She has a meeting on Monday morning."

"I will be sitting in on that meeting Monday morning, Deni. And the data reports you've been assigned to compile should take you about thirty minutes. So no, you're not missing our little expedition for work excuses."

She shook her head. "No, I can't! I don't know how to do these reports! I have to figure..." she stopped when one of his dark eyebrows went up. "What?"

"No more arguing. Sunday afternoon when we get back, I'll show you how to do the damn reports." He glanced at his watch. "Go pack up a bag. We leave as soon as Chloe comes back with her nanny from the museum in about twenty minutes."

Deni struggled, frantically trying to come up with another reason why she couldn't go. The excuse of the reports was valid and she had planned on spending the day at the bank office tomorrow to figure them out. But if he was going to help her, and she had no doubt that he could probably pull them together in a fraction of the time it might take her, then that excuse was out the window.

"Um..."

"No, Deni. You told Chloe about camping. Now she wants to try it. As a family. Since you got us into this mess, you're going to get us out of it. You're coming with us. Go pack." With that, he crossed his arms over his chest and glared at her.

She couldn't help it when her eyes dropped to his shoulders. The soft material pulled against his body and she could see the indentation where his shoulders pressed. Deni's mouth watered and she stepped back, trying to control the urge to run her fingers along his shoulder.

"Right."

She turned around, determined to get out of spending an entire weekend with Sebastian. Then something brilliant occurred to her. Spinning around, she looked back at him. "I could take Chloe camping, Sebastian. That way, you could stay here and work or relax. I promise that I'll take very good care of Chloe."

That annoyingly sexy eyebrow lifted. "You're really not suggesting that I ignore my daughter's request for a *family* weekend, are you?" he asked softly.

She heard the steel in his voice. "No," she replied, appropriately admonished. The urge to mess up his hair struck her. She didn't act on it, knowing that he wouldn't be as amused as she would be.

Instead, she turned on her heel and walked into the zombie house, as she was now referring to this house that had no soul. She almost stomped up to her bedroom, irritated that he'd won the argument. Next time, she would have to think faster.

When she walked into her bedroom, she was startled to find Martha, one of the upstairs maids, already there.

"Good evening, Ms. Stenson," she said with a bright smile. "I took the liberty of packing for you. I have four outfits ready."

Deni was stunned at the invasion of privacy but...was this just something that servants did? She wasn't sure.

Martha must have read Deni's mind because she smiled as she picked up the duffle bag. "I've already packed up Mr. Hugh's case and Chloe's, so this should be the last item needed for your weekend."

Well, that answered Deni's question! What in the world had the housekeeper packed for a weekend of camping? And should she just accept whatever was in that duffel bag?

With a sigh, Deni realized that she didn't have much of a choice. Walking over to her drawers, she pulled out a well-worn pair of jeans. Discarding the dress she'd worn to work that day, she slipped on the jeans and pulled on a tee shirt, then tied her hair up on top of her head with a band. Grabbing sneakers and a sweatshirt, she was ready to go.

Having servants seemed pretty nice right about now. Deni couldn't deny that having someone to pack and do the thinking and planning was a nice change. It certainly allowed one to head out of town on a whim, making life much easier.

If one could get past the issue of someone going through her underwear and deciding which she would wear! That was just...weird.

Slipping into her sneakers, she hurried back downstairs. Apparently, Chloe was already home if the sounds of happy yelling was any indication. Suddenly, the beautiful girl burst through the front door, her eyes lit up with excitement.

"Did you hear, Deni? We're going camping! And we're going to have s'mores! And sleep in a tent! We're really going to do it!" she shrieked, jumping up and down with her excitement.

Chloe's excitement was contagious and Deni quickly changed her thinking. So what if the three of them would sleep in a tent together? At night, Deni would be in her own sleeping bag and he'd be in his. They could have Chloe sleep in between them so there was no reason to be worried.

Deni's smile widened, really getting into the idea of camping over the weekend now that she'd worked through the scary issues. "I heard! This is going to be so fun!"

"Go change into casual clothes, Chloe," Sebastian ordered.

The girl turned and rushed over to her father, hugging his legs before giggling as she raced up the stairs. Her nanny was already at the top of the stairs, ready to help her change into clothing more appropriate for the outdoors.

Deni stood awkwardly in the massive foyer with the gloriously hideous chandelier and watched Sebastian's expression. He was looking at her as if he wanted to yell at her, but she didn't know why. She'd only changed clothes. Had he been this furious with her before?

Sebastian stared at Deni's jeans. Or more specifically, her legs encased in the soft denim that hugged her legs faithfully. The jeans looked like she'd worn them for years, the knees a lighter color than the rest. And they rode low on her hips, giving him a small peek at her stomach whenever she moved. He was already irritated that he'd be spending the weekend in close proximity with the woman who was making his body ache with a need he hadn't experienced since he was a teenager. And even then, he didn't remember the need being this sharp. This powerful!

But seeing Deni in jeans was doing it for him. And that tee shirt? Damn! The material clung to her breasts, hugging the mouth-watering mounds like a second skin. Had she chosen that tight tee shirt on purpose? Was she trying to torture him because he wouldn't let her out of coming with them this weekend?

He looked into her eyes and still wasn't sure. Her innocent gaze back at him was just too...perfect. Too innocent. And he didn't trust women.

But Sebastian didn't have a chance to figure what her look meant because Chloe was racing down the stairs, barreling towards him. He went down on one knee and caught her as she threw herself into his arms. When she wrapped her skinny arms around his neck, he closed his eyes, savoring the feeling of his daughter hugging him. There had been too many days and nights when Chloe had been with Meredith and he hadn't had this feeling. His daughter's hugs were about as close to heaven as a person could get, he thought. Not to mention, her excitement over the camping trip had completely banished the reserved, quiet child and his enthusiastic Chloe was back in full force!

When Chloe pulled back, Sebastian opened his eyes and...looked directly into Deni's startled gaze. He didn't know why, but he wanted to pull her into his arms as well. She looked like...

He stopped, wondering what the hell he was thinking. Turning away, he lowered Chloe to the floor. "Ready to head out into the woods?" he asked.

"Yes!" she replied, once again bouncing up and down.

Sebastian turned to Deni. "Are you ready?"

Deni laughed and he wanted to smile with her.

"I guess I am," she replied.

"Then let's go!"

Sebastian helped Chloe into her booster seat and Deni stepped into the passenger seat.

When Sebastian came around the car and stepped into the driver's seat, Deni looked at him curiously. "Is this car new? Or have you just not used it recently?"

He pressed the button that started the engine. "I bought it this afternoon and had it delivered here so the staff could pack the supplies that were also delivered."

She stared at his profile as he examined the dashboard, obviously for the first time.

"Let me get this straight," she began, fastening her seatbelt. "Chloe wanted to go camping this weekend, so you went out and bought a new SUV?"

He nodded absently as he maneuvered down the long driveway. He pressed a few buttons and the air conditioning system immediately blew cold air. A few more buttons, and the GPS map popped up on the dashboard monitor.

"Most of that statement is true," he pulled out of the driveway, merging into the traffic.

"What part wasn't?"

"The part about me going out and getting it."

Deni waited another heartbeat, waiting for him to clarify. "So, you *didn't* go out and get it?"

"My assistant arranged for it to be delivered. I told her what I wanted and she called the dealership."

She continued to stare at him, not sure she understood. "You mean, you needed an SUV for the weekend, for the next three days, and so you had your assistant buy one and deliver it to you. Sight unseen."

"That's what happened." He glanced at her. "Why do you sound so horrified?"

She huffed a bit. "Normal people don't have the money to just go out and buy a vehicle, especially a Land Rover, simply because they need a bigger car for a weekend trip!" she explained.

He shrugged. "It will be used for more than just a weekend. I don't like the car you're driving. It isn't safe. So, this will be your car."

Even more astounding. "You're loaning me a car because you don't think my current vehicle is safe enough?" she asked. Turning around, she noticed that Chloe was playing with her stuffed animals, having some sort of conversation with them. She was oblivious to their conversation, which was probably a good thing.

"I'm not loaning you a car, Deni. I'm *giving* it to you."

That didn't make any more sense. "You're giving me a car." She made a statement because it still didn't compute.

"Yes." He glanced at her again. "Why is this so hard for you to comprehend? It's just a car."

She shook her head, unaware that her mouth was slightly open in shock. "No, Sebastian. A Land Rover isn't *just* a car. It's a seventy-five thousand dollar vehicle with so many bells and whistles I can't even imagine needing in my life."

"I'll show you how to use the 'bells and whistles'," he explained. "Once you know how to use them, you'll enjoy them."

She laughed, then settled more comfortably into the passenger seat. "I'm not taking this SUV, Sebastian."

"Of course you are. The car you're driving is about to break down."

"Probably, but this is too much. It's too expensive."

Patiently, but with his eyes on the heavy traffic in front of him, he replied, "You're not buying it. I'm giving it to you."

She crossed her arms over her chest. "I'm not taking it."

He chuckled and the sound made her shiver. "You will," he promised. "Just consider it part of our bargain."

"No. Our bargain was you keeping my father from having his knee caps broken when he couldn't repay the loan shark. You don't owe me anything else." With that, she began fiddling with the radio. As far as she was concerned, the conversation was over. "Where are we going for this wonderful camping trip, by the way?"

"About an hour west of here," he told her. "We're going to camp in the Shenandoah National Park."

"Nice views," she murmured. Then grinned. "But if we're going to the place I think you're talking about, I hope you have lots of quarters."

He was staring ahead at the road, but her words pulled his eyes away and he glanced at her once again. "Quarters?" he asked, needing more information.

"Yep. The showers only take quarters. I think you get about two minutes of hot water for twenty-five cents."

He stared at her as if she'd said that pink elephants would be at the campsite. Deni laughed, delighted with his appalled reaction.

Sebastian shook his head and turned his attention back to the road. "You're making that up."

She laughed and snuggled down into the soft leather. "Nope. It's true."

In response, he merged over into the next lane and pressed a button on the steering wheel. There was a ringing sound and then his assistant answered. "Yes, Mr. Hughes?"

"I'm going to need several rolls of quarters brought down to me, in about," he looked at the clock on the dashboard, "five minutes. Can you make sure someone is ready with them when I pull up?"

"Of course, Mr. Hughes," she answered quickly, but Deni could hear the curiosity in her voice. "I'll have them ready for you immediately."

"Thank you," he said and pressed the button again.

"Neat trick," Deni said softly, still smiling. "It would have been hilarious to get out there and discover that though."

"Not in my mind," he grumbled and made a U turn, heading towards the bank instead of the highway.

"Depends on your perspective," she replied with a saucy grin.

Conversation halted for several moments while he maneuvered through heavy traffic on West Chestnut Avenue. When he turned right, the bank was right there and, immediately, someone came out of the building with what looked to be a bulky bank bag.

Her eyes widened as the barely-twenty-something young man rushed out. "Oh my, you are really planning on long showers, aren't you?"

But she rolled down her window and took the bag. Sure enough, it was much heavier than she'd anticipated.

"Thank you so much," she told the eager-to-impress gentleman.

"My pleasure, Ms. Hughes," and he backed up a step. Sebastian pulled back into traffic and turned around. Now they were heading towards the highway again.

"Any other tips you'd like to share with the class?" he asked, relaxing back as he merged onto the highway. Since it was early enough on a Friday, the traffic wasn't too bad. In another hour or so, this would be bumper to bumper traffic. An hour later, the highway would be a parking lot.

Deni smiled at his caustic tone, thinking about all of the wonderful adventures he was about to experience. "Oh, there are lots of tips and tricks to camping. But I don't think I can list them all right now. Camping is sort of a figure-it-out-as-you-go type of experience."

He sighed and moved over to the next lane. "Lovely," he grumbled, causing Deni to smile. But she turned towards the window so he wouldn't see her amused expression.

An hour and a half later, they pulled into the campsite that Sebastian's assistant had reserved for them. Since it wasn't a holiday weekend, the campground was only about half full, which meant that they didn't have neighbors on either side of them.

"We're here!" Chloe exclaimed from the backseat. She'd been extremely patient during the entire trip, only asking for a bathroom break once and snacks a couple of times. Thankfully, Chloe's nanny had anticipated such issues and had packed a bag filled with nutritious snack items, all of them cut up for small fingers and mouths.

"Yes, we're here," Sebastian agreed. He turned to Deni. "What do we do first?" he asked.

Deni noticed the less than enthusiastic expression on his handsome features, but suppressed another chuckle. "The first thing we need to do is put up the tent. That way, if it rains, we have a place to shelter besides the car."

Sebastian frowned at the sky, as if he were ordering the clouds to disappear.

"Tent it is," he decided, stepping out of the SUV to help Chloe out of her booster seat. They moved to the back of the truck, and stared at the wall of "stuff". It was packed right to the roof of the SUV and Deni had no idea where the tent might be.

Deni made an executive decision. "I think we need to unload everything so I know what is here."

Deni looked at Sebastian, then he looked at Chloe in his arms. She shrugged as if to say, "She's the boss," and then they both turned to Deni.

"What does a tent look like?" he asked.

Deni couldn't stop the laughter this time. "Once it is set up, a tent looks like a house, but with zippered doors and windows. It's made of waterproof fabric and the windows are screens to keep the bugs outside. Since someone went out and bought everything this afternoon," she said, looking at the supplies, "I'm guessing that the tent will still be in a box. But let's just get everything out and we'll figure it out, okay?"

He looked doubtful, but he walked over to the wooden picnic table and set Chloe down on the bench-seat. "Stay there, honey."

Chloe sat, but she craned her neck, trying to see everything.

For the next fifteen minutes, Deni and Sebastian unpacked the SUV. There was a sleeping tent as well as a dining tent, which was really luxurious. "Wow! When I was a kid, I was always jealous of the families that had these," she commented as she set the mostly screen-mesh tent next to the sleeping tent, ignoring the incredulous look from Sebastian.

"This is cool!" she exclaimed when she pulled out a plastic ball and twisted the sides, which made the ball open up into two halves.

"What is it?"

Deni grinned, looking at both of them. "Let me read the instructions before I tell you. If I'm wrong, I don't want either of you to be disappointed."

Deni burst out laughing as they gave her identical blank looks.

"Seriously! This will be awesome! Let's set up the tent," she announced now that everything was out of the truck, including three coolers filled with foods that looked to be completely prepped with recipes taped to the outside of the bags. She was super impressed with the organization of Debbie. This would save them hours of work!

She looked up from examining the contents of the coolers to find both Sebastian and Chloe looking at her expectantly.

"Right. Neither of you know how to set up the tent," she muttered and stood up. "No problem. Okay, the first thing is to find the flattest part of your camp sight."

"Why?" Chloe asked, jumping off the bench and walking over to the enormous stack of supplies.

Deni grinned. "Because you don't want to roll out of your bed," she teased.

It took the three of them about an hour to set up the tent, mostly because Chloe wanted to "help", which meant she wanted to stand inside the tent while Sebastian and Deni staked the floor and pushed through the poles. It took a bit more maneuvering to avoid poking the child, especially when she kept getting directly in line with the poles.

But she was giggling and having a good time. With each giggle, Deni would glance at Sebastian to catch the slight smile to his handsome features. It was almost as if this was the first time he'd heard her laugh, which made Deni doubly determined to get Chloe to laugh more often. Children were special and should laugh as often as possible. Too soon, life would take away that joy, she thought.

"It looks great!" Chloe announced jumping up and down inside the tent. "We did great!"

Deni laughed since Chloe had been more of a hindrance than a help, but she nodded her agreement. "Yep. It looks pretty good! Now the dining tent, right?"

She and Sebastian moved the picnic table a bit further away from the tent, with Chloe "lifting" one of the benches. The dining tent was easier to erect since Sebastian understood the process this time through. And also because he put Chloe on his shoulders this time, having her help him slide the tent poles through the top instead of letting her get inside.

"Okay, that's done."

"I'm hungry!" Chloe announced, lip quivering slightly.

Deni looked up at the girl who had her hands wrapped around her father's forehead. She looked about ready to have a meltdown and Deni gulped. Since she wasn't a full time mom, she hadn't anticipated this.

Thankfully, Sebastian carried Chloe over to the coolers stuffed with food. "How about if we figure out what is for dinner, and get some snacks for everyone? Can you help me pick out what we'll have for dinner?"

Deni brought the brand new cooking stove into the dining tent and figured out how to set that up while Sebastian lifted the heavy coolers, carrying them into the dining tent. He looked so magnificent carrying them in that she didn't have the heart to tell him that the coolers had wheels and could be rolled. Unfortunately, he figured it out with the third one and frowned at her.

Deni shrugged and turned away, pretending to figure out what they were going to have for dinner.

"You knew that those things could roll, didn't you?"

Deni jumped since his voice was right beside her ear. She didn't move, feeling the heat of him too close to her back. Instead, she swiveled her head slightly, looking up at him. "Um...yes, well, you seemed to enjoy it and I didn't want to ruin it for you."

He pulled back and she breathed a sigh of relief as she grabbed one of the big plastic bags for dinner and moved over to the cook stove.

"Anyone know where a pan is?"

Chloe jumped up. "I know!' she announced energetically and raced out of the dining tent. A moment later, she dragged a black pan that Deni recognized as cast iron. They were heavy pans!

"I'll help you," Deni called.

But Chloe shook her head. "I've got it. I'm just like my daddy! We can lift heavy things, right Daddy?" she said, looking up at Sebastian with awe in her eyes.

"Exactly!" he replied. "No weak little girls, right?" he teased, lifting both child and pan into his arms, carrying Chloe over to Deni to deliver the pan.

Deni beamed as she took the pan, but was painfully self-conscious and careful not to look up into Sebastian's eyes. Why was she acting like this? It was ridiculous to be so aware of a man who only thought of her as an employee. And if the truth were known, she felt like an employee. Okay, so she *was* an employee! Except during those times when he was close by, or when she watched him carrying something. Those muscles should be illegal, she mentally grumbled.

Deni dumped several ingredients into the pan and turned up the heat on the camping stove. Because the pan was cast iron, it would take a few moments for the pan to heat up, but once it did, the pan would be perfect for either the stove or a campfire.

"That smells incredible," Sebastian commented and Deni jumped, she hadn't realized he was so close. Immediately, he put his hands onto her hips, holding her steady. "Careful," he soothed, one of his thumbs rubbing her side. "No accidents on the first night of our adventure."

Deni couldn't stop trembling. She felt her toes curl with the heat and need that his hands ignited inside of her.

"Dinner is going to burn," he said, his voice low and incredibly close to her ear.

She looked down, startled to see smoke coming up from the cast iron pan. "No!" she gasped and turned down the heat, grabbing one of the wooden spoons to stir. Crisis averted, dinner saved. But Deni glared at the man who moved away from her with a knowing chuckle.

Sebastian sat down at the picnic table and lifted Chloe up onto his lap. He was satisfied now that he had proof that he wasn't the only one suffering a case of lust. His hands could still feel the trembling in Deni's small waist when he'd touched her. And she smelled so damn good! All soft and feminine and interesting. Those jeans were enticing! He'd been thinking about her all week, irritated that she'd stayed away from their nightly dinners after Monday night. Granted, she'd told him before each meal that she would be gone...but that didn't diminish his irritation at not seeing her at the end of each day. Over the past few weeks, he'd come to...not just expect, but anticipate her smiles and saucy responses.

If he went to bed clenching his teeth as sexual frustration gnawed at his gut for the elusive woman, he wanted to know that she was suffering right along with him.

Why that was important, he wasn't sure. It wasn't as if he was going to do anything about their attraction. He had to focus on Chloe, on ensuring that she was safe from his ex-wife's clutches. Besides, he'd never truly marry again. And Deni seemed like the kind of woman who would need marriage and the forever kind of promises that he no longer believed in. A marriage such as what they were enduring wasn't the same type of commitment.

Such a pity, he thought as he only half listened to Chloe explain the agenda for the rest of the night. He was more focused on watching Deni, on the soft pink that touched her cheeks when their eyes met while she continued to stir.

Her hands were trembling as she stirred and she kept sneaking glances at him. He wondered what she was thinking about. He'd wager big money that she was nervous about sleeping in that tent tonight. When he'd agreed to Chloe's request for an experimental camping trip, he hadn't considered that the three of them would be sleeping in one big tent. Together. No separation other than sleeping bags.

What the hell had he gotten himself into?!

"You okay?" Chloe asked, putting her small hands on his cheeks. Sebastian realized that he'd just sighed heavily and forced a smile. "I'm fine, sweetie," he said and kissed her chubby cheek.

"Dinner is ready," Deni announced. Both of them looked over at her as she lifted the skillet off of the stove and looked around. "Any idea where plates are?" she asked.

Plates. They hadn't found them yet.

"I'm hungry," Chloe whined.

Sebastian looked around, not sure where plates might be. His house-keeper had done an excellent job of thinking of various needs for a camping trip, but she apparently forgot plates.

"We can just put it in the middle of the table and take what we want," Deni announced.

He eyed her like she'd suggested stabbing someone. "Excuse me?" he asked.

"Yeah," she announced, grabbing a piece of cardboard to protect the tablecloth from the hot skillet. She set the skillet down in the center of the table and handed out plastic forks. "Here. Dig in."

Chloe and Sebastian looked at each other. This wasn't the way he ate and it bothered him. But Deni seemed to think it was a perfectly acceptable way to eat dinner. He shrugged and his adorable daughter mimicked his gesture perfectly.

"It's sliced chicken in brown rice with peas, corn and lots of cheese," Deni explained, stabbing a piece of chicken with her fork and taking a bite. "There's also some sort of cream sauce, although I have no idea what it is. But it's amazing."

Sebastian stabbed a piece of chicken and Chloe scooped up a bit of the cheesy rice. They then tasted the messy meal and...

"I like it!" Chloe whispered guiltily, as if enjoying the non-traditional meal and serving methods was naughty. She even giggled, covering her mouth with her hand.

Deni laughed as well and Sebastian stared at her, wondering why he liked the sound so much. He understood when it came from Chloe. The child was much too serious. She needed to laugh more often. But why did he also enjoy hearing the sound from Deni?

Sebastian tried to let it go, not wanting to examine his feelings. The woman was beautiful, especially with her hair pulled up on top of her head like it was at the moment. He liked that she was here. Not many women of his acquaintance would indulge a five year old's desire to experience nature like this. A thought occurred to him...he should have contacted Oz, Jayce, or Ryker. His friends were ex-special forces and lived only thirty minutes outside of Louisville. They could have given him tips on camping. In fact, those three probably would have dropped whatever they'd planned for the weekend and come with them. They all adored Chloe, including Oz and Jayce's sister, Carly.

The fact that he hadn't even thought to contact those men demon-strated exactly how far gone he was. Deni distracted him and not just at night when he lay awake in his bed, his body hard and aching for her, wondering what she was doing. He knew exactly which room she slept in each night and it was the furthest one from him. Was that on purpose? Or did she not know where he slept at night?

A giggle from Chloe snapped him back to the present and he realized that he'd been staring at Deni this whole time while she told stories of past camping trips.

"It's starting to get dark," he commented, thinking that the dim light made Deni look softer. And much more appealing. Since she was already too appealing, the light was something that needed to change. Quickly. "I'll get the lantern. I saw it with the other stuff."

Deni looked up, noticing the lack of sunlight for the first time. "We should probably get the sleeping bags ready. And blow up the air mattresses."

"Sleeping bags!" Chloe clapped, starting that bouncing thing again. "I get to sleep in a bag tonight?"

"Yes, honey," he told her. "You definitely get to sleep in a bag."

"What color is mine, Daddy?"

Sebastian stood up and carried Chloe over to the stack of stuff sitting beside the SUV. "Which one would you like?" He picked up the three rolls. "There's red, blue, and green."

"Red!" she exclaimed, clapping again. The child loved making sounds, he thought.

"Red is yours." He grabbed the three air mattresses, still in their boxes, and carried them into the tent. "Okay, how does this work?" he asked.

Deni stepped into the tent as well. "There should be a lever on the air mattresses that blows them up automatically." She picked up one of the boxes. "At least, I hope that's how they work. Otherwise, we might be sleeping on the ground."

"I don't think so," Sebastian grumbled imperiously. "I don't sleep on the ground."

She laughed and, in the dim recesses of the tent, the sound was no longer nice. It made his body spring to life. Then she did something even worse than laughing. She bent down, the soft denim tightening over her gorgeous butt and he swallowed a groan. Turning away, he focused on getting Chloe's sleeping bag ready for the night. Thankfully, the air mattress inflated perfectly and it was an easy thing to spread Chloe's sleeping bag out. She wanted to go to sleep immediately.

"How about if we brush our teeth and get ready for bed first?" Sebastian offered.

"Okay!" She launched herself into his arms.

He chuckled, thinking that the camping trip was certainly good for her spontaneity. She'd never been this exuberantly affectionate before. As a father, he loved her enthusiasm.

"I'll get her toiletries bag," Deni offered.

Sebastian stood there with Chloe in his arms as he watched Deni duck through the tent opening. Damn, she had a great butt! That denim was...

"Daddy?" Chloe interrupted his thought and he looked at his daughter. She stared back at him and he knew that he'd been caught.

"Just making sure she doesn't trip, honey," he explained quickly. Thankfully, she seemed to accept his explanation and he ducked down, exiting the tent as well.

Deni was rummaging through the equipment, trying to store it back into the trunk for the night. She glanced up at him when he approached. "I found Chloe's bag, but I can't find my own."

He reached into the back of the truck and pulled out a black duffel. "I think this one is mine," he opened it up. But when he saw pink lace, he quickly zipped it closed again. "Nope, this one is yours." He handed it over to her and looked away, ignoring Chloe's giggle.

"Daddy, can I have pretty underwear like that?" she asked.

"No!" he growled, setting her down next to the car. Reaching further into the back, he found another duffel bag, just like the first, and unzipped it. Bingo. Damn it, why had his housekeeper packed identical bags?

With a sigh, he accepted that the housekeeper had probably just gone out and bought everything quickly, trying to be efficient. He'd given her two days' notice. He was only grumbling now because he knew what the other bag contained. And he couldn't help imagining what Deni's mighty fine derriere would look like in that pink lace underwear. Going even further, he wondered if she had a matching bra. He certainly hoped so!

"Daddy?" Chloe yawned.

He looked over at his daughter, pushing thoughts of his too-sexy "wife" out of his mind. And what she was wearing underneath her clothes. And what she would look like without the sexy underwear. Or what she would look like when he....

Another yawn from Chloe brought his attention back to the present. Forcing images of Deni underneath him, legs wrapped around his waist with that look in her eyes that told him she was close to a...nope. Those were not productive thoughts. Not in any way.

"Yep. Let's hit the wash house," he said swinging Chloe into his arms. "Are you ready?" he asked Deni.

She was standing there clutching what he suspected was her cosmetics bag close to her stomach, looking up at him with an odd expression. He couldn't see her clearly in the low light, but she looked...softer. Sexier.

Headier, he realized.

"Yes. I'm ready." She handed him a flashlight and he turned it on, wishing he could shine it at her face so he could figure out what was going on in her head.

"Right," he sighed and turned towards the building he hoped was the bathhouse.

Fifteen minutes later, he'd helped Chloe brush her teeth, washed her face, and changed her into her pajamas. Since he employed a nanny, Sebastian had never done any of this with his daughter before. Chloe had always appeared ready for bed whenever she'd stayed with him. So this was a unique experience and one he had to ask Chloe to guide him through. She was patient as she taught him how to get her ready for bed.

Stepping out of the bathhouse, he looked around for Deni and spotted her leaning against a tree. She smiled when he approached and the expression landed like a gut punch.

"You two look all cleaned up!" she said, smiling and gently tickling Chloe's knee.

"Daddy didn't know how to help me but I showed him what to do."

Deni looked up at Sebastian's eyes, startled. "Didn't know how?"

"Nanny," was all he said by way of explanation.

"Ah!"

As they walked back to their campsite, Deni watched the two, almost jealous of the connection that was clearly forming between father and daughter. They looked and acted so similar, and yet, they were completely different. Chloe rested her head against his shoulder, looking like she was almost asleep already.

He carefully tucked her into the sleeping bag, kissing her cheek gently. Deni's heart wrenched at the sight of the love this hard, intimidating man had for his child. It was both sweet and confusing. Confusing because it was so unexpected.

When he backed out and came into the dining tent where she was cleaning up from dinner, Deni wasn't sure what to say.

"All tucked in?" she asked.

He sat down and nodded. "She's completely out."

"What's on the agenda for tomorrow?"

He thought about it for a moment. "There's a trail that leads up to a waterfall. Would you come with us on a short hike?"

She grinned, thinking the idea was wonderful. "Do we get to swim?"

He chuckled. "I can't imagine that swimming would be a good idea."

"Especially not with a five year old who probably hasn't swum in anything other than a chlorinated pool."

"Not true," he argued. "She's been to the Caribbean many times. I've taken her in the ocean."

"Nice!" Deni replied. "I've never been to..." she stopped and looked over at him, his hard features made even more menacing with the harsh light from the lantern. "I wasn't asking for you to bring me. I'll get to the Caribbean on my own."

His eyes were mysterious in the dim light. "I know you weren't asking, Deni. We're just talking."

"Exactly," she said, then looked down, wrapping up the food and storing it all carefully in the coolers. "We need to put heavy items on these coolers so the bears don't get into them."

"Bears?"

She looked at him over her shoulder. "We're in the forest, Sebastian. Of course there are bears."

"Not here in the campgrounds, I would imagine."

She smiled at his disdain for the wildlife that dared to interfere with his weekend. "Yes, in the campgrounds. Although raccoons would be more likely. Even so, putting something heavy on top of them would make it more difficult for the critters to get into the food."

"Raccoons," he replied, sounding resigned and irritated. "Raccoons and bears. Any other issues you might want to warn me about?"

She laughed softly, aware that sounds traveled further at night for some reason. "I can't think of any off the top of my head, but as soon as I think of them, I'll let you know."

"Great." He stood up and lifted several boxes, placing them on top of the coolers. "Is that sufficient?"

"Probably," she teased.

"Probably?"

She shrugged, wondering about this new tone. "We'll know in the morning."

"Outstanding." And then he was closer. "The perils of camping are interesting to discover as I go along."

She didn't dare turn around, thinking he was too close. "Yes, it's a lot of fun," she told him, her voice sounding a bit breathless.

He sat back down on the wooden picnic table that wasn't made for comfort. "So...what do we do now?" he asked.

She smiled, but bowed her head. "It's nighttime, Sebastian. We talk. We play cards. We read, go to sleep. Drink wine or beer or...whatever is quiet."

He sighed and she wanted to laugh. "I don't play cards," he told her with what sounded like revulsion. "Unless it's poker."

Deni perked up, thinking about the lessons she and her friends had been working on over the past several months. "I can play poker!" she exclaimed, sitting up straighter on the bench.

He looked at her, the dim light from the lantern making his features appear almost sinister. "Really?" His doubts were clear.

Tilting her head slightly, unconsciously challenging him, she nodded. "Yeah. I know how to play poker and I'm pretty good."

He chuckled. "Unfortunately, we don't have any poker chips. But perhaps tomorrow night."

She nodded. "Fine! We'll drive back to town and, if they don't have poker chips, we'll use something else. You're going to regret doubting me, Sebastian!"

His grey eyes widened and Deni stiffened. "What?"

Sebastian looked across the picnic table at Deni, startled by how much he liked hearing his name spoken in her gentle voice. "Nothing," he replied, thinking that if he admitted how much he liked hearing her say his name, she'd...well, he wasn't sure what Deni might do. She'd think he was crazy but...damn! His name sounded sexy the way she said it!

"Nothing," he snapped, sounding harsher than he'd intended. "Perhaps we should turn in as well. I understand that the sun rises early and I doubt that there's a great deal of protection from the morning sun in a tent."

They got up and he allowed her to enter first, once again, gritting his teeth as he watched her bend down, her adorable derriere just within arm's reach.

"Good night," she whispered and stepped over to her sleeping bag, climbing in.

Looking around, he realized that his adorable, sweet daughter had gotten up after they'd tucked her in. Deni's sleeping bag and air mattress were right next to his, with Chloe's on the other side of him.

Cute, but...damn it! Now he'd be closer to Deni than he'd thought.

Sighing, he slipped into the sleeping bag, rolling onto his back as he stared up at the ceiling. It was going to be a hellishly long night, he thought.

Chapter 13

Deni stared at the wall of the tent, listening to the squirrels or chipmunks rummaging through the dry leaves. She had no idea what time it was, probably in the early hours of the morning. But she couldn't sleep. Not with Sebastian so close. She could feel him breathing, sense the heat of his body.

And the hard ground.

Her air mattress was completely useless. It had deflated as some point. Since she was lying on the hard earth with only the sleeping bag to cushion her body, she could feel every rock and pebble. She'd be bruised tomorrow from all of these stupid rocks. She knew better. Clear off the site before setting up one's tent. Now she was paying the price.

"What's wrong?" Sebastian's deep voice asked.

Deni jumped, surprised to hear his voice.

"Nothing!" she whispered before she could think better of it. She should have pretended to be asleep. "I'm fine."

"You're not fine," he argued. "Your air mattress deflated."

Mentally, she groaned. "I'm fine. The sleeping bag is enough."

A moment later, strong arms lifted her, sleeping bag and all, onto his cushy air mattress. Instantly, her body rejoiced. But then Deni felt his arm go around her waist as he pulled her closer.

"Relax," he soothed, his voice too close to her ear.

Deni was more tense now than she had been before. Just because she wasn't on the rocks anymore, that didn't mean she was more comfortable. Besides, Sebastian's chest and arms were rock hard as well. The two layers of sleeping bag material between their bodies didn't stop her from being hyper aware of every inch of him. Or of his warm breath drifting into her hair.

This was Sebastian! He wasn't supposed to be this hot! He was cold and heartless. He was a master manipulator!

So, if all of those things were true, why did she feel like this about him?

Because she'd seen another side of him. She'd seen the man who sacrificed his own comfort to make his daughter smile. The man who teased his daughter to get her to try new foods. The man who spent hours playing with his little girl in the pool each night, talking with her, teaching her to swim and encouraging her in sweet, gentle ways. Not to mention, he was here, camping in a tent. That was something Deni suspected Sebastian Hughes, banker extraordinaire, never would have consented to do in a million years. He looked like the kind of man hoteliers fawned over when he stepped through the doors of a resort. He demanded the best and wouldn't settle for anything less.

And yet, he was sleeping on an air mattress in a newly purchased tent. He'd eaten out of a communal skillet. All for the love of his daughter.

And now, he was sharing his air mattress. Which she suspected was a huge sacrifice for the man because he was a big, tall guy! Was he on the edge of his side of the mattress? She couldn't tell and was afraid to reach out to determine how far from the edge she was. She didn't want to move, afraid that if she did, Sebastian would know that she was still awake. He might wonder why and she couldn't explain that she wanted to roll over and run her hands all over his muscles and...a lot of other things!

So, she remained as still as possible. Not even breathing, for fear that any sort of movement might wake him up.

"You're not relaxing," he muttered sleepily into her ear.

"I know," she sighed, then deflated. "I'm sorry. I'm just not used to sleeping with someone so close to me."

"Good to know," he teased. "But regardless, you're going to be useless tomorrow if you don't get some sleep."

She knew that was true. Deni didn't cope well during the day when she had trouble sleeping. But nor could she figure out how to relax enough to fall asleep.

"Tell me what's on your mind."

She laughed, shaking her head but then stopped doing that because she'd bumped his chin. "I'm just...nervous about being so close."

"I promise I won't bite."

She laughed again, but wasn't sure that his assurance helped. Especially when she immediately wondered where he would bite her. And if she'd like it!

Oh good grief. This was ridiculous!

"Tell me about the reports you have to create on Sunday," he encouraged.

She started listing the various reports her boss had assigned to her for the Monday morning meeting. By the time she was five minutes into the litany, she was yawning. And a few minutes after that, she was sound asleep.

Sebastian curled his arm around Deni's now-sleeping body, wondering how long it had been since she'd been with a man. She'd said she wasn't used to sleeping with a man, so he assumed it had been a while.

Damn, she felt good, he thought. He'd been lying here imagining her naked like this. And then his body had reacted too strongly with the images that flashed through his mind. Thankfully, the sleeping bags hid the evidence of his lustful thoughts – but he couldn't seem to relax and get to sleep himself, even though he'd managed to get her to sleep.

She felt incredibly good. Not nearly as thin as his last mistress, but not fat either. She was soft and curvy and fit against his body perfectly. Or she would if these damn sleeping bags didn't hinder his body from curling around her. Hell, he couldn't even press his leg between hers. They were adequately cocooned and it pissed him off!

Tomorrow was going to be a long day!

Chapter 14

Tents were awful at blocking out the morning sunshine, Deni thought. Pressing her eyes closed, she tried hard to snuggle deeper into the sleep that seemed to be escaping her hold. There were some strange sounds, but she didn't recognize them so she tried to ignore them. She didn't want to wake up. Waking up meant she'd lose this incredible warm place and she wanted to savor that warmth. Her pillow was a bit hard though and she shifted, trying to find a softer place. But everywhere she moved, her head was on a hard surface.

A giggle broke through her hazy mind.

When her eyes fluttered open, she found Chloe sitting at the end of their air mattress, a hand covering her mouth as she giggled in the early morning chill.

"You're sleeping on Daddy!" she whispered.

Deni lifted her head and looked around. Sure enough, she was almost lying on top of the man. No wonder her head was on something hard! It was his chest!

"Good grief," she muttered, and slid off him onto the air mattress. The movement jostled him, which woke him up. When he lifted his head, his grey eyes took in Chloe's laughing expression and Deni's horrified one. She must look a fright with her hair going every which way, she thought, sitting up and trying to run her fingers through her hair while not falling off the edge of the stupid air mattress.

Deni shifted quickly, scooting off the air mattress completely. The hard ground was just as painful as she remembered it. She flinched, squirming away from the sharp rocks that her sleeping bag couldn't protect her from.

"Are you okay?" Sebastian asked, sitting up and revealing more of his glorious chest.

"I'm fine," she mumbled, trying to pull her eyes away. But his chest... and...well, no sane woman would look away, she told herself.

"Deni, that isn't helping," he warned her.

She pulled her eyes upwards to find his grey eyes laughing at her. He glanced down pointedly and she gasped when she realized that he was fully erect, pretty obvious even through the thick sleeping bag. Had he been like that before?

Deni had no idea but she scrambled out of the sleeping bag hurriedly. "Let's hit the bathhouse and brush our teeth, Chloe," she said, slipping her feet into her painfully cold sneakers without socks because she was flustered.

Chloe jumped off the air mattress to her own sleeping area and found her shoes, stuffing her feet into them and standing up, looking proud of herself as she pushed her tangled, blond hair out of her eyes.

"Ready!" she announced.

Deni smiled, extending her hand even as she heard Sebastian's low, rumbly laughter behind her. She grabbed sweatshirts for both herself and Chloe, and headed out. The air was chilly and, once they were outside, she helped Chloe put on the sweatshirt, donned her own, and then hurriedly grabbed their toiletries, heading towards the bathrooms. It was still relatively early so not many people were up and about yet. Thankfully, they were able to wash their face and brush their teeth without a huge crowd. In an hour or two, there would be a long line of people trying to shower and get ready for their day. That was the downside to camping. The upside was that in that same amount of time, the air would be filled with the smells of everyone making their breakfasts. Bacon and sausage, eggs and pancakes were staples at most campgrounds.

There were the brave souls who camped out in the wild, but Deni hadn't ever ventured that far off the beaten trails. She might enjoy camping, but she also needed her creature comforts such as a private, flushing toilet and showers. She couldn't even imagine how to go to the bathroom without a toilet!

During the whole walk, Chloe chattered on about anything and everything. Her enthusiasm and energy were exactly what Deni needed that morning to banish the cobwebs and images of Sebastian's chest from her mind.

Okay, that was a lie. Sebastian's chest wasn't leaving her thoughts. That image was permanently plastered in her mind and she wasn't letting that one go. Nope! She was going to enjoy that image. Replay it over and over again.

When they returned from the bath house, Sebastian was gone. She suspected that he'd gathered his toiletries and was doing the same thing, and she was grateful for the reprieve.

"Okay, let's figure out what Martha prepared for our breakfast, okay?" she suggested to Chloe.

"Yeah!" she agreed, excitedly running over to the coolers, waiting until Deni took the heavy bins down that had protected the food from the wild animals last night.

Deni was concentrating on what to make for breakfast when she felt the air change. Sebastian was back. A moment later, Chloe squealed as she was lifted into Sebastian's arms as he hugged her, making her giggle with delight.

"Daddy! Your face is scruffy!"

Deni looked over her shoulder at Sebastian. Sure enough, he hadn't shaved. Wow! She'd thought he looked good with a bare chest. But looking at him now, all rough and rugged...her heart began pounding. Hard! He literally took her breath away.

What was it about a man who could make a little girl squeal with delight while looking like he'd just carved out a mountain?

It wasn't fair, she thought as she grabbed what looked like pre-whisked eggs in a plastic container and a bag of cheese. As soon as the cheese and eggs were out of the way, Deni discovered another with bag filled with chopped peppers and onions. With a sigh, she picked up the skillet, surprised to find that it was clean. Her eyes glanced over at Sebastian and that beating in her chest became a pounding. He could make Chloe laugh, carve out a mountain, AND clean a pan?

Damn!

Flipping the dials on the stove, she started heating the pan while she looked for oil, trying to keep her eyes away from Sebastian and Chloe as they moved in and out of the tent. Obviously, they were cleaning things up and she wanted to rush over to him and...do wicked things to him!

She'd read a funny sign once that said there was nothing sexier than a man in a well-tailored suit. Deni would have to disagree. There was nothing sexier than a rugged man who could also clean the dishes. A man who could clean without having to be told!

The oil in the skillet started sizzling and she focused on cooking breakfast. Dumping the onions and peppers into the hot oil, she stirred while they sizzled. She didn't look up. She didn't peer over at the man and his daughter as they searched through the boxes, coming up with the missing paper plates.

It didn't take long to pour the eggs into the vegetables and add the cheese. The cook stove was top of the line and produced a good amount of heat.

"Breakfast is ready," she announced, taking the skillet off the heat. She looked over at the picnic table to find that Sebastian and Chloe had discovered fruit and cut it up, with Chloe creating a pretty design with the pieces. "That looks beautiful!"

Chloe grinned, preening under the praise. "Daddy helped."

Deni looked over at the man with a scruffy jaw. "I bet he was a great helper in making the fruit flowers."

He rolled his eyes. "I only cut it up. I didn't suggest the flowers."

"That's what they all say," she taunted as she spooned scrambled eggs onto three plates.

She almost dropped the skillet when she felt his hands on her waist. "Are you maligning my masculinity?" he asked, his voice low and dangerously sexy. She could felt his lips incredibly close to the shell of her ear.

"Trust me, Sebastian. Your masculinity was never in question," she admitted, hoping he couldn't read between the lines.

"Good," he replied, his hand slipping lower, as did his voice. "Because that would force me to validate my masculinity."

A moment later, his hands and his heat were gone and Deni was left trembling as she watched him move over to the table, taking an apple slice. He bit into the juicy fruit as he locked eyes with her, his eyes conveying that yes, she'd understood his message perfectly.

The skillet hit the stove with a loud thunk. "Sorry," she muttered as she sat down at the picnic table.

"This is delicious," Sebastian said. "Thanks."

Chloe looked at the eggs with her nose squinched up. "I don't like it."

Deni looked down, her fork halted in mid-air. "Vegetables!" she gasped. "Oh, sorry!"

Sebastian looked at her curiously.

Deni thought quickly. Chloe obviously was uneasy about the green peppers and onions in her eggs. Deni should have thought about that before making the batch of eggs. She hadn't cooked for a little girl until last night so she'd forgotten children's aversion to vegetables.

"They aren't vegetables," Deni announced, giving Sebastian a meaningful look. "They are worms."

Chloe looked doubtfully at Deni, then back down at her eggs. "Worms?"

"Yep! And they are delicious!" Deni announced.

Sebastian's eyes sparkled at her with a strange, undefinable light.

Chloe picked up her fork and stabbed a bite of the green peppers. "I didn't know that worms were green."

"Only the icky ones are green," Deni took another bite.

Chloe was fascinated. Taking a tentative bite, she chewed, looking at Deni, then at her father. "They don't taste like worms," she announced.

"You've never eaten worms before, have you?"

"No," Chloe admitted, taking another bite.

"Then how do you know what worms taste like?"

Chloe took another bite, bigger this time. "I like them!" she finally announced, and dug into the eggs with gusto.

Deni grinned across the table at Sebastian. The shock as he lifted his eyes from his daughter's quickly vanishing food to Deni made her heart thud. And then the stunned look turned to admiration and that thudding just about caused her heart to break a rib.

But he silently ate his eggs, accepting that his daughter enjoyed eating worms.

They finished breakfast with a great deal of fanfare since Chloe decided that she and Deni needed to dance. Obviously, Chloe had remembered Deni's stories about her parents dancing in the kitchen. Sebastian declined, and took the skillet over to the campsite sinks to clean.

When Sebastian came back with a clean skillet, Deni and Chloe were inventing silly ballet moves to the Sleeping Beauty soundtrack. Deni had just spotted Sebastian when he pulled her into his arms and twirled her around, then dipped her low. Chloe laughed, bouncing up and down as she clapped.

"My turn!" she announced.

Sebastian lifted Chloe into his arms and swung her around and around, letting her back arch against his arms so that her hair swung out. The girl had such complete confidence in her father's strength that she let her hands fly over her head as she laughed, delighted with the new game.

Deni pulled out her phone and took several pictures of them dancing. Several other campers were walking along the road, either going to or coming from the bath house and they all stopped to watch. There were dips and lunges, twirls and hops until, finally, Sebastian turned his daughter upside down and danced with her like that before ending the song with a dramatic dip, just as he'd done to Deni.

The crowd clapped and cheered. Chloe was laughing so hard, she could barely stand, but she managed to grab her father's hand and encouraged him to bow for the crowd.

Deni watched it all, taking more pictures as she watched.

When they turned and walked back to the picnic table, Deni stared. If anyone had told her a week ago that Sebastian Hughes would dance in the woods with a giggling little girl, she would have scoffed, not believing it. But Deni flipped through the pictures, laughing.

"I wanna see!" Chloe called, racing over to Deni and tilting her head way back.

Deni went down on one knee to show Chloe the pictures. They flipped through them and Deni almost choked with emotion when Chloe's little arm creeped around Deni's neck as she leaned against her.

"Daddy looks very handsome," she whispered.

Deni and Chloe both looked up, spotting Sebastian coming around from the back of the Land Rover.

He stopped when he saw them staring at him. "What?" he demanded.

"Nothing," Deni replied, stuffing her phone back into her pocket. A moment later, Chloe giggled and Deni felt the small child's hand slip into her own. "Are we still going to hike up to the waterfall?" she asked.

Sebastian had no idea what was going on, but he suspected that it was better not to know. "Do you want to hike to a waterfall?" he asked of Chloe.

"Yes!" she exclaimed, bouncing excitedly. He chuckled, thinking that the bouncing seemed excessive, but it was a hell of a lot better than the sedate child he'd picked up from his ex-wife's house two weeks ago.

"Then we'd better get started!" he announced, tossing reusable water bottles into the back seat of the SUV. The water was fresh from the water station and he added some snacks as well.

Ten minutes later, after packing a backpack with snacks and "locking up" the tent, they were driving towards the trailhead that would take them to the waterfalls. The parking lot was filling up with cars but they found a good parking spot.

As they walked through the woods, Chloe chatting about everything and bouncing on her toes, Sebastian walked next to Deni, his hands in his pockets. "Thank you for breakfast. For everything," he said, and meant it. "Chloe has really come out of her shell."

"I got some great pictures of you two dancing this morning," she told him.

Chloe heard that and turned around. "Will you teach me how to take pictures?" she asked.

"Sure!" Deni replied. "I'm not very good, but I'll show you what I know. I took a class in college and loved it."

"Will I go to college?" she asked her father.

"Absolutely!"

For the next two miles, they walked and talked. Deni learned more about Sebastian as he patiently answered Chloe's steady flood of questions. Deni took more pictures of them as Sebastian helped Chloe over the rocks or cuddled her when she stumbled on an "invisible" tree root, causing a minor tearful moment.

"Can I take some?" Chloe asked, distracted by the enticement of photography.

"Sure," Deni handed the little girl her phone. "Here's what you do," Deni explained how to focus and press the dot on the screen that would capture an image.

"Will you go over to that rock so I can try?" Chloe asked eagerly.

Deni settled on the rock, she hated having her picture taken but would do it for Chloe. She could always delete the pictures later, she told herself.

Sebastian crouched behind Chloe and helped her through the initial picture taking process. "Will you go over to sit behind Deni?" Chloe asked. "Just like you were this morning."

Deni looked at Sebastian, thinking of their position this morning. Instantly, her heart went into overdrive, blood thrumming through her veins. It was one thing to accidentally wake up in a man's arms. Would it be just as intense if they did the touching intentionally?

She was reminded that Chloe was only five and nothing could happen during the photoshoot. But that was before Sebastian moved to sit behind Deni on the rock. When they couldn't seem to get comfortable, he shifted so that his legs were on either side of Deni's hips. He wrapped his arms around Deni's waist, pulling her close.

While Chloe clicked happily away, Sebastian tightened his arms around Deni. "Why do you tense up when I'm close?" he asked.

Deni lowered her head, choosing her words carefully, trying to find an answer that wouldn't reveal how she felt towards this man.

"I guess I'm just... out of practice," she finally admitted.

"I guess you need more practice, then," he teased and Deni felt his words all the way down to her toes. Was that intentional? Was he trying to make her crazy by teasing her like this?

A moment later, she felt his thumb shift against her stomach and she gasped, turning her head to look at him over her shoulder. Deni was startled to find the same heat echoed in his eyes. Was she imagining it? Was he just...she couldn't know.

The heated look in his eyes was so intense, she wanted to turn around and kiss him, feel his lips touching hers. She wanted to wrap her arms around his neck and press her body against his. She wanted...him.

He'd gotten under her skin in ways that she didn't quite understand. He melted her heart and heated her body. The scruff on his face and his love for his daughter just...everything about him made her want him in the most primal way.

"Deni," he groaned, his arms tightening around her waist.

"Kiss her, Daddy!" Chloe directed imperiously. Chloe's command pulled her out of the hazy lust that had wrapped itself around both of them.

Realizing what was happening, Deni shook herself mentally. "Okay, I think that's enough pictures," Deni announced pulling out of his arms abruptly. She reached for her phone, but Chloe pulled it back. "Can I take more pictures of the trees and leaves?"

Deni shrugged, relieved to have some space between herself and Sebastian. "Sure. Why not?"

And Chloe was off, heading towards the nearest tree to take pictures of bark.

"Are you okay?" Sebastian asked, close by her side.

She sighed and glanced up at him. He kept an eye on Chloe, ensuring that she didn't go too far, but turned back to her and she saw it again. The same heat that still bubbled inside of her was reflected in his no longer icy grey eyes. Just now, they were molten silver, watching her carefully.

"I'm fine," she whispered.

"Yes. You are. Very much so."

And then he turned and headed down the pathway after Chloe. His words caused her heart to skip a beat and she stared after him, stunned and fighting the heat in her veins that was just...silliness.

He'd made it a few steps before he turned back to her, lifting those dark eyebrows. "Coming?" he asked.

"Yes! Definitely." She jerked back into motion, relieved to focus on not tripping and falling on the roots that studded the hiking trail.

They made it to the waterfall in what must have been the slowest pace ever recorded for that trail. Mostly because Chloe wanted to take pictures of everything. There were several people already at the waterfall when they arrived, most in swimsuits and almost all of them teenagers or in their early twenties. Right below the waterfall was a small reservoir where the water pooled before toppling down the next set of rocks and several families dipped their toes into the water.

"Can I swim?" Chloe asked immediately.

"No, it's too cold for little girls," Sebastian told her. "But you can take off your shoes and socks and wade in the area where fuzzy rocks are."

Chloe didn't understand about fuzzy rocks but she was intrigued. Moments later, she had her shoes and socks off and was racing towards the water.

Deni was already there, sitting on a rock because she didn't want to get her feet wet. The water looked painfully cold. She was just in time to catch Chloe before she barreled into the water while Sebastian pulled off his hiking boots and socks. He'd just bent to roll up his pants when Chloe broke away. He called to her, but it was Deni who jumped off her perch and caught the small girl.

"Wait for your dad," Deni warned.

Chloe sighed in resignation. "He's so slow!" she groaned.

Sebastian heard her words and rolled his eyes, scooping up his daughter. "You didn't listen, honey. You have to listen to me."

"Sorry Daddy," she replied contritely as she looked wistfully out at the rocks. But as she looked down, her contrition turned to fascination as she noticed the rocks right by the water that were covered in moss. "They *are* fuzzy!" she exclaimed.

Deni climbed back up on the rock, snapping pictures of Sebastian holding Chloe's hands as she stepped carefully onto each rock. It looked like Chloe was asking her father questions, but with the roar of the waterfall, Deni couldn't hear their words. But she snapped several adorable pictures of the pair and laughed when Chloe began dancing in the water, splashing her father's jeans in the process – which caused him to lift her up into the air pretending to toss her away.

It was possibly the first time that she'd heard Sebastian laugh outright. And the sound was magical. The smile transformed his harsh features and...well, it melted Deni's heart just a little bit further.

Okay, a lot!

Chapter 15

"How about if you build a fire?" Deni suggested, pointing to Sebastian as they parked back to their campsite after the hike, "And you," she pointed to Chloe as they all stepped out of the Land Rover, "need to help him because I doubt he knows what to do. I'll get dinner started and then," Deni bent down low, whispering in Chloe's ear, "you can help me get ready for s'mores!"

Chloe's mouth formed an excited O. "Really?" she whispered back. "Really?"

"Yes," Deni laughed. "Tonight, we'll have a campfire and one of the main reasons to have a campfire is to roast marshmallows. And if you're going to roast them, we might as well make them into s'mores!"

Chloe turned serious, her blond eyebrows going low over her grey eyes as she tried to anticipate issues with this newest adventure. "Is it hard to roast a marshmallow?"

Deni feigned seriousness too. "Yes. It's very hard. You have to watch your marshmallow very carefully. Sometimes they roast too fast and sometimes, the coals aren't hot enough and they don't roast and a person is just sitting there, waiting and wondering and hoping that they can find a hot spot."

Chloe nodded, taking it all in. "But..."

"Don't worry," Deni promised, touching the child's cheek softly. "I'm an expert marshmallow roaster. My mom and dad taught me well and I will train you to be an expert too."

Deni's words seemed to allay Chloe's concerns and her face brightened. "Okay!" Chloe replied earnestly. A moment later, she was gone, off searching the woods near the campsite for kindling.

Deni stood up, watching Chloe for a moment. Then she felt Sebastian move closer. She felt his gaze on her and glanced over in his direction.

Sure enough, he was leaning against the Land Rover, his arms crossed over that magnificent chest as he watched her. Was that amusement in his grey eyes? Admiration?

A warm sensation melted over her as she took in his gaze. But it was too intense and she couldn't hold it for long. In the end, she broke contact and hurried into the dining tent, opening the coolers to figure out what Martha had prepared for their dinner. Deni lifted a foil covered object labeled "dinner". Carefully, she peered inside. Instantly, her mouth started watering.

"Oh wow!" she whispered, amazed at Martha's creativity. Or her internet search skills. Either way, dinner was going to be easy and delicious!

"What's in that?" Sebastian asked as he loaded the iron fire circle with logs, twigs, and other kindling in a triangle.

Distracted, Deni watched his hands, fascinated with the length of his fingers as well as the skill of his fire-making. "Where did you learn to build a fire?" she asked, staring at the perfectly organized campfire.

He looked at her as if to say, "You doubted me?", then turned back to finish building the fire. With a flick of the lighter, he got the twigs started and slowly fanned the fire until more twigs caught.

In a few minutes, he had the beginnings of a perfect campfire going. "Have faith," he teased.

She chuckled, shaking her head. "You looked it up, didn't you?"

His eyebrows lifted with a look of disdain that only a man of his elite status could pull off. "Whatever gave you that idea?"

Deni shrugged casually, although she didn't feel casual in any way. He was hot and grubby and that scruffy beard was doing things, dangerous things, to her libido! "The bank job. The tailored suits. The horror at the idea of camping. The thousand dollar shoes." She looked at him with raised eyebrows. "Should I continue?"

"Only if you want your cute butt spanked," he growled and reached towards her menacingly. Deni laughed, and quickly danced out of range. With an arch look, she glanced back over her shoulder. "Since you're such a brilliant camper, I'm putting you in charge of dinner." And she tossed the foil wrapped loaf to him. He caught it, but winced at it as if it were coal. "*This* is dinner?" he asked.

She nodded. "Yep. Figure it out."

He stood up and wrapped his arms around her waist. "I think you're getting a bit *too* sassy, Ms. Hughes," he teased.

Deni laughed, trying to wiggle out of his embrace, but he didn't allow it. "I'm not!" she gasped, but she was laughing so hard, it was difficult to catch her breath.

"Explain what I'm supposed to do with this," he demanded, brandishing the foil-wrapped blob.

She laughed so hard she gasped for breath, but his hands tightened around her waist and all laughter died. She felt him...everywhere! He was so hard and so amazingly strong, it was difficult to remember what they were talking about. For a long moment, she just stared up at him. Her eyes dropped to his lips and...she was lost. So lost!

"Are you guys gonna kiss?"

Deni heard Chloe's question and jerked out of Sebastian's arms. Looking down, she realized that Chloe was standing right next to them, her arms filled with kindling, a curious and almost hopeful look in her shining grey eyes.

"No, honey. We weren't kissing."

"You were *gonna*," she insisted, dumping her sticks right next to the stack of firewood her father had bought at the camp store.

"Um...s'mores!" Deni announced. "Your dad is going to figure out dinner while we get the stuff for s'mores!"

Chloe was easily distracted, but Deni peeked at Sebastian, saw the smirk in his eyes, and cringed. His gaze told her their interlude was not over. Postponed, perhaps, but not over.

She shivered, thinking how nice it would be to be kissed by that man. He wasn't...she shouldn't...but...she did! Oh, goodness, she did!

"I found them!" Chloe announced.

Chloe held up a package of giant marshmallows. Not a giant bag of marshmallows, although the bag was huge. Nope, these marshmallows were literally four times the size of a normal marshmallow.

"Good grief!" Deni breathed as she took the bag from Chloe. "These are mutant marshmallows!" she laughed.

"Will they work?" Chloe asked, eyes widening with concern.

Deni laughed. "We'll have fun trying, right?"

Relieved, Chloe threw her hands up in the air. "Yes!" Chloe exclaimed.

"Dinner is ready," Sebastian announced.

Deni stood up, looking out through the mesh and, once again, their eyes clashed. Deni suddenly remembered their sleeping situation. Her lack of an air mattress...this was going to be an interesting night, she thought.

"Right," she whispered and grabbed plates and napkins as well as the leftover fruit from breakfast.

The foil wrapped meal was actually a sliced loaf of crusty bread with slices of pre-cooked steak, cheese, and a special sauce that Deni didn't recognize, but it smelled amazing as it heated over the campfire. Sebastian used tongs to pull it off the fire and they sat in their camp chairs, pulling off slices of the delicious meal, devouring almost all of it.

By the time they'd finished dinner the sun had set. They moved their chairs closer to the heat of the fire to roast their marshmallows and laughed uproariously as they jousted for the best spots in the lower level coals. Deni explained that one didn't want to put the marshmallow too close because it would catch fire. But not too far away, because the marshmallow would just melt and not become crusty on the outside.

When they finally roasted the perfect marshmallow, she showed them how to put it between the chocolate and graham crackers. Chloe was too impatient to try her first bite of a s'more, so her chocolate wasn't completely melted. But she fell in love anyway, her pretty eyes wide as saucers as she bit into the messy, gooey treat.

Deni watched with painful awareness as Chloe roasted another marshmallow. Sebastian was right next to her and every few moments, his leg would brush hers. The first time, she looked at him, wondering if he'd done it on purpose. But she couldn't see his eyes clearly in the dim glow of the fire. So the next time it happened, she kept her eyes on Chloe. But somehow, he seemed to move closer. He was roasting yet another marshmallow, this one probably for Chloe because she kept lighting hers on fire. But now he was so close, his shoulder would occasionally bump her arm. Or his leg would press against hers.

Deni knew she should shift away. Becoming involved in any way with Sebastian Hughes would be a mistake. He was rightfully focused on Chloe and Deni should just move away.

But she didn't. Instead, Deni enjoyed the brief contact.

And then the contact wasn't brief any longer. He leaned forward to help Chloe slide the marshmallow between the chocolate and crackers, but when he sat back up, he didn't move away.

She peered at him, trying to determine what was going on. But just as had happened before, as soon as she looked at him, Deni couldn't look away. His gaze was hypnotizing.

Swallowing hard, she tried to look away. But somehow, she felt herself shift closer. And closer. Chloe was talking about something, dancing and hiking, while Deni and Sebastian leaned into each other. So close, she could feel his breath on her lips.

And then he kissed her. His lips were hotter than the fire and she turned slightly, wanting to deepen the kiss. It was wonderful and shocking and the touch made her head spin. Deni wasn't aware of lifting her hand up, cupping his jaw. But suddenly, her fingers were exploring the hard lines of his jaw, feeling the rough beard and moving lower.

Over and over, he slanted his mouth over hers, kissing her until she opened her mouth. And then she gasped when she felt his tongue moving into her mouth. It was explosive and she wanted to climb up onto his lap and find out more, touch him more. Find all the places on his body that might make him feel the way she felt.

The giggling was her first clue that they had an audience. Pulling away ever so slightly, Deni turned at the same time Sebastian did. Chloe was standing in front of the fire with a huge grin on her adorable face as she watched them kiss. Her marshmallow was slowing burning to a crisp, but the little darling hadn't even noticed.

Sebastian snatched the marshmallow-torch out of her hands and tossed the gooey mess into the fire.

"Time for bed," he announced and scooped Chloe up into his arms. "Bath house first, I think. A good brushing of those teeth is in order."

Deni stayed by the fire while they walked up to the bath house, trying to get herself back under control. Looking around, she noticed that it was much later than she'd thought. Goodness, it was close to ten o'clock! Chloe's normal bedtime was eight thirty! They'd been so absorbed in making dessert, playing games, and being silly...and kissing...that she hadn't noticed the passing of time. Of course, Chloe was probably hyped up on sugar, which is why she'd had so much energy well beyond her normal bed time.

Chapter 16

Deni watched Sebastian carry Chloe into the tent. He gave her a gentle kiss on the forehead, then backed out of the tent. As soon as Sebastian laid her down, tucking her into the sleeping bag, the little girl was out, her head lolling to the side as she sank into exhausted oblivion.

From the light of the fire, Deni could see the intent in his eyes as he approached and she tensed, painfully aware of the man. Gone was the father and in its place was the man and all of his intensity, but it was different now. Purposeful.

He straddled the log so that he faced her and they stared into one another's eyes, tension building, heat rising, and not from the fire.

When he reached for her, she twisted her body, needing the kiss, his touch, and anything else he could give her.

She felt his lips, hard and firm as he pulled her closer. Deni knew that this was exactly where she wanted to be and wrapped her arms around his neck, opening her mouth to his kiss. He tasted wonderful! Minty and fresh and so male that she needed more, tilting her head slightly to deepen the kiss. In response, she felt his hands on her back, moving lower to cup her bottom and lift her higher. She was somehow straddling the log with her legs over his, her core pressing against the very large, very intriguing erection. Shifting against him, she moaned as she found exactly the right spot.

"Deni!" he growled, but his hands clenched around her bottom, pressing her against him as he kissed her over and over again. By the time he lifted his mouth away, they were both panting.

"We can't finish this," he groaned. "Chloe is only a few feet away."

She pulled away from him, laying her head on his shoulder as she felt his hands sliding up and down her back. "I know. No privacy," she whispered, wishing he would kiss her again. But kissing was dangerous because it led to wanting more. And they couldn't have more. Not right now.

He looked down at her, his eyes burning with desire. "Can you wait until tomorrow when we're home?"

She thought about that for a long moment, unaware of her teeth biting her lip. "I think so," she said, but she didn't sound convinced. And her body shifted again, drawing a groan from deep inside of him.

"Don't move, Deni," he ordered, his hands tightening on her bottom. "Not even an inch."

She stilled, but it took all of her effort. "Okay. I think I'm okay now."

He laughed, lowering his head so that he could nibble along her neck. "I don't think I am."

She chuckled, but tilted her head back. "We have to stop," even as she gasped with the incredible sensation of his teeth against a spot just under her ear. "Do that again!" He did and she shivered.

Sebastian pulled his head away with a groan. "Deni, we have to stop. Otherwise..."

"We're in a tent," she finished for him. Tents. Small children. Lusting after one's "husband". The combination seemed wrong somehow.

He went very still as they stared at each other, the implications of what their night would be like flowing between them.

"Hell!"

She laughed but pulled away. "We can get through this."

"I'm not so sure about that," he replied but they both stood up. "I'll bank the fire. You go ahead into the tent and get into your sleeping bag. Make sure that you're fully clothed."

She wanted to ask him what would happen if she *wasn't* clothed, but figured that might lead to answers that were better left unanswered. So she moved into the dining tent to ensure the food was properly stored away and safe from curious creatures, and ducked into the tent. For a long moment, she stared at the air mattress. It was a big one, queen sized at least, but Deni's was rolled up, shoved off to the side. Sebastian had spread her sleeping bag out next to his and it all looked so enticing! She should pull her sleeping bag off the air mattress and just sleep on the ground. It would be safer that way. And she'd probably get just as much sleep as if she were sleeping next to him.

Movement behind her spun her around. Sebastian stepped through the door and then he crouched down to zip the tent closed for the night. When he stood up, he pulled her into his arms. "We can get through this, Deni," he promised, his strong hands sliding up her back and into her hair, holding her gently to his chest.

She could hear his heart pounding, but it wasn't nearly as loud or as hard as her own. She was trembling with awareness and need. Her eyes moved to Chloe, sleeping innocently on the other side of the tent, mere inches from the big air mattress and Deni sighed.

He'd promised that they could finish this tomorrow night. Did she want that? Yes! Would she have the courage to go for it? Probably. That was a question for tomorrow, she decided.

"Let's go to bed."

Deni smiled at the husky tone. It soothed her slightly because it told her that he felt the same way she did. He took her hand and led her to the sleeping bags.

With a sigh of resignation, she slipped into the sleeping bag, trying to keep her eyes away from Sebastian as he did the same. She curled up on her side, facing away from him. But the moment he was settled, he reached out and pulled her close. Deni smiled, enjoying the feeling of being in his arms. She doubted she'd be able to sleep at all, but she liked it.

A moment later, she shifted so that her head rested against his shoulder and...she was out. Sound asleep.

Chapter 17

"Leave everything," Sebastian ordered as they stepped out of the Land Rover. They'd taken another hike this morning after a pancake breakfast, then broke down the tents and packed everything up. Chloe made them promise to have another camping trip "really soon!" and they both agreed.

The sweet darling was completely unaware of the tension that continued to increase throughout the morning. On the drive home, she sang songs and had her stuffed animals "dance" around her legs, happy in her own world. Which was good because Deni could barely breathe. Every time she glanced over at Sebastian, his gaze told her what would happen as soon as they were home. She smiled tightly, her body tensing with need, fear, hope, and desperation.

But now they were back at Sebastian's house and she felt the tension increase even further. They'd slept last night on that air mattress, but woken up again to a grinning Chloe standing at the end of their bed.

She glanced over at Sebastian, wondering if he would follow through on his promise to finish what they'd started last night. She still wanted him and knew his limitations. This was still just a temporary marriage, for the sake of Chloe. And if Deni could keep that in her mind, she could enjoy a hot and heated affair with a man she found more fascinating with every moment.

But as he walked into the house with Chloe, he didn't look her way, and her heart sank. Maybe it had just been the romance of the campfire. Last night had been dreamy and romantic. They'd both been tired after a long day of camping and hiking, their guards lowered. She looked down and tried to figure out what to do with her time now.

"How about a swim?" Sebastian suggested.

"Yes!" Chloe replied, doing her now-usual jumping up and down to reinforce her answer.

Deni stood off to the side of the foyer, thinking that his invitation had been just for Chloe. But when he looked at her, his eyebrows lifted in silent question.

He wanted her to join them? Really? Suddenly, her heart lifted and she felt...free! And happy! "Um...okay," she replied, thinking about the reports she still needed to get done for tomorrow.

He must have sensed her hesitation because he looked down at Chloe. "Hey, Deni and I need to get a little work done. Would you go find Jenny and tell her that you're back? We'll meet you in the pool in an hour, okay?"

Chloe grinned. "Jenny must have been lonely without me all weekend!" she exclaimed. "I can't wait to tell her about the s'mores!" She raced up the stairs, eager to tell her nanny about their weekend adventures.

Sebastian looked over at Deni. "You ready?"

She opened her mouth, not sure what he meant. "Umm....?"

"Let me show you how to run those reports." He moved closer to her, taking her hands in his. "I want to get any distractions out of the way, so that we can finish what we started last night."

"Yes," she whispered, feeling the tension morph from insecurity to white-hot desire.

He looked at her carefully as he said, "Unless you've changed your mind."

She shook her head, looking up into those silver eyes that had previously been so cold and sardonic. But now they promised...heaven! "Not even a little."

He hesitated. "Deni, I can only offer you sex. This won't change the future. I just don't have it in me to feel emotion any longer."

Deni's heart ached, but she understood. "Meredith really hurt you," she murmured, laying her hand gently over his heart. "I get that."

"And you're okay with where this is going? And where it won't go?"

She wished it were otherwise, but she'd take what he was offering and savor every moment. "I understand what you can give me."

He moved closer, cupping the back of her head. "Have no doubts about this, Deni. I don't want to hurt you. But I can't offer you flowers and forever. That part of me died a long time ago."

She nodded. "I understand. I'll protect myself."

He lowered his head, giving her a light kiss that she felt all the way to her toes.

All too quickly, he lifted his head, almost-smiling down at her. "Let's get those reports out of the way then. Once Chloe is asleep, I don't want any distractions."

Deni gulped, shocked by the heat in his eyes, the determination. It made her more than slightly wobbly, but she followed him into his office. She'd passed by this room a couple of times, but had only stepped inside it that one time he'd told her to meet him there. That day had only been a few weeks ago, but it seemed like forever. Looking around now, she felt as if the room was an extension of the man and stepping inside was an invasion of his privacy.

"Come on over here," he waved her to the other side of his desk. "I have this computer set up to connect directly to the bank system, so anything you need, we can download from here." She leaned over his desk when he sat down in the big, leather chair, but he put his hands on her hips and pulled her over so that she sat on his lap. "You can't see from over there," he explained, as his hand smoothed up her back, silently telling her that their position wasn't only because of the view.

She smiled, enjoying the fact that he wanted to touch her.

"Okay, so you have to pull up this data first..." and he explained how the reports worked, and went into detail about the data and how to analyze it. In less time than she would have thought possible, the reports were not just ready, but she'd written up the analysis of the data, going far beyond what she normally would have done.

"Thank you!" she said, turning to face him. He had his hands on her hips and they shifted, pulling her closer.

"You're welcome," he told her a moment before he kissed her. This kiss started off as just a gentle, teasing touch. But it soon burned hot. She opened her mouth at his urging and she moaned when his hands slipped under the material of her tee shirt. The almost-painful desire that had been banked last night along with the fire, flamed back to life, hotter than before, heating her up and making her almost dizzy with the need for more. So much more.

"Daddy!" Chloe called out.

Deni jerked out of his arms, jumping away from him as she turned to face the little girl who was standing in the doorway to Sebastian's office. Chloe's hand was over her mouth, giggling at what she'd just seen.

"I have your phone," Chloe announced, waving it to her. "I kept taking pictures on the drive home. I'm sorry."

Deni hurried over to the girl, noticing Jenny standing just outside the room, looking into one of the other rooms, demonstrating that the nanny had definitely seen Sebastian and Deni kissing. "That's fine. Thank you for returning it."

Her grey eyes glowed hopefully up at Deni. "You're coming swimming with us, right?" she asked.

Deni looked over at Sebastian who sat behind his desk, looking like a king with an amused smile on his handsome features. He knew exactly what she was thinking and Deni hoped that he was in the same state she was in.

"Please?" Chloe begged.

Deni couldn't resist her. "Of course I'll go swimming with you! Let me just bring these reports up to my room and get on my bathing suit. I'll join you in a few minutes."

Five minutes later, Deni walked into the indoor swimming pool, smiling when she found Sebastian and Chloe already in the pool. Chloe was jumping into the water, right into Sebastian's arms. Over and over again, she'd jump, then he'd help her swim over to the edge, and then do it all over again.

Deni understood that Sebastian was teaching her how to swim while she was enjoying spending time with her father. It was ingenious and she felt that melting sensation once more.

"Coming in?" Chloe asked, wiping water from her eyes as she looked at Deni.

"Absolutely!" she replied and tossed her towel onto one of the chaise loungers.

She pulled off her tee-shirt and dumped that too, then dove quickly into the water. It was a heated pool so there was no shock upon entering. Goodness, it felt divine to swim through the clear water, glorying in the sensation of floating and being free.

For the next hour, they swam and played. Chloe decided that she was going to throw the ball and they had to catch it. Then she climbed onto her father's back and rode through the water while he swam from one end of the pool to the other. She squealed with delight when Sebastian swam over to Deni, grabbing her legs and lifting her up. Chloe hung onto his neck while he held Deni in front of him.

When Chloe started to get a bit cranky, Deni and Sebastian decided it was time to get her out of the pool so she could eat dinner. She whined a little, but when her nanny showed up, she willingly went with her to change, but only because Sebastian promised to get out as well so that they could all eat dinner together.

As soon as Chloe was gone though, Sebastian pulled Deni into his arms and kissed her until she melted into him. When he lifted his head, she clung to him.

When he lifted his head, they were both panting. He smiled as his hands smoothed along her slick back. "Just wanted to remind you of what's on the agenda tonight."

She laughed. "I don't think I could have forgotten."

"Good," and he took her hand, leading her out of the pool area. They walked up the steps silently, but separated at the top of the stairs to get to their rooms.

Deni quickly showered, put on makeup, and blow-dried her hair. It seemed a bit nonsensical to get all glammed up for a casual meal, but it also felt right. Very right!

Dinner was a bit quieter than usual since Chloe was pretty wiped out. Between hiking in the morning, packing up their camping equipment, and swimming in the afternoon, she could barely keep her eyes open.

Before Martha brought out dessert, Sebastian laughed and picked his half asleep daughter up. "Time for bed, honey," he told her.

"I'm not ready for bed," she announced, even as her head dropped onto his shoulder.

Deni helped clean up with Martha, who kept trying to shoo her out of the way. "I can handle this, ma'am. You go and relax with Mr. Hughes."

"I don't mind helping," she told the friendly housekeeper. In reality, it helped keep her mind off of what was to come. Even though she wanted very much to make...uh...have sex...with Sebastian, it still terrified her. She wasn't exactly sure what to do, how to handle herself. When she was in his arms, she instinctively moved, kissing him back and enjoyed herself. But their interludes up to now were spontaneous.

She knew what was going to happen tonight as soon as Chloe was tucked into her bed.

"Deni," his deep voice called.

She turned, found him standing in the doorway to the kitchen.

"May I speak with you?" he asked softly.

She might have nodded. She might have simply floated over the tile floor. Deni had no idea. But he took her hand and led her out of the kitchen and up the stairs. Neither of them said a word as he led her into his bedroom and closed the door.

When they were alone, he turned to face her, his eyes again a smoldering silver. "Are you sure?"

"Yes," she told him, but she was terrified. If he would just...kiss her, then she wouldn't be so nervous.

"You don't look very sure, Deni. This isn't torture. But you're looking up at me as if I'm going to beat you."

She laughed, but the sound came out as a burst of nervousness. "I'm nervous. I just..."

He took her hand and lifted it to his chest, pressing it against the material of his shirt. "I'm the same man as yesterday and earlier today."

"I know." She shifted her fingers against his shirt, feeling the heat through the material. "If you could just...kiss me. I don't think I'd...."

He interrupted by kissing her, covering her mouth with his and lifting her up into his arms. That was all it took for her to lose her nervousness and get into the kiss. His lips were demanding and she gave in to his silent command, kissing him back even as her hands crept up his chest, her fingers tangling in his hair. She noticed vaguely that his hair was softer than she would have thought, but then his hands cupped her breasts and she gasped, closing her eyes to savor the sensation.

Her shirt was tossed onto the floor and she stood before him as he admired her. Deni was relieved that she'd donned her prettiest bra after her shower this evening. The look in his eyes told her that he appreciated the sight.

"You're so beautiful," he groaned, lifting her back into his arms, high enough so that her breasts were even with his mouth. He latched onto her nipple through the lace of her bra.

Deni cried out, the heat rippling through her and she wrapped her arms around his head, pulling him closer, needing so much more. She wasn't aware of her legs wrapping around his waist but she sighed when her back touched the mattress. He stood up and moved to the edge of the bed, pulling her pants off and tossing them onto the floor as well. It took him only seconds to discard his own clothing. Deni lifted up onto her elbows, wanting to view him in his full glory.

When he tossed his slacks and boxers to the side, Deni gasped at the size of him. He was amazing and awesome and she unconsciously licked her lips in anticipation.

"You okay?" he asked, as he slipped his fingers into the lace of her underwear, pulling them down and tossing them onto the pile of discarded clothes. He pressed her legs apart and moved his body between them, settling so close, she couldn't believe the intimacy already.

"You're trembling," he commented as he braced his hands on either side of her head. "Why are you nervous?"

She didn't answer, not wanting him to know. "Kiss me," she begged, caressing his arms and shoulders, sliding her fingers over his muscles like she'd imagined doing all weekend.

With a growl, he lowered his head, his muscles straining and she let her fingers glide everywhere, not stopping to ask permission. She needed this, felt that it was very right.

Deni closed her eyes when she felt his lips nuzzling her neck, her body shivering with excitement. "More," she whispered, her legs tightening around his hips as she strained to get closer, to feel more of him. Her hands moved along his arms, his shoulders and back as her inner thighs reveled in the feeling of his hips.

She was too absorbed in her own exploration so when his hands moved up, cupping her breast, she gasped in shock, stiffening for a short moment, then arching against his hand when his thumb scraped over her already-taut nipple. "Yes!" she hissed, unaware of her hips shifting against his. She heard the deep groan come from him and loved it, needing another.

"You're so gorgeous!" he whispered into her ear as his thumb teased and she closed her eyes, trying to control her reaction, but the sensations were too much, too intense. She let her desire sweep her away.

When the heat of his mouth closed over her nipple, she gasped, her fingers moving to his head to pull him away. But when his teeth scraped, she couldn't stop him. In fact, her fingers tangled in his surprisingly soft hair, holding his head in place as she arched again, pressing her breast into his mouth.

"Sebastian, I don't ...!" his mouth pulled against her nipple and whatever she'd been about to say was lost as she moaned.

He moved to the other breast while his hands continued to tease, driving her wild with need and Deni was lost in a sea of desire and sensation. Lower and lower, he moved down her body and her fingers slid against his shoulders...

Sebastian inhaled the scent of her arousal, needing to taste her and feel her. Sliding one finger into her tight, hot sheath, he closed his eyes as he discovered how ready she was. He knew that he could press into her right now and take both of them over to oblivion, but he wanted more. He wanted to taste her, to feel her throb against his mouth. Because he couldn't give her his heart, he wanted to give her as much pleasure as possible to compensate.

So instead of grabbing a condom and burying himself in her heat as he so desperately wanted, he moved lower and lower, his finger moving in and out of her body. Her fingers in his hair were soft and he could feel her desperation. She was so damn close already! So responsive! Everywhere he'd touched her, it felt like she was on fire and that turned him on further, made every touch hotter.

Something inside of him needed her surrender. He wouldn't stop until he had all of her, her body melting in his arms.

The first touch of his lips against that nub was almost all it took. He pulled back, not ready to let this taste end. He smiled at her whimper. "Oh, no, my dear. This isn't going to be over that quickly," he warned her.

She gasped, most likely unaware of how wanton she looked at this moment. That was so damn erotic and Sebastian took a moment to admire her from this angle. So hot! So beautiful! His finger continued its rhythmic torture and he smiled, but the glistening temptation was too much for him and he moved in for another taste.

And that's all it took! She was so tightly wound up now that the smallest touch against that nub had her body arching, tightening...then throbbing with a beautiful release and he absorbed it all from the most perfect angle.

When she fell back against the mattress, he moved away, grabbing a condom and looking down at her completely relaxed body as he rolled on the protection. Her eyes were closed, that sexy tongue darting out to wet her lips. Everything about her right now made him feel...powerful. She was replete and he'd done that to her! No, he might not be able to love her as she deserved, but he could damn well give her this!

Moving back to the soft, sensuous curve of her stomach, he kissed her, sliding his hands against her shockingly silky skin. "Are you okay?" he asked her, and Sebastian could have sworn that he felt her sighs against his back. Hell, even that turned him on!

"Yes!" she replied, laughing as her hands moved back to his shoulders. Damn, he loved the way she touched him. It was as if she needed to touch him almost as much as he needed to feel and explore every part of her.

That word, just one word, and he could barely hold back the need to thrust into her, bury himself deeply into her heat.

She wrapped her legs around his waist again, beaming at him. "Thank you for that."

"It's not over," he teased, bending his head to kiss her nipple. But that just wasn't enough, he took that tip into his mouth, enjoying the moans coming from Deni as her body tightened, the sensuous relaxation leaving her. She bent her knees and the action cradled his hips, pulling him in closer. Exactly where he wanted to be!

Shifting, he moved so that he was poised right at her core and looked at her. "Deni, look at me," he urged.

When her long lashes fluttered open, he looked down into her eyes, needing that connection as he pressed into her this first time.

She was so tight! So hot and tight and perfect! As he pressed deeper into her heat, he watched her eyes widen. He might have grinned, but he felt like a wild lion, needing to roar.

Moving in, then pulling out again, he watched, trying to be gentle as he pulled back on the intense need to press into her fully, to feel her inner muscles around his shaft. She was so slight! So tender and amazing. He didn't want to hurt her.

Her hands explored his back and he groaned, pressing in deeper and deeper, looking into her eyes to determine if he was hurting her. When he was finally fully embedded in her heat, he shuddered, pulling her closer. "You feel so good!" he groaned before starting the rhythmic thrusting that would take them to that pinnacle.

Slowly, trying not to hurt her, he pressed into her. Again and again, shifting until her eyes widened, silently telling him that she liked the movement. Too soon, Sebastian knew that she was right on the edge. She felt so good like this and he wanted to savor the moment, enjoy the feelings. But she was too tight. When her body arched, stiffening as she exploded with her second climax, the feeling and the sight of her like that, her body arching against him as she tightened even more...her orgasm pulled him right over the edge as well.

Thrusting harder, he couldn't hold back and didn't try. Again and again, he pressed into her body and...the mind-blowing climax was so intense, he held onto her, trying to gentle his thrusting but he couldn't. He needed...all of her!

A long time later, Sebastian pulled his face out of the curve of her neck, surprised by the tender feelings rolling over him as he slowly slid his weight off her. Kissing her shoulder, he rasped, "I'll be right back," and he left the bed, going into the bathroom to clean up. Sebastian took a look at himself in the mirror, shocked to find a ferocious expression on his features.

He paused, but his mind couldn't process his expression. Especially when he knew that Deni was still in his bed, her body replete. Immediately, his body reacted to that image and he turned away from... whatever was going on inside of him. He didn't care at the moment. He just wanted to get back to Deni, to hold her. After what he'd just experienced in her soft arms, he...?

Hell, he didn't really understand any of it. But he knew that he wanted to hold her, to feel her naked body pressed against his.

Walking out of the bathroom, he grunted slightly when he noticed that she'd pulled the covers up over her nakedness. Oh, no, my beauty! Not tonight!

Sliding into the bed, he pulled her against him, trying to tamp down the surge of lust he felt as she curled against him.

"I should..."

"Stay," he commanded, and reached out to turn off the light.

Chapter 18

Deni woke up with a start and looked around, trying to figure out why she felt so...different. Then the arm around her waist brought her fully back to the present and she sighed as her head dropped back onto the pillow. Uhhh...Sebastian's shoulder. She'd slept in his arms last night, had made love to him so many times, she couldn't even count them. And she was sore! But sore in a good, amazing way.

Unfortunately, morning was creeping up on them and she needed to get back to her bedroom. She probably shouldn't have slept here last night.

With a sigh, she carefully slipped out of the bed, moving slowly so as not to wake him, grabbing her clothes and slipping into his shirt. Deni hurried out of the room, padding barefoot down the long hallway to her own bedroom. She felt her muscles in ways she'd never thought possible before last night. It felt good but strange.

Once she was safely back in her own room, she sighed and leaned against the closed door with a smile. "Goodness, who would have thought a man like Sebastian knew those moves!" she whispered to the empty room.

Pushing away from the door, she shook her head as she walked into the bathroom. Unfortunately, she didn't have a lot of time to savor last night. Monday morning meant meetings, work, and stuff that she wanted to just ignore.

Stepping into the shower, she smiled dreamily, thinking that she'd love to do some of those things again. Right now, actually. Even as she soaped up her body, she could still feel Sebastian's hands on her.

Pushing her fantasies aside, she finished her shower and quickly got ready for work. She had a big meeting today and she was excited to present her findings to her boss. The tips Sebastian had given her yesterday evening were swimming through her thoughts and she wanted to put them to work, needing to wow her boss after last week's difficult meeting.

Two hours later, she was hard at work, trying to find more ways to present the data. When she stepped into the meeting, copies of the report in her hands, she was excited. Never had she been this excited for a Monday morning briefing.

Sebastian walked into the office late, furious with Deni. She hadn't been in his bed when he'd woken this morning. Hell, she hadn't even been in the house! He was so furious, he could barely speak, so he simply walked into his office.

Unfortunately, Margaret followed him in with his messages, none of which he retained as he sifted through his schedule for today.

"Get me the time and conference room where the mortgage update meeting is happening," he snapped, cutting off his assistant in mid-sentence. But Margaret was always professional and turned around, prepared to immediately obtain that information.

Five minutes later, the message popped up on his computer screen, a strong indication that Margaret was irritated with him. Normally, she would hand him a slip of paper with the information on it. Knowing that he owed her an apology, he thanked her via reply text for the information.

The meeting was in two hours and he was ready to tear off heads by the time he walked into the conference room. Perhaps he should have called Deni up to his office and yelled at her, gotten all of his frustrations out on the correct person. But he wasn't in the mood to be fair. He was irritated and furious and just...irritated!

"Go!" he snapped when everyone came into the meeting and settled down. His presence was making everyone nervous, but not Deni. She gave him several curious glances, but otherwise, she kept her attention on the speaker until it was her turn to present her data.

When she started speaking, he spoke up to ask something, but she'd already answered it in the text of her reports. He skimmed through the papers, trying to find fault. Unfortunately, he'd taught her too well yesterday afternoon. And she'd even gone beyond what he'd explained to her yesterday. Any other day, he'd be impressed. But today he was too furious.

When she finished speaking, he stood up and walked out, not offering any explanation.

Yes, he knew that he was being an ass. But he couldn't help it. He felt off kilter and ready to roar. But without a target, he couldn't release his pent up anger. Sebastian thought about calling Ryker Thune, his friend who lived in LowPoint, about thirty minutes away. After work, they could run through Ryker's obstacle course and maybe expend some of this frustrated energy, get rid of his anger. But in the end, he went home instead, wanting to confront the object of his frustration instead.

Until he walked into the house that night and found her in the kitchen with Chloe and Martha. They were snacking on vegetables and hummus, laughing about something but Sebastian was so angry, he couldn't think rationally.

Throughout dinner with Chloe, he bided his time, glancing at his watch to see how long it was until Chloe was tucked into bed. And even that infuriated him further! This whole marriage issue was so that he could be with Chloe! Now his fury at Deni was causing him to want to be alone with her? This was infuriating! And as soon as he got her alone, Sebastian vowed to demand that Deni stop doing this to him! He didn't want to be distracted! He was normally cool, calm, and controlled!

Right after he'd kissed Chloe goodnight, tucking her into bed, he turned and walked out of her bedroom, determined to find the woman who had infuriated him all day.

He wrapped his fingers around Deni's upper arm and pulled her into his office.

Once they were alone, she spun around on him, obviously furious. "What is wrong with you?!" she snapped, pulling her arm out of his grip and backing up. "You were rude in my meeting today and you're being rude now."

Again, the need to howl and roar hit him. He was feeling primal and he didn't know how to handle it. So he went right to the heart of his fury. "You left my bed this morning!" he snapped, leaning in, his hands pressing against the wall behind her, trapping her right where he wanted her.

Her eyes widened, as if she had no idea why he would find that upsetting.

Some of the anger left her shoulders. In fact, her whole body softened, even her eyes as she looked up at him and that softening, that look of understanding melted some of his anger away. He tried to hold onto it, but she laid her hand on his arm. "Of course I left your bed this morning. Is that why you've been such a grouch today?'

No! He was furious about...he wanted...! What the hell?! "Yes! Why did you leave? Why didn't you wake me up before you left?"

She wrapped her arms around his neck and kissed him. He pulled her into his arms and gave her the kiss he'd been needing all day long.

Afterwards, when she was soft and melting in his arms, only then did he lift his head, looking down at her with almost savage satisfaction roaring through his body. He realized that he'd spun her around so that she was sitting on his desk and he was now between her legs. Exactly where he'd wanted to be earlier today.

"I left your bed this morning in an effort to be discreet, Sebastian. I didn't mean to hurt your feelings." She kissed him again and he noticed that her lips were swollen and soft from his kisses. "I was worried that Chloe might burst into your room. You said that you didn't want her to know about our relationship."

He sighed because she was right. He had stipulated that condition when he'd presented his terms to her. "Well don't."

She blinked, but he barely noticed because her hands slid up, caressing his neck and he loved it! Love it too much, but he wouldn't ask her to stop. No way!

"Don't what?" she asked, her head tilted slightly to the side.

"Don't leave my bed again. Chloe saw us sleeping together this weekend. She wasn't traumatized by it then, so she can handle seeing us together in the future."

His stomach loosened when she smiled up at him. "Okay. I won't leave your bed."

He pulled her closer. "I mean it Deni. Tomorrow morning, I want to wake up with you in my arms. It didn't feel right waking up alone this morning. Not after last night."

She kissed his throat, the only place she could reach. "I promise to wake you up before I leave, if you're not already awake."

"Good," he said, then tilted her head back so that he could kiss her properly.

With that, he carried her up the stairs. He kicked the door shut and placed her in the middle of his bed, then pulled back and stripped off his clothes.

Deni pushed up onto her elbows, watching him, fascinated by every inch of skin revealed to her. Licking her lips, she sat up. "Would you do me a favor?" she asked, still staring at his chest, then lower as he pushed his slacks and boxers off.

"Yes."

He came closer, his hand reaching up to curl softly around her neck.

She leaned into his hand, a sexy smile hovering over her lips. "Just yes? Aren't you going to put some restrictions on that promise?"

He lowered his head and kissed her neck. "Anything, Deni," he vowed reverently as he teased that sensitive spot he'd discovered the night before. "Just ask."

She shuddered, moving closer to him, needing skin to skin contact. "I want to make love to you this time," she whispered.

Sebastian stilled, his lips hovering a breath away from the skin of her neck. A moment later, he lifted his head and looked down at her as she smiled tremulously up at him. "Please?" she whispered. "Last night, you were in control, which was beyond amazing. But, tonight..." she licked her lips as her fingers slid down his hair-roughened chest.

The hiss that followed told her that he liked the way she was touching him. But would he let her do more?

"I don't think..."

Her fingers slid lower, wrapping around him as she watched as his eyes closed tightly. "I'll be gentle," she teased, her fingers caressing him in the most intimate way.

"That's what I'm afraid of," he groaned. But he didn't pull her hands away. Deni took that as permission to venture forth and she lifted her hands to his shoulders, turning him so that he was on his back on the massive bed.

A moment later, she stood up beside the bed and pulled off her own clothes, smiling shyly when he lifted up to watch, his erection telling her that he liked the view. So she slowed down, giving him glimpses as she did a strip tease.

"Deni, you're going to lose the upper hand if you keep that up," he growled, and the taut muscles in his abdomen tightened further as he sat up.

Deni laughed, shaking her head. "Fine, I'll hurry," she promised, pulling off the rest of her clothes and tossing them to the side. When she joined him on the bed, her eyes took in the man in all his glory, amazed that he was allowing her to take control like this. But she knew from the look in his eyes that her control wasn't going to last very long. Besides, Sebastian wasn't really the kind of man who relinquished control easily, so this was a special treat.

Unaware of her tongue sliding out to moisten her lips, she slid her body next to his, but that wasn't good enough and she moved higher, straddling his stomach as she stared down at him. She felt his hands on her thighs, shivering when they moved up her waist. Taking his hands, she pressed them to the thick, luxurious comforter spread out over his bed. "No touching, Sebastian."

"Why not?"

Her eyes moved over his chest, enjoying this moment. "Because you'll distract me and I want to explore you," she told him moments before she bent and pressed a kiss to the side of his neck, exactly as he'd done to her only moments before. Last night, he had been so powerful, so demanding, that she hadn't had a chance to taste him. He'd over-whelmed her with desire and need. But now, she could take her time and enjoy this man, explore him at her leisure.

With each touch of her lips or tongue against his skin, she felt his muscles tighten. As she moved lower on his body, her mouth exploring his chest, the flat male nipples that were so different from hers, but at her first touch, she felt his hands dive into her hair, his fingers tangling and holding her in place. She smiled, hoping he was feeling what she experienced last night when he'd done that to her.

But her goal was lower still, although she didn't want to miss any interesting spots along the way. Inch by inch, she let her fingers slide over his skin, slowly followed by her lips, her tongue darting out to taste occasionally. When she moved even lower, kissing his abdomen, his fingers tightened in her hair, starting to pull her back up.

"Please?" she whispered. "Let me. I allowed you last night."

He chuckled. "If I remember correctly, I had to pin you down," he replied.

"Well, maybe I wasn't ready."

"You were ready by the time I finished."

She laughed, nodding her head. "Yeah, I liked it by that point," she replied and heard his laugh when her cheeks turned pink. At that same moment, her fingers curled around him, tightening as she moved her hand up and down, her thumb exploring even as her eyes watched his face. "Will you like it as much as I did?"

He let out the breath he'd been holding, dropping his head back against the mattress. "I don't think I'll live through it!"

"I think you can take it," she didn't give him any additional warning. Her mouth closed over him, exploring and tasting, enjoying the hiss as she teased him. But she was only able to explore him for a few mo-ments before he pulled her higher onto his body.

"I think that's enough," he warned, pulling her legs into place. "Take the condom!" he ordered, his hands moving up her waist, cupping her breasts as his thumbs teased her nipples into tight buds. "Now, Deni!" he snapped.

A few weeks ago, that tone would have terrified her. And possibly angered her into saying something just as snappish back. But her lips curled into a seductive smile, knowing that she'd taken him beyond the limits of his control.

"Deni! Damn it!" He grabbed the condom he'd tossed onto the bed earlier, ripping the package and shifting her again. But this time, he was in control and he rolled the protection down over his shaft, then pulled her hips back into place. With one finger, he soothed the passage, finding her wet and ready for him. "Damn, Deni!" he groaned, pulling her forward, bracing her hips over him. Slowly, with excruciating slowness, he lowered her down onto him until she'd taken him fully into her body. Then he held her hips still, not letting her move. "Hold still," he ordered roughly.

By this point, Deni wasn't able to obey him. Nor did she even try. Shifting her hips, she gasped, trying to relax her inner muscles to accommodate his size. "I need to move, Sebastian," she moaned, her hands braced on his chest, eyes closed.

"Fine. Move," but he lifted her hips up, maintaining control. She might be on top, in the position of power, but Sebastian was completely in control. Deni wasn't exactly sure what to do in this position, so she didn't fight his grip, especially when he guided her up and down his shaft, showing her how to move, how to give herself maximum pleasure.

Deni loved every moment of it! She couldn't believe that anything could feel better than last night. When his hands released her hips, she understood and continued the rhythm. As she felt that spiraling need, her eyes snapped open and she looked down at him, not sure what to do now.

"Just go with it, love," he urged, his voice strangled and she understood that he was trying to hold back so that she could find her own release first. With that reassurance, she shifted again and again, trying to find her rhythm again, but she was too close and it wasn't working. His hand moved lower, giving her some help and that was all it took! Her back arched, her mouth fell open and she was unaware of the sounds she made as the pleasure hit her in intense waves. She'd thought it was all over, but that's when Sebastian flipped their positions, holding her in his embrace as he pulsed into her until he too groaned out his climax moments before collapsing down against her.

When she could breathe again, Deni opened her eyes and stared up at the ceiling, smiling as she felt his warm breath against her neck.

"I want to do that again," she announced.

Sebastian stopped breathing, then lifted his head and, gently, tenderly, kissed her. "Not going to happen, honey."

She laughed, feeling giddy and happy and amazing! Her arms and legs curled around him as she hugged him, her happiness overflowing at this moment. She knew that it wouldn't last, but for this moment, she was in lo...happy. So very happy.

Chapter 19

"Can I help Gramps again this weekend?" Chloe asked as she climbed into her chair for dinner the following night.

Sebastian was unfolding his napkin, but froze at his daughter's question. "Excuse me?"

Chloe was unaware of her father's sudden anger, but Deni understood and cringed. "She's talking about my dad, Sebastian. Remember when Jenny was sick a few weeks ago, I took Chloe over to help me fix dinners with my father? We made cookies and Chloe was a huge help."

Chloe was concentrating on spreading her napkin out perfectly over her lap, unaware of the increasing tension between the adults.

Sebastian frowned at Deni and she wasn't sure what to say. Deni hadn't given Chloe permission to call her father "Gramps". She'd come up with that all on her own. Turning away from Sebastian's glare, she smiled across the table at Chloe. "Why don't we find out if he needs our help this weekend before making any plans?" Deni offered, hoping that Sebastian wasn't too angry with her.

"But Gramps said that he *always* wants us to come over. He said that he likes for us to help him make dinners."

"Yes but..."

Her grey eyes widened with worry. "Should I not call him Gramps? Will he not like that? I know that he didn't tell me that I could, but I was learning about families with Jenny today and the book said that the parents of my parents were grandparents." Then, in expected child-mind fashion, Chloe was off on another question. "Do I have any cousins? I should have cousins, right? And aunts? I want aunts and uncles too." Martha came in with dinner. "Martha, do you have aunts and uncles?"

The kind woman stopped, looked at her employer, then at Deni, then finally back at Chloe before she resumed her progress, placing a plate in front of each of them. "Yes. I have many aunts, uncles, cousins, brothers, sisters, and..."

"Brothers and sisters?" Chloe asked in a whisper of reverence at the thought. Then her grey gaze shifted to her father and Deni. "Can I please please please have a brother and a sister? Or more than just one?"

"Eat your dinner," Sebastian ordered in a tone that warned his daughter that he wasn't going to answer the question.

Immediately, Chloe looked down at her plate, but all three of them could see that she wasn't happy about her father's command. Martha, darn her, escaped back into the kitchen, a sneaky smile on her face. Deni was stuck with an irritated Chloe and a furious, exasperated Sebastian.

"Chloe, what else did you learn with Jenny today?"

Chloe picked up her fork and started eating. "Well," she said in between bites, "we learned that..." and she went into a long litany of subjects that she and her nanny had gone over during the day. Apparently, Jenny was an extremely good tutor, if the range of subjects Chloe listed were any indication.

"So, can I?" she asked, when Martha brought in small bowls of fruit covered sherbet for dessert.

"Can you what?" Sebastian asked, leaning back and glaring at both of them.

"Can I go to Gramp's house this weekend to help him make dinner and cookies?"

He sighed, rubbing the back of his neck. "We'll talk about that later."

Deni understood the unspoken message, even if Chloe didn't. Sebastian was irritated and worried about Chloe's feelings being hurt after he gained full custody of his daughter and Deni moved out of their house.

As soon as the meal finished, Deni excused herself. "I'm sorry, I have some work that needs to get done," she told Chloe and Sebastian, then hurried out of the dining room. She didn't have any work. In fact, she worked hard all day long so that she didn't have to bring anything home. She wanted her evenings to be free so that she could enjoy spending time with Chloe and Sebastian.

As she pressed her shoulders back against the wood of her bedroom door, she wondered if those lovely evenings were over now that Chloe had innocently decided to call Deni's father "Gramps". It wasn't Chloe's fault that she wanted an extended family. It wasn't Deni's fault either! The child wanted relatives that she could count on, people in her life that she could spend time with, who didn't judge her. Mark was one of those people and Deni was furious that Sebastian would deny the desperately lonely girl the interaction with a similarly lonely old man!

So, when the knock came on her door that night, she was spoiling for a fight!

Sebastian stepped into her room and Deni was already pacing the long width of her lovely bedroom.

She walked over to the door and whipped it open, glaring at him as he stepped through and closed the door once again.

"I didn't encourage her to call my father 'Gramps' Sebastian," she began, not stopping as he leaned against the doorway. "She did that all on her own. But it doesn't matter because Chloe wants to spend time with my father and my father is just as lonely as she is. He won't hurt her!"

"I know that."

"And no matter what happens between you and me, my father will still be there for Chloe. As will I! She's a sweet, wonderful child who needs people in her life that won't force her to sit still!"

"I know that."

"And we need her too! I never knew what fun it would be to be around a childlike Chloe. She's blossomed in the past few weeks!"

"I know that."

"And my father would love to have her around. He lights up when Chloe is with him. And Chloe giggles when he teases her. You should have seen them making cookies last time! She loved it and they ate the cookies right out of the oven, not the raw cookie dough, but I'd eat it that way if I weren't so wary of your temper."

"I know that."

Deni froze as his words penetrated her brain. Turning around, she faced him warily, her mouth hanging open as his words finally broke through to her frazzled brain. "You know?"

"Yes, Deni."

She stammered, her hands lifting slightly in helpless confusion. "So... if you know that my dad won't hurt her and they need each other, why are you angry?"

He pushed away from the doorway, moving towards her. "I wasn't angry, Deni," he said softly. "I was just startled."

She backed up a step, not sure she fully understood. "Okay, so..." she let out a breath. "Sebastian, you confuse me. I keep expecting you to be angry, but then you...well, you're *not*!"

"Why did you expect me to be angry?" he demanded as he pulled her into his arms.

She looked up at him suspiciously, feeling better now that he was touching her. "Because you seemed like such an angry person when I first met you," she told him honestly. "You were the most terrifying man I'd ever met."

"And now?"

She reached up, her hands resting on his chest. "Now..." her head tilted slightly, "you're different," she whispered.

He kissed her then. It wasn't that overwhelming passion that he'd stirred in her the previous nights. This was a slow, gentle kiss that stoked the fires inside of her. The passion arrived, but it was more of a slow, intense burn than an explosion. It was just as sweetly wonderful when he took her over the edge, holding her in his arms afterwards.

Deni's head rested against his shoulder as they lay sprawled amid the mess of her bed. Her fingers sifted through the rough hair on his chest as she tried to sort out her impressions. She was right. Sebastian *was* different now. He was still terrifying, but in a different way. He used to scare her because...because he had been her boss and a wealthy, terrifying, cold and seemingly emotionless man. Now he scared her because...?

"Stop thinking," he ordered gently, as he turned off the lights.

Deni tried to obey. But the reason he scared her now was because she loved him. She loved him and this was only a temporary marriage. Nothing had changed, except they had sex in addition to providing a secure home for Chloe.

But this would all end. And Deni would leave this horrible, soulless house and go back to her previous life. Her father would be fine. He was out of debt. Sebastian hadn't just paid off the loans and the medical bills. She'd discovered that he'd also paid off her father's mortgage completely. Her dad owned his house outright now. He was still going to grief counseling and he had found a new job.

Yes, her father was going to be okay.

Chloe was laughing and smiling, wiggling and being her adorable self. She was going to be fine too.

Sebastian? She sighed into the darkness, wondering what went through his mind. Most of the time, she had no idea what Sebastian was thinking. He was so basic, and yet, such a mystery.

She needed Carly's advice. She needed her friends! But Sebastian was such a private person, Deni couldn't...she wouldn't violate Sebastian's privacy by talking about him. Maybe there was some way she could ask her friends' opinions on what she should do, without letting any of them know that the man in question was one of the wealthiest men in the world and owned the biggest bank in history.

How had her life become so complicated?

Chapter 20

Deni's cellphone chimed as she stepped through the door at the same moment as Martha stepped out of the kitchen and into the foyer. "I just heard from Mr. Hughes, ma'am. He said he has a dinner meeting but will be home in time for Chloe's bedtime."

"Oh, well..." Deni tried to hide her disappointment. She'd come to look forward to their dinners together. She knew that they weren't a real family, but with Chloe's eager discussions, Deni could pretend that they were for a while. And she knew that those memories would last her well into the future when she found herself alone again.

Sighing, she nodded and smiled at Martha who took Deni's purse and jacket. "Thank you."

Looking at her phone, she saw that her father had just texted her, but she didn't want to read it, afraid that it was something horrible. Right now, Deni couldn't face more bad news.

Chloe raced into the foyer, Jenny trailing more sedately behind. "Did you hear?" Chloe gasped.

Deni's heart lightened at the excitement in Chloe's eyes. "No! What's going on?"

"Gramps is coming over here for dinner!" she announced, clapping her hands together. "It's going to be just like a holiday!"

Deni cringed, then pulled up the message on her phone. Looking at her phone, she realized that her father was simply *asking* if Chloe needed a babysitter for the night. He was offering his services. Meanwhile, Chloe must have heard about the offer somehow and was all ready to have a fabulous night with her "Gramps". Oh boy.

"Chloe, I don't know if..."

"Do you think he knows how to play checkers?" she asked. "Daddy taught me to play checkers last week. He was teaching me strategy or something. I don't really understand, but I liked the game. And next he's going to teach me to play chess. That game has horses and kings and queens in it," she chattered on.

"Chloe, I don't..."

"And I know how to play Go-Fish too! Daddy said that it would teach me memory skills, but it's just a fun game and Daddy makes a funny face every time I guess correctly and he has to give up his cards. Do you think Gramps will make a funny face too?"

Deni looked helplessly at Jenny. Jenny seemed equally stunned, shrugging her shoulders with an odd smile.

"Right. Well, how about if we call your dad and ask him if he's okay with you spending an evening with my dad, okay?" Deni offered.

"Daddy will say yes," Chloe predicted, that strange confidence that seemed to run in the family. Chloe took Deni's hand, her small fingers wrapping trustingly around Deni's and her heart lurched. It was such an innocent gesture, but it was also one that shouted out that the adorable girl trusted Deni.

"Let's call your dad, shall we?" Deni suggested and led Chloe over to the stairs. They sat on the bottom step as Deni dialed the phone, but as soon as it started ringing, Chloe took it out of Deni's hands, lifting it to her ear. The small girl looked just like her father! The girl's eyebrows narrowed, her lips tightened, and she looked off into space, as if her mind were working and she was waiting impatiently for the rest of the world to catch up.

Deni heard Sebastian's deep voice and Chloe instantly perked up. "Daddy? It's me!"

"Is Deni okay?" he asked, and Deni's heart did another little twist. He was concerned for her? Wow!

"Yes. But listen. Gramps asked if I wanted to play games with him tonight. And Deni said I had to ask you if that was okay. Jenny said it's okay with her. And Deni didn't say no. Will you say yes? Please Daddy?"

There was a long silence at the other end and Deni pictured Sebastian sitting in an elegant restaurant with very important people, trying to figure out how to protect his sweet daughter from "games" and a stranger.

"Let me speak with Deni, Chloe."

Chloe handed the phone to Deni, not bothering to warn anyone.

"Hello?" Deni greeted Sebastian, startled by the change in course.

"Deni, does your father want to come over to play games with Chloe? I don't want her to be a burden."

Deni chuckled, looking at Chloe who grinned as if she needed to be cute in order to be loved. Deni then looked away, nodding. "If my father offered to come play games with Chloe, then he genuinely wants to play games with her. He never would have offered if he didn't want to do it."

"Okay, fine," he said, sighing and Deni could picture him rubbing a hand over the back of his neck. "If it's okay with you, then I don't have any objections."

"Great. I'll give him a call."

"Just..." he hesitated. "Don't let her be a burden."

Deni looked down at Chloe and her face instantly sprang back into a gamin smile. Deni laughed. "She's never that, Sebastian. I promise."

The call ended and Chloe jumped up. "Yeah!" she exclaimed, throwing her arms up in the air. Jenny laughed as well, walking away.

"Call Gramps now!" she urged Deni.

Deni rolled her eyes, and wrapped an arm around Chloe's back as the girl leaned against Deni's side. Again, as soon as the phone started ringing, Chloe took the phone out of Deni's hands. "I'm not sure that's a good thing to get used to," Deni grumbled.

But Chloe was doing her phone-face thing and there was no way Deni could admonish the child. She was so much like her father, which was going to be a huge issue as Chloe got older.

"Gramps!" Chloe exclaimed. "Daddy said its okay for you to come over and play games with me!" she announced, bouncing slightly. "So, when can you get here?"

Deni heard her father tell Chloe that he would be there very soon. "Okay, but hurry, okay? We have a lot of games that we need to play." And before her father could say anything else, Chloe ended the call, but didn't relinquish the phone. "He'll be here very soon," she said. Pulling away, Chloe took Deni's hand in hers, pulling her off the step. "Let's hurry up and have dinner. That way we won't have to make Gramps wait while we eat." And then Chloe was off, yelling down the hallway to Martha who had disappeared back into the kitchen.

Deni followed at a more leisurely pace, smiling at Chloe's enthusiasm. They ate dinner in the kitchen tonight, since Sebastian wasn't around to object. Deni hated the formality of that miserable dining room anyway, and the kitchen was a warm, welcoming area. Plus, Martha was there and the housekeeper didn't have to carry the plates into the dining room and then back.

Her father arrived just as they were finishing up dinner and Chloe could barely contain her excitement. In fact, as soon as the doorbell sounded, she leapt off her chair and raced for the front door. It took Deni racing after her in order to stop her from pulling the door open.

"Honey, you never, *ever* answer the door by yourself, okay?"

"Why not? It's just Gramps," she replied, perplexed.

Deni didn't want to tell her about the issues surrounding being the daughter of an extremely wealthy man. There was no value in frightening Chloe, although she'd have to learn that lesson someday.

"It's just a rule," Deni told her sternly, while Martha opened the door.

Deni's father beamed as soon as he spotted Deni and Chloe, stepping into the massive house. "There are my girls!" he announced, immediately bending down to take Chloe into his arms for a hug. Then he stood and hugged Deni as well. "Ready to play?" he asked Chloe.

The three of them settled in one of the smaller living rooms, one that was a bit less formal than the others, but in this zombie-house, that wasn't saying much. The house could use a bit more comfort and a lot less formality, in Deni's opinion.

For the next two hours, they played Candyland, Chutes and Ladders, and a few other board games that Mark brought over. They moved on to Go Fish and they laughed, enjoying the faces that Deni's father made. Chloe had retained possession of Deni's phone and snapped pictures. As soon as Chloe realized that there was another phone available to her, she snatched up "Gramp's" phone and started taking pictures with it too. By the time Jenny showed up to announce that it was time for her bath, Mark and Chloe had taken probably fifty photographs of themselves with various silly faces and odd poses.

Chloe begged to stay up later and it was only "Gramp's" offer to tuck her in that got her up the stairs for her bath time and bedtime rituals.

After Chloe had disappeared, Deni turned to look at her father. "How are you doing?" she asked, thinking that he looked much better.

Mark sighed, leaning back against the formal sofa, putting his arm around Deni's shoulders. "I'm getting there, honey. I'll tell ya though, that girl is helping me more than the grief counseling group."

Deni smiled, leaning her head against her father's shoulder. "Yeah, she's pretty special."

"How are you doing?" he asked, looking into her eyes.

Deni lowered her lashes, not wanting her father to know how desperately she'd fallen for the father of the girl. "I'm doing okay too," she assured him. "I miss Mom, but you're right, Chloe makes me feel better every day."

"And Chloe's dad?" he asked softly.

Deni didn't answer immediately, trying to find the words without giving her feelings away. "He's a good man, Dad," Deni replied honestly. "He was so terrifying at first, but he loves Chloe and that girl seems to weave some sort of magic when it comes to helping all of us. He's a different person around her."

"And you love him," Mark said. It wasn't a question.

Deni wiped at the unexpected tears that escaped from her lashes. "I... well..."

"Stop it, honey. Your old man knows you better than you think. You love him. What does he feel for you?"

Deni shrugged and turned away. "He's complicated."

Mark sighed. "Life is complicated, honey. It's our job to simplify it and make sense of it."

Deni snorted. "Right. Like I'm doing that so well at that."

Sebastian slipped silently out of the room, not sure how he felt about being labeled as complicated. But the assurance from Deni's father that she loved him...? Hell, several months ago, those words would have irritated the hell out of him. But for some reason, the news that Deni had feelings for him... felt damn good!

At that moment, Chloe raced down the stairs, literally jumping into his arms. "Did you have a fun evening?" he asked, holding her close.

"Yes!" she replied, and went into a litany of the games they'd played and how many times she'd beaten "Gramps".

But Sebastian could see that she was fading fast. It was about twenty minutes past her bedtime. "Gramps promised to tuck me in, Daddy," she told him, punctuating the statement with a yawn. "He promised. Has he already left?"

"No, honey. He's waiting for you." He kissed her forehead and carried her back into the living room where Mark and Deni were straightening up the games.

"You're still here!" Chloe muttered sleepily, but her fatigue was evident in her lack of exuberance.

"I promised to tuck you in," Mark said, as he followed Sebastian up to her bedroom.

Deni didn't go upstairs immediately, but instead, waited for her father to come downstairs. "Everything good?" she asked.

Mark chuckled, shaking his head as he pulled on his jacket. "She's such a cutie," he replied. "But yes. Everything's fine. She's in bed and fast asleep already."

"Thanks for coming over tonight, Dad. Chloe really enjoyed tonight."

He sighed, glancing at the top of the stairs. "She needs more of these kinds of nights, doesn't she?"

"Yeah," Deni nodded. "Her mother...well, she doesn't like wiggly children," Deni finished.

"I'll see you Sunday if you have time. If not, don't worry, honey. I can manage."

Deni kissed his cheek, then closed the door, locking it and making sure to activate the house's alarm system. But for some reason, she was wary about going upstairs. What had Sebastian's look meant?

Deni should have anticipated him coming down to find her. They'd spent their nights in each other's arms, meeting in either his room or hers to make love well into the early hours of the night. He only left moments before the servants started moving about, so that there wasn't unusual talk.

"Was she okay?" he asked, taking her hand in his.

"Chloe is always fun, Sebastian."

"You say that, but she can be a bit exhausting."

Deni didn't deny that. "How was your dinner meeting?"

"Boring," he said, then took her fingers kissing the tips of each one. "How was your dinner?"

Deni smiled, trying to hide the shivering those slight kisses caused. "Martha always makes a delicious meal. We ate in the kitchen. I hope you don't mind. The dining room is a bit...formal for my taste when you're not here."

"This whole house is a bit too formal for you, isn't it?" he asked, then put his hands on her waist, pulling her in closer.

Deni hesitated for a moment, but then shrugged slightly. "It was intimidating at first, but I'm getting used to it." She forced a bright smile onto her face. "Besides, I won't be living here forever." Her heart ached as she spoke, but she had to remind herself of their deal. "Once you have full custody of Chloe, I'll be out of your hair."

His features tightened for a moment, just a flash of an emotion. Deni didn't have time to decipher it before the emotion was hidden once again.

His hands slid off of her waist. "Quite right," he muttered. "I think I'll retire early tonight," he said and stepped back. "Are you going up soon?"

Startled, Deni looked up at him and he had to toughen his resolve at the surprise in her pretty eyes. "No, I um...I was going to read."

He nodded slightly. "Well, goodnight then."

Deni was so startled by his retreat that she didn't know what to say. For the past several nights, he'd made love to her as if he couldn't get enough. As if he wanted to imprint himself on her in some way.

But not tonight. Instead, he walked up the ornate stairway without looking back.

Hurt, she headed back into the room where she'd spent the past several happy hours with Chloe and her father. But after reading the same paragraph in her book several times, she gave up. Turning off the lights, she moved through the horrible, ugly, museum-like house, walking up the stairs to her own bedroom. At the other end of the house from Sebastian.

What had she said to turn him off? He'd been so sweet only moments before she...before she'd said that her staying here would only be temporary. Was that what bothered him? Deni sat up in bed, looking around at the darkness. Was he mad because he didn't want their relationship to end?

Her heart pounded as she contemplated that possibility. Was it true? Could he want more from her than just a steamy affair and a convenient person to demonstrate a steady home life for the courts?

But as soon as she thought that, Deni pushed it away. No, Sebastian had been quite clear. He didn't want a wife. He'd married her for the sole purpose of gaining custody of Chloe. Reminding herself of that stiff, horrible man she'd met so many weeks ago, the man who had blackmailed her into marriage...!

The man who had not only paid off her father's debts, but his entire mortgage as well.

The man who adored his daughter and lived to hear her laugh.

The man who had taken his daughter camping, danced with her in the dirt and rocks, oblivious to passersby, simply because Chloe was happy. As long as Chloe was happy, Sebastian didn't care about anything else.

Falling back onto her pillow, she stared up at the dark ceiling. That last thought was the most important. Deni was here, living in this house, because Sebastian loved Chloe more than anything else. That was his goal. His purpose for everything.

Rolling over, she punched her pillow and forced Sebastian out of her mind.

Chapter 21

Deni sighed and snuggled closer to the warmth, ignoring the alarm that kept going off. She didn't want to wake up, she was so comfortable, she wanted to just...sleep and revel in the blissful morning.

Unfortunately, her "pillow" shifted, grabbing her cell phone to shut off the alarm.

"Go back to sleep," Sebastian muttered, but slipped out from under her head.

His deep, sleepy voice startled Deni and she lifted her head. "Sebastian?" she whispered, her voice hoarse from sleep. "I thought..."

"Yeah, I know, but..." he sighed and pulled on a pair of silk pajama bottoms. "I have to get into the office," he told her and, without even bothering to kiss her, he turned and walked out, leaving Deni confused, but still admiring the rippling muscles on his back.

With a huff, she flopped back down. "He wasn't here last night," she said into the morning air. "So...?"

But Deni acknowledged that she'd slept like the dead last night. After tossing and turning, trying to figure out the man, she'd finally fallen into a fitful sleep. But at some point, he'd come to her and her fitfulness had disappeared.

"Well, I'm not going to be able to sleep now!" she muttered and climbed out of bed. Padding barefoot into the shower, she turned on the water and stepped into the instantly hot water. For a long moment, she simply stood underneath the water, trying to revive herself enough that she could make sense of her morning.

But in the end, she just...Sebastian was too much of a mystery. A part of her suspected that she should be irritated that he'd come to her bed last night. But the majority of her brain told that small part to shut up because she'd slept well and was now able to start her day with a bit more energy.

Pulling on a black sheath dress, red cardigan, and her favorite pair of red suede pumps, she pulled her hair back into a neat twist, applied a bit more makeup than normal and added gold earrings. Looking at her reflection in the mirror, she felt better. If her body hummed with a bit of unsatisfied longing, well, that was the price one must pay for a good night's sleep.

But...she wasn't going to allow him to get away with slipping into her bed at night. He had some 'splaining to do! Deni refused to be used and discarded by the man, no matter how wealthy and mysterious he was.

Chapter 22

"Hello Martha," Meredith's smooth voice called.

Martha cringed, recognizing the voice at once. Meredith Hughes was about the vilest, most horrible, and repugnant woman that Martha had ever known. The woman had manipulated Mr. Hughes, used Chloe as a weapon and demoralized the child to suit her own status in the world.

As far as Martha knew, the beautiful actress hadn't even attempted to see Chloe over the past several weeks. Which, in the broad scheme of things, was a godsend. Meredith had a chilling effect on people. Unless she was on screen, the woman was vicious! There wasn't a charitable bone in the woman's perfect figure.

So it was with reluctance that Martha turned to face the woman. "How do you do, Ms. Hughes?" she asked politely, but really didn't give a damn about the woman.

"Fabulous, of course," the actress replied. "It's fortuitous that I found you here," she said, looking around at the exclusive shops. "I didn't think that you shopped in this district."

"You're right," Martha replied flatly. "Just shopping for Chloe."

"Ah!" A few tears welled up in the woman's perfectly made up eyes. But the tears didn't dare spill over and mess up that perfect make up job! Oh no, the tears wouldn't dare. They were a nice touch though! "How is my darling girl? I haven't been out to see her lately. Just finishing up with a movie and it's been terribly hectic!"

Martha tilted her head slightly. "Chloe is doing extremely well."

"And Sebastian? Is he good? Not lonely, I hope. That house is just too big for the two of them, I suspect."

Oh, how Martha hated this woman! "He's fine. Perfectly fine. Happily married now to a lovely woman."

Meredith's eyes fired up and Martha felt a spike of pure evil split the air.

"Right. Deni something or other," Meredith mused. "I can't believe that the slut moved into my place. I suppose she's out there spending my husband's money and manipulating Sebastian horribly, isn't she?"

Martha didn't reply, just stared at the actress with a bland expression.

Meredith laughed. "Well, you can't blame me for being jealous! I mean, that woman married Sebastian so soon after my divorce was finalized. She's a money grubbing slut, in my opinion." She sighed, shaking her head, all traces of the crocodile tears were gone. "Did she redecorate Sebastian's bedroom? I so loved that red wallpaper I found! It was beautiful! It would be a shame if anything changed in that perfect room!"

Martha moved away. "If you'll excuse me, I'm in a hurry."

Meredith didn't take the hint. "Of course! Well, I'll just go with you. If you're shopping for my sweet Chloe, then you'll need my help."

Martha couldn't tell the woman that her opinion wasn't needed or wanted in any way. Martha walked into the store where Jenny normally purchased Chloe's clothes. Martha looked around, frantically trying to find a dress quickly so she could leave the horrible woman behind.

"This one is perfect for Chloe!" Meredith exclaimed, picking up a formal dress with layers and layers of silk so that the skirt puffed out. There were perfectly embroidered roses at the edge of the neckline and a matching hat.

It was so completely not right for Chloe! The girl loved to run around and dance now that she'd gotten away from her mother's desperately strict household.

Martha and Jenny were intensely protective of Chloe these days, not wanting her to go back to that place. Ever! Chloe smiled and laughed and was one of the most amazing students! The child absorbed information like a sponge! Chloe truly was an amazing child! No thanks to this vile woman!

"Here," Meredith urged. "Get this one!" She walked over to another dress, just as frilly and inappropriate. "This one too!" she said, exclaiming over the velvet and satin dress. "Oh, Chloe would look perfect in this dress!"

Thirty minutes later, seven more frilly dresses were piled up on the counter. Martha had snuck a dress under the others, not wanting Meredith to see the pretty, but less frilly cotton dress that Martha knew Chloe would love. Plus, it was short enough for the girl to run around in and it would be easier to clean. Deni had taught Chloe how to slide along the hardwood floors, and now they had competitions to see who could slide the furthest. Even Jenny took part in the competitions occasionally. But those silly competitions meant that a longer dress would be dangerous because Chloe couldn't see her feet.

The cashier rang up the sale and Martha handed over the credit card that she used for household expenses. The eight dresses added up to several thousand dollars. The total made Martha gasp with horror at the amount, but Meredith didn't even blink.

"Now we should accessorize, don't you think?" she announced.

Martha shook her head. "I'm sorry, Ms. Hughes, but I need to get back to work. My task was simply to purchase the dress and…"

"Fine!" Meredith snapped. "Just give me the credit card and I'll finish off the outfits." The woman extended her hand, but Martha carefully tucked the credit card back into her purse.

"I'm sorry, ma'am, but I can't allow that."

And Martha turned, hauling the boxes with the carefully packed dresses away. It was irritating, since she'd be back here tomorrow to return the ridiculous seven dresses. But Martha had learned over the years not to argue with Meredith. Life was just easier that way.

"You're kidding, right?" Meredith laughed, but the sound was harsh, not humorous. "Martha, I demand that you give me my husband's credit card so that I can have my daughter appropriately dressed!"

Martha nodded her thanks to the cashier, then turned and walked out of the store, Meredith huffing angrily beside her.

"You're going to be fired for this!" Meredith snapped angrily, and brushed past Martha in a fury.

Martha watched as the horrible woman stalked down the street in the opposite direction. "Oh, thank goodness!" And she turned, heading back to the cashier. "I apologize for that nastiness. And I'm going to have to return seven of these dresses. They aren't appropriate."

The cashier looked confused. "You don't want them?" she asked, looking towards the large windows at the front of the store. "But…wasn't that the mother?"

Martha sighed. "Yes. It's complicated!" she explained. "But the little girl will never wear those frilly dresses. I bought them simply to appease her."

The cashier reversed the purchases, backing out the charges for all but the cotton dress, which was only a couple hundred dollars.

"Thank you so much," Martha said when the cashier handed back the credit card.

"What will I say if Ms. Hughes comes back?"

Martha chuckled. "Tell her to buy the dresses herself if she ever gets custody of her daughter back. But she won't!" Martha laughed with hopeful delight and turned to walk out of the store. "They might not sleep in the same bed, but they had the same mission," she muttered to no one as she carried the one dress out of the store.

Chapter 23

Sebastian sipped his scotch, then tossed several more poker chips onto the pile.

"Call," Jabril announced to the men sitting around the table.

Jayce and Oz chuckled, shaking their heads. "Remember that one night when Kazar lost something like four million dollars on a single hand?" Jayce commented, releasing a puff of cigar smoke into the air.

Tarin chuckled as he sipped his bourbon. "You mean the night that he lost four point six million on a pair of nothing?" he clarified.

Oz grinned, leaning back in his chair as he looked at the others. "Yeah, that would be the night."

Tarin, Jabril, Oz, Jayce, and Kazar all laughed. The only man missing from their group was Ryker, who was home with his wife, Oz and Jayce's baby sister, who was due to give birth any day now. Which was also the reason why Jayce and Oz were here. Their baby sister, Carly, was the managing director of their company and she was a force when she wasn't pregnant. Add in that she was now complaining about swollen ankles, swollen feet, heartburn, backaches, and a slew of other complaints as her pregnancy came to the last few days...or week...and they felt that they were better off far, far away from their beloved, but cranky sister.

"I liked that night," Jabril commented, downing the rest of his scotch. "It's always profitable when one of you gets emotional. Your lack of attention is a great boon to my bank account!"

The others laughed, but all of them had been there at one time or another. Except for Jayce, who was smarter than the average bear and had avoided their poker games when he'd been trying to figure out how to keep his lovely lady, Jessa, from kicking him out of their bed and explaining to her that he wanted to be a full time father, not just the sperm donor to her child.

Thankfully, all of their sometimes frantic and always irritating romances had ended happily. Now there were lots of babies and happiness seemed to bloom everywhere.

As Jabril revealed his cards, including three kings, the rest of the men groaned. All of them, that is, except for Sebastian. He tossed his cards down onto the pile, not even bothering to turn them over. He had an ace, a two, and a five. In other words, he had nothing!

"Oh no, my friend!" Tarin chuckled, picking up the cards. "We've all been in your shoes. And we've all lost fortunes on a bad hand. Now it is your turn," and he turned the five cards over to the astonishment of the other men.

"Damn, Sebastian! I thought you out of all of us would be immune after your first marriage."

Disgusted, Sebastian walked over to the bar and poured himself another scotch, needing a bit of fresh air. In fact, not even their wives knew about the poker games. The men all assured their wives that their meetings were strategy sessions.

Which wasn't exactly a lie. A great deal of business was conducted in this room. During the months when there was no romantic crisis happening among one of the men, they discussed business issues, political crises, economic problems, and brainstormed solutions. A great many problems had been resolved over the years that they'd been friends.

"So, what's bothering you?" Oz asked, swiveling around so that he and the others could watch their latest "victim" squirm. When one of them blew a huge amount of money on a bad hand, they all knew that it was most likely a romantic problem. Business and financial issues these men could handle. It was the ladies that got under their skin and made them do stupid things. It was always the ladies, the ones that got under their defenses, which boggled the men's normally logical minds.

"Nothing," Sebastian snapped, taking a large sip of his scotch, studiously not looking at his friends.

"Right. So, what's her name?" Jabril asked, turning slightly as well.

Sebastian didn't want to talk about it. He wanted to...hell, he wanted to be with Deni. But she was still assuming that their relationship was temporary while he acted like an idiot and...!

"If you won't tell us her name, what's she like and how did she get to you so completely?" Jayce asked. "You're normally the cool cucumber of our group."

Sebastian glared at him. Sebastian might have the power to financially ruin Jayce, but the man was muscular and...well, he knew things. Dangerous things. How-to-hide-bodies types of things. If the man wasn't his friend, and if Sebastian didn't know what a good guy Jayce was, then Sebastian might actually...well, he'd stay far away from Jayce.

"Icy," Tarin corrected. "A cucumber has warmth but Sebastian? Nah!"

A chuckle went around the table, the others enjoying the teasing now that it wasn't their turn to be involved in these horribly annoying, gut-clawing emotions.

"Are you quite finished?" he drawled, looking over his shoulder at his friends and wondering why he was here when Deni waited at home. Exactly where he wanted to be. With her. But she...hell!

"What happened?"

"Meredith," he sighed, but he wasn't sure why his ex-wife's name came out of his mouth.

"Damn! I thought she was gone!" Kazar snapped, then stood up and walked over to the bar to pour himself some more liquor. "What's she done now?"

Sebastian sighed. "Might as well tell you all and just get it over with," he muttered, looking bleakly at the ceiling.

"Exactly," Oz commiserated. "We're going to find out anyway. It's just better to give us all of the information up front so we can torment you with it later."

Jabril chuckled. "So we can get all of the facts straight, distort them, and rile you for the next several months."

"Exactly!" Jayce agreed.

Tarin laughed, but didn't say anything else. He simply leaned back in his chair, waiting for Sebastian to explain.

Sebastian sighed and gave in to the inevitable. "Chloe was becoming more and more withdrawn," Sebastian finally explained. "She didn't laugh or wiggle. She rarely even spoke when I had her over the weekends."

"The hell you say!" Oz snapped, leaning forward in his chair, his muscles tense, ready for battle. "Chloe laughs all the time."

Sebastian clenched his glass, remembering his silent daughter. "Not after Meredith convinced a judge to give her weekday custody. Chloe just...she pulled into herself. I found out that Meredith snapped at her whenever she wiggled. She spent most of her time at Meredith's house in her bedroom, taken care of by irritated and bored nannies who didn't give a damn about her."

"So, you got Chloe back, right?"

Sebastian rubbed the back of his neck, walking over to look out the window. "Yes. I got her back, but because Meredith had slept with so many of the judges in our jurisdiction, I had to go about gaining custody of Chloe in a rather...unconventional manner."

"What did you do?" Jabril asked, but his tone indicated that he wasn't overly concerned about any action taken if it protected a child. "And I don't care what you had to do, Meredith was toxic."

"Agree!" several of the others announced.

Sebastian nodded. "Yes. She was. But..." he sighed, deciding to admit it all to his friends. "In order to convince the judge that I was the more stable parent, I found a woman in a difficult situation and convinced her to marry me."

There was a long silence. Sebastian wasn't proud of what he'd done, but he would have done anything to keep Chloe safe.

"Okay, so...what's the problem? Is the woman demanding money from you?"

Sebastian shook his head, still looking outside, but his mind was focused on Deni's features. "She's lovely, actually. Truly a good person. Inside and out, she's beautiful."

More silence as the men absorbed what he'd said. And what he hadn't said.

Oz was the first to voice their thoughts. "And you fell in love with her."

Sebastian heard the words that he'd avoided saying, even to himself. But they were right. He was in love with Deni. She was smart and funny, a bit goofy, which was exactly what he needed in his life. His world was too serious and Deni brought a bit of whimsy to his world, to his days. She was light and happiness and...he loved her.

"Damn it!" he snapped. "After Meredith, I'd vowed never to put Chloe in danger!"

"Do you *really* think that this woman would hurt Chloe?" Jayce asked.

Sebastian thought about Deni. "No. She wouldn't. That's maybe part of the problem. This woman...I married her just as a show for the judge. But..."

"She's more than just a prop now, isn't she?" Tarin filled in the silence.

"Yes," Sebastian answered after a long moment. "She's...much more than just a prop. She's lovely and amazing. But she keeps reminding me that our marriage is only temporary."

"Perhaps you should take her to bed and make her..." Kazar stopped at the look in Sebastian's eyes. "Right. You've already gone there."

The men chuckled, they had each taken that same route to convince their lady loves of their sincerity. It had never worked though.

"So now I have an ex-wife who is definitely maneuvering to get Chloe back so that she'll get my child support payments again and the house that I provided for her. And a current wife who can't wait to get away from me and go back to her hovel of an apartment."

"Are you sure that your current wife feels that way?" Tarin commented.

Sebastian's eyes sharpened on the man. "What do you mean?"

He shrugged. "Well, sometimes, Zuri tells me stuff just to see my reaction. But she doesn't actually believe what she's saying. She's simply testing the waters, so to speak."

Sebastian considered that. He thought about Deni's eyes when she'd commented on their one year contractual term. Yes, now that Tarin had said it, Deni's eyes sometimes looked...questioning. But at night, when he pulled her into his arms, Deni gave herself to him completely. There was no hesitation in her touch or the passion inside of her. She gave of herself and her body generously.

He thought about the first time he laid eyes on her, when she'd danced in the rain. Even then, he'd thought her a carefree spirit, but also one that was innocent of guile and manipulations. At that moment, he'd thought her just a woman in love with being alive.

There was no evilness in Deni. She was bright and unsullied, she was freshness and happiness. She gave herself to Chloe, giving the small girl attention and laughter. And Deni gave herself to him. Not just in the bedroom, but she listened to him. Truly listened. She didn't try to solve his concerns. In fact, most of the time, she simply snuggled up closer to him when she told him about his day.

"So, you're saying that she might not...?"

Tarin stood up and came over to clap Sebastian on the shoulder. "We're saying sometimes women, and men, actually, test the waters and wait for a reaction instead of actually coming out and saying what they want. And if she's looking up at you with hope in her eyes when she says something stupid, such as not wanting to truly be married to a guy like you, then she's testing you."

Jabril wasn't as kind, "And it sounds like you're failing!" The other men laughed, indicating that they all agreed.

Sebastian looked around at his friends, chuckling at their wisdom. "After my experience with Meredith, I never thought that I'd ever want to tie myself to another woman."

"But this one has changed your mind?" Jayce asked, his voice a bit more contemplative now.

Sebastian hesitated, but then an image of Deni came into his mind and he sighed. "Yeah. She's different."

There was silence as they each thought about the beautiful women they knew who also were "different".

"It's nice when you find the kind of woman who changes your life," Jabril commented.

"For the better," Tarin added.

Oz nodded, picking up the cards. "What the hell are we doing here instead of with our ladies?"

Jayce slapped his brother on the shoulder. "Hey, Sebastian has solved so many of our problems over the years. Now, it's our turn to help him solve his."

Oz brightened up. "You're right. So what are you going to do?" he asked, turning to look at his friend.

Sebastian took the cards that Oz dealt, shifting them in his hand as he worked up a plan in his mind. "I'm not sure."

"Not sure?" Tarin laughed. "You're not going to fly back to your lady love and prostate yourself on the floor, begging her to stay married and give you lots of babies?"

Sebastian's dry look caused the rest of the men around the table to laugh. "Laying myself out on the floor isn't really my style."

Sebastian was planning. As he won the next several hands of poker, he put the pieces together to form a plan that might...just might get him Deni permanently!

Chapter 24

Deni was in hell.

Yep, a personal hell of her own making. She was madly in love with Sebastian and yet, she knew that her love was not returned. Even worse, she knew the exact date at which her one-sided love affair with Sebastian would end.

Was it better to know the ending? Or would she be happier if she were blindsided when Sebastian told her their relationship was over?

Maybe it was better to know. If she didn't know, then she couldn't try to make the most of every moment with Sebastian and Chloe. Deni had come to look forward to their family dinners together, laughing at Chloe's active imagination as she described the events of her day as well as hearing about Sebastian's meetings. At first, he'd simply say that he'd been in a series of meetings, then change the subject or ask her about her own day. But as the three of them eased into a routine, with Chloe and Deni sharing the funny or irritating parts of their days, Sebastian slowly started sharing more of his workday.

And Deni was fascinated! She told him that hearing what he did during the day helped her to understand the bigger picture of her job. And in return, Sebastian explained more of the financial and management aspects of running an international financial organization. In response to his generous guidance, Deni worked even harder at her job, finally understanding how all of the smaller pieces worked together to help the customers. Sometimes, international clients simply came to Sebastian for his expertise, and even that amazed her! She couldn't imagine knowing so much about issues that people came to her for advice.

With each passing day, Deni fell more deeply in love with the enigmatic man. And every night, they tucked Chloe into bed before moving to either his room or her own, making love in a way that wrenched her heart at the tender passion that he brought out in her.

Right now, waiting for him to come to her, Deni surveyed the silk negligee she'd purchased today. She'd been walking down the street to meet Carly and Charlotte for lunch. Jessa usually joined their group lunches, but as a writer, she sometimes lost herself in the plots of her stories. So, she she'd been at home describing a nefarious character's evil intentions.

Deni had been in a hurry, running late to their lunch when she passed by a shop that she'd seen before, but had never entered. Looking in the window, she'd spotted the sexiest piece of silk draped over the mannequin. But since she'd been late, she'd pulled her eyes away from the negligee and hurried on to meet her friends.

But on the walk back to her office, she couldn't resist going back to the store. Sliding her fingers over the amazing champagne silk, she nodded her head. Without even looking at the price, she'd picked it up and carried it to the cashier. There was a small cringe when Deni handed over her credit card, but she smiled in anticipation as she walked out of the store.

Now, standing in her room, she surveyed her appearance in the long mirror and wondered what Sebastian would say when he saw her in the silk. It was a simple, smooth cascade of silk over her body, the only embellishments were the stiff points of her nipples.

Sebastian burst into the room after a cursory knock. His jaw dropped as he took in her appearance.

Deni smiled, her body tingling with desire as she watched his reaction. In that moment, she forgot about the price of the silk negligee, thinking that it was worth every penny!

"Deni!" he groaned, frozen in the doorway, drinking in the sight of her. "Where the hell did you get *that*?" he demanded, moving closer. He reached out, running gentle fingers over the silk.

"At a store by the office," she replied, lifting her hands to his chest, sliding over the tailored fabric of his dress shirt. He hadn't bothered to change after he came back from the office and, for some reason, she really enjoyed seeing him like this. He looked so stiff and formal in his business clothes, but as soon as she touched him, he lost the stiffness and became ravenous. For her! It was a wonderful transition, and one that she looked forward to every night.

He cupped her breasts and rubbed his thumbs against her nipples. Deni gasped as the passion flared inside of her like an inferno! It was always fast, but with his hands on her like this, or maybe it was the silk, she didn't know nor did she care. She loved it!

But her eyes flew open when she heard something tear and, looking down, she barely had time to gasp in horror before his mouth covered one taut nipple. After that, she had no concerns for the silk that she'd paid so much for because Sebastian was almost out of control! Deni loved it!

The bed was only a few feet away, but they couldn't make it that far. Nope! Sebastian's mouth was hot and heavy on her nipple and, perhaps it was the tearing of the material, or perhaps it was something else in the air that night, but Deni couldn't get enough of him either! With his mouth covering one tip, his thumb and forefinger teased and tortured the other and Deni's knees could no longer hold her upright. Sebastian followed her down to the carpet and he tore the rest of the silk away as his mouth found her core. Always, she was ready for him but when his mouth covered her there tonight, she couldn't hold back. In almost no time at all, she was screaming her release, the silk sliding against her skin, making her even hotter. She wasn't sure if it was the silk or the heat of his tongue against her like that, but her climax came hard and fast.

Before she had time to even come down from that wave of intensity, Sebastian was inside of her, thrusting with a furious passion that ramped her body into an inferno of heat so intense, she could barely breath! When her body burst into another climax, all she could do was hold on, and scream her pleasure.

Sebastian barely held himself back. He hadn't even taken the time to undress tonight. There hadn't been time. He thrust into her, feeling the sensuous silk of both her skin and the material brushing against him. Looking down at her, he could see the flush of intense pleasure, and that only heightened his own. In no time at all, he felt her inner muscles clench around him and he released his control, thrusting into her again and again. Too fast, his own pleasure hit him and all he could do was hold on.

When it was all over, he rolled to his side and collapsed against her, holding her close so that he didn't crush her. For a long moment, neither of them could speak, their breathing labored. He felt Deni's hand on his chest, her breasts brushing against his chest as she breathed, but other than that, he couldn't think. Only feel as his body came down from the most intense orgasm he'd ever experienced.

A long time later, he felt her shoulders shake and lifted his head. "Are you laughing?" he demanded sternly.

Deni lifted her head as well, looking at him from on top of his chest where she was still intimately connected to him. "Yes," she admitted, but there was a look in her eyes that made his body tighten with renewed desire.

"I don't think that you are in a good position to be laughing, Deni," he groaned, but he couldn't stop his body from hardening again. Then she wiggled, her eyes widening as she realized what was happening to him. His hands slid down her bottom, the silk still covering that part of her anatomy even though the rest of that negligee lay in tatters. The sight of those torn pieces, the realization of what he'd done, stunned him. And turned him on all over again.

Deni gasped as his body responded.

"Hell!" he groaned, but he couldn't stop. "I'm sorry, Deni!"

"Don't stop," she whispered, shifting her hips ever so slightly. He watched her eyes widen, then she shifted again, rocking back and forth with her hands braced against his chest. When her eyes closed, his body almost exploded at the image of pure, wanton bliss on her face.

But because he was so turned on, again, he couldn't wait for her to take her time. He tweaked her nipples, causing Deni to gasp. But when he started to pull his hands away, she grabbed his wrists, holding them to her breasts as the rocking of her hips intensified. So he continued to tweak her nipples, watching her face. Deni simply closed her eyes and...rocked his world!

Sebastian had always disdained the term, but as Deni ground her hips back and forth against his erection, he finally understood it. With increasing enjoyment, Deni found her release, those soft sounds of exultation spurring on his own pleasure. When she was almost finished, he lifted her hips and thrust into her, harder and faster, taking her higher. Deni threw her head back, rocking with him and finished just as his own climax started.

Afterward, Deni collapsed against his chest and Sebastian had to remove his hands from her silk covered derriere for fear the whirlwind would start all over again. Damn, he liked the way she looked in silk!

What the hell? He tangled his hands in her soft tresses, remembering the initial moment when he saw her in the negligee. And when he'd torn the material...! He couldn't remember ever finding another sound more erotic than the sound of silk being torn off of Deni to reveal the treasures hidden beneath.

Other women in his life had worn silk and he'd never reacted like that. What was it about seeing Deni in the silk that had made him crazy?

He didn't know and, at the moment, she just felt too good to try and figure everything out!

Lifting his head up, he looked down at their intertwined bodies and realized something. "Deni...is there any chance that you are on the Pill?"

He felt her stiffen. Over the past several weeks, he'd taken control of their contraception, not willing to trust someone else. A pregnancy would be...well, he'd thought it would be bad, which is why he used condoms religiously. Unfortunately, seeing her in the silk had...well, he hadn't thought about anything. Touching her like that, feeling her body in the silk and tearing it off of her had been...explosive. He hadn't thought about contraception and he was...stunned.

But now...thinking of Deni pregnant with his child...the thought wasn't as abhorrent as he might have thought a few weeks ago! Damn, what the hell was happening to him?! Did he really want another child?

Yes. His sudden certainty stunned him. Especially since the idea of Deni growing big with his child popped into his mind. She'd be a wonderful mother, he thought.

"No," she whispered and he noticed the worried expression in her eyes.

"How likely is it that you might be pregnant?" he asked, carefully extricating himself from the warmth of her body. He stood up, and lifted her gently into his arms, pushing the torn negligee out of the way. He couldn't have her in silk, he decided. It was too much of a turn on for him.

Deni nibbled her swollen lower lip and he groaned as he carried her over to the bed, placing her in the middle.

"Um...I don't know. My cycles...aren't always predictable."

Sebastian stared down at her for a moment, the image of her pregnant flashing behind his eyes. His body hardened again and he sighed, running a hand over his face. His desire for this woman was getting out of hand, he thought.

He started peeling off his clothes. "You'll tell me if anything comes of tonight's..." he glanced over at the shredded remains of her silk negligee.

"Of course," she replied without waiting for him to finish his sentence. "I doubt that anything will happen, but I'll let you know."

He kicked off his pants. "Good." Then he realized something else and walked into the bathroom. Wetting a washcloth with warm water, he cleaned himself up, and carried the washcloth back to her.

"I can do that," she told him, scooting back and extending her hand to take the cloth.

"I created the problem," he told her with increasing heat in his eyes. "I'll fix it." A moment later, he took her ankles and pulled her mercilessly towards the edge of the bed. With a gentle touch, he cleaned her, watching as her body shivered with reaction. And when he was all done, he couldn't resist the beautiful pink folds, or her reaction to his touch. His mouth moved over her, tasting, teasing. Touching. Sucking.

After two rounds, her body took a bit longer than the first time, which was good. Because Deni tasted like nectar and he loved making her body shiver.

And when he entered her this time, he remembered protection, but as he thrust into her, he was still picturing her body big and beautiful with child. That was all it took him over the edge.

Chapter 25

There was a skip to her step as Deni entered her office the next day. She should be exhausted. Sebastian had taken her to the heights of pleasure several more times over the course of the night. By this morning, when dawn's light started to filter in through the filmy curtains, he'd kissed her shoulder and whispered "Good morning!" before he left her room, fully clothed, to shower in his own bedroom.

Things were good, she thought with a hop to her step. "Very good," she whispered as she settled into her desk and started working.

Around midday, a delivery person approached her desk. "Ms. Deni Hughes?"

Deni's fingers hesitated over her keyboard as she blinked up at the man holding a stack of boxes. Some thick boxes, but many thin ones.

"Yes. I'm Deni."

"I have a delivery for you," he announced, extending the clipboard to sign.

"What is it?" she asked, signing the electronic clipboard. She hadn't ordered anything in a long time.

"I'm just the delivery guy," the man shrugged, taking back the clipboard and handing over the tall stack of boxes. "Have a good day!"

And then he was gone, leaving a confused Deni. She picked up the first one, a slender box with the name of a store she'd never heard of. As soon as she lifted the top of the box and pushed the tissue paper away, Deni knew exactly who had sent the delivery. Inside of the box lay the most beautiful silk negligee she'd ever seen. Last night's silk piece had been destroyed by Sebastian. Today, he'd replaced it?

Her body throbbed with awareness and...lust. Yeah, there it was, that desire that seemed to be ever present whenever she thought about Sebastian! But at the idea of him ripping the beautiful piece of silk...every part of her body throbbed with need! Good grief, she wanted to ride the elevator up to his office, strip off her clothes and pull this on, just to see if he had the same reaction as last night!

Wow!

Opening up the second box, she found another silk negligee, this one in black.

Oh my!

How in the world had he...! No, Deni decided that she didn't want to know how he'd ordered these pieces. And no way would she open any more boxes here at the office. Her boss could walk in at any moment and there wasn't any good way to explain a delivery of silk negligees during the middle of the work day.

Shoving the silk back into the boxes, she covered them up and stuffed them under her desk. But all afternoon, she kept thinking about the end of the day when she could leave the office and hurry home to investigate what the other pieces might be!

Chapter 26

Sebastian whistled as he walked into his office several days later, feeling more powerful than he ever had. His eyes widened as he walked behind his desk, surveying the information laid out by his assistant. The woman was incredibly efficient and he appreciated her efforts. He made a mental note to contact the personnel office and tell them to give her a ten percent raise.

He'd just picked up a file, ready to tackle his first meeting, when his door burst open and Ryker Thune came in.

"Ryker? What are...?" he stopped, registering the man's expression. It only got worse. Oz and Jayce Cole stepped in right behind Ryker.

"Is Chloe okay?" he demanded immediately, thinking the only reason these three would be here was if something had happened to his daughter.

Oz knew where Sebastian's mind went and lifted his hand up to stop him. "Chloe is fine. Our team watches out for her and Jenny whenever they leave the house. They are safe."

Sebastian breathed a small sigh of relief. "Deni?" he demanded next, his voice hoarse.

The three men looked at each other, then back to Sebastian. "Your wife?" they asked.

Sebastian understood the look in their eyes.

"It's complicated," was all he said. "Is she...?"

"Deni is fine," Oz reassured him. "She's in her office, working diligently. We did another background check on her, by the way."

Sebastian leaned against his desk, closing his eyes for a moment as relief surged through him. "They're both fine," he muttered, mentally needing to hear the words out loud. "Thank you, God," he whispered, sincerely thanking his maker for keeping the people he loved safe.

154

"But there is some bad news," Ryker said, stepping forward.

"What's going on?"

"We received information about your ex-wife," Oz explained and laid a report down on his desk. "She's been maneuvering in the background. It wasn't much at first, but we've discovered that she might have some information that could sway the judge against your custody of Chloe."

Sebastian's gut tightened with the news. "What is it?" he demanded, not hesitating. When it came to protecting his child, he didn't delay.

"Meredith has information that your marriage is fake. That you sleep in separate rooms," Jayce explained.

Oz snorted, shaking his head in disbelief.

Sebastian stared at the men, not saying a word for a moment. "How could that influence custody?" he demanded.

Jayce and Oz stared at Sebastian hard and hid their reactions. Ryker, the most subtle of the three men, didn't react in any way.

"We have word that the judge is contemplating punishing you for lying about having a real marriage."

"The marriage is real." Although, by design, the marriage was supposed to be temporary.

Oz hesitated, looking at Jayce, then Ryker before turning back to him. "Our sources tell us that he's going to revoke custody, saying that Chloe's interests aren't being served." He sighed, shaking his head. "We haven't heard that Meredith has slept with this judge, but we're still investigating."

Sebastian nodded, but from the look in their eyes, he knew that there was more. "What else?" he demanded.

Ryker stepped forward. "Nothing substantiated. Let us get more information first."

Sebastian looked at Oz and Jayce, both of whom looked back at him with worried expressions.

"Tell me," he demanded, every muscle in his body tightening with dread. Whatever it was, it wasn't good, that much was clear.

"Tentatively, someone told us that the news about your fake marriage came from Ms. Stenson. That she told Meredith. At least, that's what she's telling the judge."

Oz stepped closer. "Before you do anything, Sebastian, let us confirm this information."

A cold sensation surrounded Sebastian as the news that Deni had leaked information to Meredith. Impossible! Deni wouldn't do that! No way!

But the look in his friends' eyes warned him that it was possible, although not confirmed.

"Sebastian, we're tracking this down. We'll figure out what happened."

For a long moment, Sebastian stood there, not moving as the cold seeped into his bones. He hadn't felt this sensation since...since that afternoon he'd seen Deni dancing in the rain.

He looked up, noticing that the three, big men were watching him with concern. He nodded sharply. "Thank you."

Ryker stepped closer. "Don't do *anything* until we've confirmed the information," he cautioned.

Sebastian smiled, but it was a tight, sardonic smile. "Thank you for your warning. As soon as you have more details, let me know." He looked around. "If you'll excuse me, I have a meeting in a moment."

The men nodded, but it was obvious that they didn't want to leave him like this. But he picked up a file and walked out of the office.

For the next hour, he tried to focus on work but he couldn't stop the pain lashing at him. Why would she have done that? Why go to Meredith and give her the ammunition the vile woman needed to regain custody of Chloe?!

Chloe had come alive over the past few months! She was vibrant and cheerful, talkative and eager for each new day. Dinners had become a happy event where Chloe and Deni shared stories of their days. Hell, even he'd started sharing!

A thought occurred to him. Had Deni passed along information about the bank to his competitors? Every night, Sebastian discussed details of bank business, trusting her. Thinking she was interested in learning more about the industry.

Had she actually been selling off that information?

Abruptly, he stood up and walked out of the meeting, unaware that he'd cut someone off midsentence.

Out in the hallway, he dialed Oz's number. The man picked up immediately. "What's wrong?"

"I need you to dig into some other issues concerning Ms. Stenson. I've discussed bank business with her. See if she's been passing that information along to my competitors and get back to me."

There was a long pause. "Will do."

Sebastian ended the call and walked back into the meeting, nodding sharply to the woman who had been speaking as he'd walked out. She began again, but Sebastian heard none of it.

Heading back into his office, he picked up his phone. "Martha," he said to his housekeeper, "I need you to pack up Deni's things and have them by the front door before she walks into the house today," he told his housekeeper.

There was a pause, and he could picture the woman's confused frown.

But he didn't relent, reminding himself that Chloe was his first priority. If the cold, aching sensation filling his body was any indication, he should have done this a long time ago. Marrying Deni had been a monumental mistake.

"Yes, sir. I'll get it done."

"Thank you." He hung up the phone and walked over to the bar in one corner of his office. With precise movements, he poured himself a finger of scotch, and took the drink over to the windows in his office. But Sebastian didn't see the beautiful Appalachian Mountains in the distance. He didn't see the city of Louisville stretched out in front of him or the warm, summer sunshine sparkling over the horizon.

He only saw Deni, her eyes lit with an inner fire. He'd thought that the fire had been for him. Now he knew better. That fire had been for something else: the money that his competitors would pay for information about the inner workings of his bank.

He suspected that Meredith had paid Deni for the information on their marriage. Had they been laughing about him? Had they compared notes on their bedroom antics? He doubted that. His sex life with Meredith had been...fine. Nothing to brag about, he mused. But his life with Deni...!

He turned and threw the crystal glass against the glass shelves containing high-end liquor, causing the entire mess to crash down to the floor.

Revulsion swamped him for the embarrassing display of emotion. Turning away from the mess, he straightened the cuffs of his dress shirt, adjusted his tie, and took a deep breath.

After that, he walked over to his desk and picked up the file for his next meeting, walking out of his office.

Pausing by his assistant's desk, he said, "Have maintenance come and replace the shelves in my office," and then he walked away, not even noticing the stunned expression in the ever-efficient woman's eyes.

Chapter 27

Deni hurried home that evening, excited to see Chloe and Sebastian. In her mind, she was thinking about which silk nightie she'd pull on for Sebastian after Chloe went to sleep that evening. He really seemed to love seeing her in silk and it turned her on just as much. It was like a light switch and she meant to flip it on as often as she could.

Stepping into the foyer, she was just about to toss her purse onto the table when she spotted something in the corner. "What in the world?" she muttered, seeing her suitcases lined up against the wall. Looking up, she saw Margaret standing by the doorway, tears in her eyes as she wrung her hands. "Martha, what's going on?" she asked.

Before the kind housekeeper could say a word, Sebastian stepped out of his office and glared at her. "Could I have a word with you?"

The coldness in his eyes warned her that something was wrong.

"Of course," she replied, putting her keys down on the polished table. Sebastian disappeared into the office and Deni followed. She didn't bother to close the office door, thinking that he just needed...something. She had no clue.

"Are you okay?" she asked, moving closer to him. But as soon as she was halfway across the carpet, he moved to stand behind his desk, making a point of putting a physical obstacle between them.

"Yes. I'm fine. But I need you to leave. Tonight."

Deni froze. "I'm sorry...could you repeat that?"

"You need to leave. I will not allow you to put my child in danger."

There was a stabbing pain in her heart. "Chloe is in danger?"

"Yes. You've been telling Meredith about our private lives. She's suing me for permanent custody of Chloe. So, if you could just leave, I will keep trying to protect my child."

Deni shook her head. "But Sebastian, I haven't even *seen* Meredith.

How could I have told her anything?"

He tilted his head, looking at her as if she were a cockroach. "Really? Then how does she know we sleep in separate bedrooms?"

"I don't know!" She shook her head. "I haven't said anything! I would never! Our nights together are private!"

She took a step closer, trying to reassure him that she would never, ever, say anything to anyone. Especially not that they didn't sleep in the same room! That had always been a bit embarrassing to her. A married woman that didn't sleep with her husband? It was ridiculous. Especially considering that they spent their nights together. In fact, it was one of the things she'd meant to bring up with him – that perhaps they should start sharing a bedroom. But after what he'd gone through with his ex-wife, Deni hadn't wanted to rock the boat, loving him too much to scare him away.

"Then how does she know?" he demanded harshly.

"I have no idea, but she didn't hear it from me," she vowed. "I would never say anything, Sebastian!"

"Sure you didn't," he snapped, obviously not believing her. "Well, it doesn't matter who told her, she knows that ours is not a real marriage and the judge is demanding another hearing. So your services will no longer be needed. Thank you very much."

Deni felt as if he'd slapped her. *Services*? What the hell did he mean by that? She hadn't offered him any "services" other than standing in front of a judge to give his adorable little girl a stable home life.

"You...I'm sorry..." she blinked, fighting back the tears. "I don't understand."

"You are no longer needed, Deni. Please leave my house immediately. I know that you kept your apartment. So, it isn't as if you don't have a place to live." He paused for a moment, turning away from her. "Your bags are packed, but if there is anything that Martha missed, give her a call and let her know. She'll deliver it to you. But I don't want to see you in this house. Ever again!"

Deni cringed, feeling like a leper. There were so many things that she wanted to say, too many questions crowding her throat. But the stabbing, piercing pain in her chest was too painful. So, she turned on her heel and walked out of the office.

Out in the foyer, she looked around, still unsure of what she should do. Leave? Go back and try to talk to him?

But the way he'd looked at her! Dear God, she'd never seen such contempt in a person's eyes!

So, Deni did the only thing she could think of. She grabbed her purse and her keys and hurried out of the horrible house. Away from Sebastian. Away from Chloe.

She jumped in her car and drove. And drove! She wasn't sure where she was going, so she just drove away, out of town. Away from Sebastian and the horrible things that he'd said to her. She couldn't even process right now. It hurt too much.

Thirty minutes later, she found herself in LowPoint, staring at the lake and the mountains and the setting sun, but feeling nothing. There was no warmth in the world now. No happiness. No color. Everything was just...blank.

Deni parked her car near one of the parks in LowPoint and started walking. She should go to one of her friends' houses, but at the moment, she couldn't even think to figure out how to get there. They didn't live far, because nothing was very far in LowPoint. The town was small but growing, quaint and beautiful while retaining a quirky quality that drew people here on the weekends like a Mecca for foodies and anything artsy.

Deni saw none of it. For the first time since she'd discovered this wonderful town, she didn't smell the delicious scents coming from "Desire", Tony Itola's flagship restaurant or Jane's chocolate scones. Of course, Jane probably wasn't baking right now. She'd be closing up and heading home to her handsome husband, a trauma surgeon who worked in the hospital located only five minutes from her office. From Sebastian's headquarters.

She didn't notice Ms. Scarlett walking down the street with her adoring posse of men behind her. She didn't see Sheriff Jansing across the street, his eyes narrowing as he watched her head towards the swing set on the playground. She didn't see or feel anything, her whole body numb.

For a long time, she just walked, her arms closing around herself.

But finally, she looked up and realized that she'd walked over to Jessa's house. It stood overlooking the water, a beautiful old, Victorian house with red siding and white trim. A massive house that her husband had refinished, piece by piece.

Would Jessa be home tonight?

She couldn't do it. Didn't want to see anyone right now. So instead of bothering her friends, she turned around and walked back to her car, which she'd parked behind the old church. Driving back out of town, she drove to her old apartment. For some reason, she was surprised that she still had the key on her keychain. But then, why wouldn't it be there? Her marriage to Sebastian had been pre-determined to last only one year after he regained custody of Chloe. A little less than half that time had passed, so of course she'd retained the keys to her apartment.

Unlocking the door, she stepped inside and looked around. Everything was covered in a fine coating of dust. It was dark too, the sun having set...well, a while ago, she supposed.

Instead of turning on the lights, she walked into her bedroom and curled up on the bed fully clothed. Sleep, she thought. In the morning, she'd figure out what had happened. She'd go back to Sebastian and ask him to explain. She'd...

Tears fell silently from her eyes, dampening the pillow. Deni didn't even bother to wipe them away. He'd kicked her out of his house. Out of his life. Did she even have a job? Deni wasn't sure, and didn't even try to think about it just now. It hurt too much to think.

She tried to sleep, but her eyes wouldn't close. Instead, she stared at the wall, trying not to think. Because thinking only made her more confused. Numbness descended over her and she curled her arms around her stomach. Staring.

Chapter 28

Four days later, Deni stepped out of the shower. Her suitcases had been delivered the day after she'd been kicked out of Sebastian's house, but not by anyone she recognized. The man carried her suitcases up to her apartment, and nodded politely before leaving. Deni had called in sick to work that day, making sure that she called in early enough that she wouldn't have to speak with her supervisor. Her voice cracked as she left a voice mail for her boss, ensuring that her boss would believe her lie of being sick. Although, it wasn't really a lie. She was sick, with heartache, pain, confusion, and a slew of other emotions.

Today was the big day though. For four days, she'd hidden away in her apartment, not speaking to anyone, barely eating, just...thinking. She hadn't even unpacked her suitcases.

By Sunday night, she'd finally been able to think. And Sebastian's words came back to her. He'd said that Meredith was suing him for permanent custody? Of Chloe? No, that couldn't happen! No way would she allow her to get her clutches into that sweet child! Chloe had only recently recovered from her last confinement in Meredith's grip!

Deni had no idea how to find out when the hearing would be, but that was an issue for another day. Today, she was going into her office and hope that she still had a job.

Her grey slacks and plain, white shirt were boring, but they matched her mood perfectly. Deni didn't bother to do anything with her hair, just pulled it back with a tie and grabbed her purse. As her hand rested on the doorknob of her apartment door, she contemplated grabbing something for breakfast, but since she hadn't been to the grocery store yet, there wasn't much in the apartment. She'd subsisted on frozen meals over the weekend when the ache in her stomach became too much to ignore, but even then, she'd only been able to eat about half, tossing the rest away in revulsion.

But the thought of trying to figure out what to eat this morning was just too much for her, so instead, she left her apartment, driving to the office. She parked her old car in her usual place, getting to work earlier than normal. She suspected that there would be a great deal of work to accomplish, since she'd missed Thursday and Friday of the previous week.

Well, there would be a lot to get done IF she still had a job. Until her boss told her that she was fired, she was going to get her work done. Sitting down behind her desk, she sorted through the stacks of files that had accumulated in her absence, organized everything by priority and then...got to work.

Deni was oblivious to the rest of the department staff coming in and getting to work, grabbing a cup of coffee, and talking about their weekend. Nothing mattered but focusing so she didn't think about Sebastian, worry about Chloe or wonder what might happen to that poor child. Every time Chloe's smile popped into her head, or Sebastian's annoyance, she pushed herself harder. She didn't take time to eat lunch that day, but her boss came in around midday, bringing a sandwich with her. "Here," she said, putting the sandwich and diet soda down on Deni's desk. "You look horrible, Deni. Are you sure that you're okay to work? You can take more time off. You haven't used a sick day in the past few years, so you're definitely due some time off if you need it."

Deni tried for a smile and hoped it looked better than it felt. "I'm fine," she lied, then pulled the next file forward.

She ate about half the sandwich, but couldn't stomach any more of it. The thought of eating made her feel nauseous and she pushed the sandwich aside and focused on working.

Hours later, she realized that her back hurt and she looked up, stretching sore muscles. She realized that everyone had gone home. Looking at the clock on her computer, she noticed that it was almost ten o'clock at night. Good grief, had she really worked for sixteen hours?

Packing up, she went back to her apartment. But still, nothing in her freezer appealed to her. That night, as she tried to sleep, she wondered what Sebastian was doing. Was he okay? Was Chloe? Had Meredith won custody back? Deni hoped not. Meredith didn't want Chloe at all. She only wanted the child support payments from Sebastian. Not once in all the time she'd lived with the two of them, had Meredith even asked to see her daughter. There'd been no frantic calls, no desperate pleas for just a few hours with Chloe. And Chloe, bless her heart, hadn't asked about her mother either. Not once! That spoke volumes for how much that child missed her mother.

For the next three weeks, Deni followed the same pattern. Waking up early, showering, dressing, skipping breakfast and heading into the office as soon as possible. Working until she couldn't sit at her desk any longer, then going home to her tiny apartment and staring at the wall as she desperately tried to sleep.

She knew that she was losing weight, but couldn't stomach anything. She was getting more work done than three other employees, and her boss came in and asked what was wrong. "Nothing," Deni had replied, unable to explain that she'd fallen in love with the wrong man. A man who was unwilling to explain what she'd done wrong, accusing her of breaking promises and shattering trust. Saying something to Meredith? A woman Deni hadn't seen or heard from since the day they'd "met" in his office? What would she have said? And what about the "secrets" she'd told to his competition? What secrets did she know? Deni worked in the mortgage department. There weren't any secrets here! At least, nothing all that important to his competition!

Over those weeks, there were spurts of anger. But mostly, she simply existed. She couldn't think. She couldn't eat. And she didn't feel a whole lot. Because every time she started to feel, it was anger, hurt, and that horrible, stabbing pain. It was better to feel numb. Better to just...exist.

Chapter 29

Sebastian watched Deni from his office window. He could barely see her from this height, but he knew it was her. He recognized the way she walked, the way she carried herself. She drove to work these days and he hated...everything! Why had she done it? Why had she spied for Meredith?

He'd called her supervisor to find out if she'd actually shown up for work and was told that she'd missed only two days. He'd expected her to be living large, going on shopping sprees with all of her newfound wealth.

Something occurred to him and he whipped around, walking over to his computer. Pressing several buttons, he remembered that he'd set up a monthly transfer of forty thousand dollars. He'd have to stop those payments. No way would Deni live off his money as well as her ill-gotten gains from spying on him and Chloe!

But as soon as he pulled up the account, he noticed the amount balance: one hundred and twenty thousand dollars. No, not quite. There was actually more in the account. Interest! Damn her! She hadn't spent any of it? She'd take money from Meredith and his competitors, but she wouldn't spend his money?

And then he stopped. Why wouldn't she spend his money? She'd never driven that damn SUV he'd bought her, preferring the ridiculously old, weather beaten and barely useable car that she owned. Then another thought occurred to him. Where the hell had she stored the money from Meredith?

He'd dismissed the possibility that she'd given corporate secrets to his competitors. He had absolutely no evidence to support his belief, but he was certain that she hadn't done so. Which was why he hadn't fired her the same day he'd kicked her out.

Still, he stared at the amount in the bank account. What game was she playing? Why hadn't she spent his money? Why was she working? There was more money in that account than she earned in a year! She should be living it up!

Instead, she was walking around like a zombie!

Damn her! What game was she playing? And he damn well knew that she was playing at something. He'd been around manipulative women for too long and knew their tricks. He hadn't figured out exactly what game Deni was playing, but he would eventually. They always showed their hands eventually!

"I don't have time for this!" he snapped and walked away from his computer. Checking the time, he noted that he had a meeting in fifteen minutes.

He shouldn't go, he thought. His entire staff was terrified of him lately. He snapped at anyone who made even the slightest mistake, his fury over Deni's betrayal too deep and raw to keep completely in check.

And he hated that she'd gotten past his defenses. He'd known for too long what women would do to gain his money!

But Deni didn't want his money, he reminded himself, thinking of that damn bank account.

Okay, so if she didn't want his money, what did she want? She was already married to him. And no, he hadn't started divorce proceedings. Although, why he hadn't informed his lawyers to start that process was still a mystery to him.

"Hell!" He had a meeting with his lawyers this afternoon to discuss strategy for overcoming Meredith. Oz had already put a watch on the judge for the case to ensure that Meredith didn't try to use her numerous wiles on him, which is how she'd gained initial custody. So far, Oz's guards hadn't spotted Meredith anywhere near the judge or the judge's family, another one of her tricks – get to the family in order to manipulate the judge.

The woman had no morals, he thought with increasing frustration.

"Sir?" his assistant asked, holding the reports for his first meeting.

Sebastian sighed. "Send my apologies," he told her with resignation. "Tell Desmund to take over for me," he told her, referring to his executive vice president.

The woman left. Sebastian caught the relieved expression as she pulled the door closed behind her, leaving him alone.

Alone. Damn Deni for doing this to him! He hated this cold sensation that enveloped him. It never seemed to dim. Dinners with Chloe lately were the only times that he seemed to come out of his anger and fog. And even then, Chloe kept asking if Deni would ever come back, or if she could visit "Gramps". What the hell was he supposed to tell her?

So far, he'd only told her that Deni had gone on a business trip. Since he'd done the same many times over the years, she didn't question it. But lately, she'd been asking when Deni would be coming back.

Sebastian didn't have an answer for that one. Soon, he was going to have to tell his little girl the truth.

But what was that truth? Fifteen minutes ago, he would have said that the truth was that Deni, like Meredith, was a money grubbing liar who had snuck into his life and torn it apart.

But the untouched bank account. The strong work ethic. The Land Rover still sitting at his house.

So if she wasn't after the money, what was she after?

Oz had confirmed that a brunette woman had met with Meredith in a dress store several weeks ago. He didn't have pictures and the store didn't have security cameras, but who else would it be? According to the store manager, who had looked up the sales for that day, there had been a large sale. Eight dresses costing over four thousand dollars.

Oz's man had reported that the brunette had muttered something about "not sleeping in the same bed" and "they had the same mission". The store manager hadn't understood at the time.

Sebastian had understood. And the words confirmed his suspicions. Although, that bank account balance brought those suspicions back into question.

Rubbing his forehead, he tried to focus on work. But thoughts of Deni kept intruding. At night, he'd walk around his house, looking at the various things that had changed since Deni's arrival. There were soft throw blankets on the couches in the small living room. The space looked much more inviting that way. He and Chloe preferred eating in the kitchen now, listening to Martha bustle around as they chatted about their days.

There were other things too. Like when he wandered about after kissing Chloe goodnight. Too often, he found himself in that room on the opposite end of the house from his own. Deni's room. It still smelled like Deni, her soft perfume floating in the air. When he'd walked through the room one night, he'd discovered that it wasn't her perfume, but actually her shampoo.

That's when he'd discovered the silk negligees he'd chosen for her. Sebastian had handpicked all of those gowns, picturing her in them. Picturing him ripping them off of her.

She'd left them behind.

Damn her! What did it all mean?!

Chapter 30

The date of the custody hearing approached and Sebastian still didn't have any answers about Deni or how to keep Meredith away from Chloe. For a man who prided himself on controlling the details, this situation was getting to him. He hated not being in control. He hated being vulnerable.

And he hated that he was still thinking about Deni, wishing she were by his side for this damn hearing! It was all her fault that they were here, and yet, he still craved the sight of her. He wanted a smile from her. A smile of reassurance. Something that told him that everything would be okay and Chloe would stay with him forever!

Instead, he walked into the courtroom next to his lawyer, furious with the circumstances that had brought him here. And he had no one to blame but himself!

Meredith swished into the courtroom, beaming, even signing autographs for a few people who dared to approach her. Then she moved over to the defendant's table, taking the seat next to her lawyer and perching on the edge, looking regal and exotic. Sebastian watched as she looked at him, his skin crawling as her smug smile curled those perfectly made up lips. She'd had surgery, he realized, her lips looking fuller somehow.

He didn't care. Not anymore! His only goal was to keep Chloe away from her. He had to protect his daughter!

Mark Stenson stepped into the judge's office and looked around. The judge's assistant wasn't at her desk and the door to the judge's chambers was open. So instead of waiting for permission, he simply walked into the office.

"Your Honor?" he asked.

The judge was pulling on his black robes and spun around at Mark's query. "I'm sorry, but I have court. I can't talk right now."

Mark smiled and bowed his head slightly, pulling his phone out of his pocket. "I know, Your Honor. I just...would you look at this picture?" and he showed one where he and Chloe were laughing while making cookies one afternoon. "This little girl..." Mark began. "She's happy now, Your Honor. When I first met her, she was silent, sitting as still as possible." The judge looked stunned by the adorable face. Chloe was pretty, but more than that, she was sweet and innocent, her exuberance glowing from the photo. "She used to count carbohydrate and calories." At the judge's shocked expression, Mark nodded. "That's right. She's five years old and her mother had already taught her to count calories and carbs, telling her that women can't get fat or they are useless to the world."

The judge pulled back, horrified. Then he shook his head. "This is inappropriate," he told Mark. "You can't be in here. This all needs to be..."

Mark ignored the judge's comment and continued, showing the judge a different picture, this one of Chloe peeking out from behind a hand of cards, looking mischievous. "She giggles now. Her father is so good to her. And my Deni, that's her stepmother, loves her like she were her own child. Chloe calls me 'Gramps'. She smiles and laughs, I've taught her to dance and her father teaches her numbers by playing dominoes and Go Fish with her. The child didn't even know how to play games before she lived with her father. Please, don't send her back to that evil woman!"

The judge sighed, shaking his head slightly. "I can't discuss this further," he insisted and turned, buttoning the black robe. He rested his hand on the door to the courtroom. "I'm truly sorry. But the law...I have to follow the law."

Mark's shoulders sagged and he looked at the man, defeated. "I had to try, Your Honor."

The judge paused, then pushed through, disappearing.

"All rise!" the bailiff called out.

Everyone in the courtroom stood up as the judge swept into the room. "Be seated," the judge said, not bothering to look up. He seated himself, and sorted through the papers in front of him while the bailiff read the issue in front of the court.

Deni sat in the back of the courtroom, trembling as she watched. Her father had discovered that the hearing was today and she should have stayed away, but this was Chloe's future. It was her life! Okay, not literally. But Chloe's personality would die a slow, painful death if she was forced back into Meredith's home.

The judge sighed and looked briefly out at the courtroom. "So we're back again in court to determine which parent should have custody of Chloe Hughes," the judge commented, then straightened his glasses as he looked up, surveying the crowd. "Seems we've been here before, haven't we?"

Deni watched as Meredith preened, trying to get the judge's attention. Thankfully, this judge was a bit more discerning and he kept his focus on the lawyers as both stood.

"Your Honor," Meredith's lawyer began, "the court awarded custody to Mr. Sebastian Hughes during the last court appearance simply because the court decided that his recent marriage would provide a more stable environment for the child. But..."

The judge interrupted, "I thought the court awarded custody because the mother couldn't be bothered to show up to fight for custody of her daughter. Wasn't she in Paris shopping?"

The lawyer hesitated. "Ms. Hughes was in Paris bringing back the French culture, Your Honor. Since the court stipulated that Chloe Hughes was not allowed to leave the country."

"Culture?" the judge snorted. "Is that what she's calling it these days?"

Deni almost laughed, but that wouldn't be appropriate. Her father stepped through the doors of the courtroom, startling her. He slipped into the row and sat down next to her, looking grim and frustrated.

"What are you doing here?" she whispered, glancing at her father, then up at Sebastian, worried that he would see her here and order her to get out.

"My granddaughter is in jeopardy," he whispered right back. "I had to do something!"

Deni's heart swelled with love. "That's so sweet of you, Dad," she hugged him briefly.

"I'm not giving up."

She took his hand, squeezing his fingers. "Neither am I," she whispered back.

The judge listened for several moments. "Your Honor, Mr. Hughes married under false pretenses," her attorney argued. "It was a sham marriage. I have an affidavit here that certifies that the couple wasn't even sleeping in the same bedroom."

The judge rolled his eyes and lifted a dismissive hand. "You understand that I'm not overly impressed with that argument, right?"

"But, Your Honor...!"

"Shut up, Joe," the judge snapped. "About half of the married couples in this country sleep in separate bedrooms. Even my own wife sleeps in a different room because I snore like a hibernating bear. Are you going to tell me that the woman I've been married to for the past thirty years isn't a true wife to me?"

The attorney stopped, stumped until Meredith hissed something at him.

The judge was having none of it. He lifted his hand, stopping the next argument. "Right. So, the issue here is who is the better parent. Who is going to give the child a better, more stable, and healthy home life, right?"

"Yes, Your Honor," Meredith's attorney agreed. "And my client..."

"Stop, Joe." He looked at Meredith. There was a long pause and Deni watched with confusion as the judge looked at Deni's father, then down at his papers. The silence in the courtroom was intense. When the judge finally looked up, he stared straight at Meredith. "Ms. Hughes, do you have pictures of your daughter on your phone?"

Deni was startled by the question, not sure where the judge was going with it, but she felt her father's fingers tighten around her hand.

The room turned to the beautiful woman who looked shocked and confused. But she rallied quickly, pulling up a smile. "Of course, Your Honor. My daughter is beautiful. I have many pictures of her on my phone."

The judge didn't look impressed. "Show them to me."

Meredith blinked, but then leaned down and pulled her phone out of her purse. She flipped to the gallery of her pictures and pulled up an image, then handed the phone to the bailiff. "You see? She's a perfect angel," Meredith preened.

The judge looked down at the picture, lifting his glasses to see better. He flipped through the other pictures. "There are only these posed pictures, and you only have three of them." He handed the phone back to the bailiff who brought the phone back to Meredith.

"Well, when you have a perfect daughter, one doesn't need a slew of pictures, Your Honor," she replied, laughing as if she'd said something hilarious. No one joined in.

The judge turned to Sebastian and Deni sat forward, understanding where this was going. "Mr. Hughes, do you have any pictures of your daughter on your phone?"

Sebastian already had his phone out and pictures of Chloe's laughing image could be seen even back here in the gallery.

The bailiff brought the phone to the judge who flipped through several pictures, smiling at some of the images. "Where did you go camping?" he asked.

Sebastian stood up, buttoning his suit jacket. "A small campsite in the

Shenandoah Park, Your Honor."

He chuckled at something else. "How long did it take you to get the marshmallow goo off her face? S'mores?"

Sebastian smiled slightly and nodded. "Longer than I'd expected."

The judge laughed and nodded. Then his eyebrows shot up. "How many dog ear filters did you apply to these?" he asked.

Deni watched, fascinated as Sebastian nodded again, cringing slightly. "Uh, Chloe did that one night when we were playing Go Fish. Every time she got the numbers right, she got to take another picture and play with the filters. She uh...she likes the dog filter the best."

The judge nodded. "My granddaughters prefer the tiara filter," he commented and handed the phone back to the bailiff who brought it to Sebastian.

"Is your current wife here in the courtroom?" he asked, looking out at the others.

Sebastian was about to shake his head when Deni interrupted, standing up. "I'm here, Your Honor!"

The judge pulled his glasses down, looking at her from a distance. "Ms. Hughes, do you have pictures of Chloe on your phone as well?"

Deni ignored Sebastian's startled glance, pulling her phone out of her purse and moving forward, unlocking the device and pulling up the pictures. "Pictures and videos, Your Honor." The bailiff brought the phone to the judge and Deni resisted looking at Sebastian. This was all for Chloe, she reminded herself. Sebastian could...well, she had no idea what he could do, but she had to save Chloe.

The judge chuckled as he flipped through the pictures on Deni's phone. "Looks like she beats you at the hardwood floor sliding contest every time," he said.

Deni smiled, brightening at the memories of their silly game. "She's lower to the floor, Your Honor. And fearless. But I have some fuzzy socks that might give me an advantage for the next challenge."

The judge handed her phone back, then sighed. "Meredith Hughes, it appears that you prefer the pristine images of your daughter taken by a professional photographer rather than the reality of a small child."

Meredith's mouth opened and closed. She looked at Deni, then at the judge. "Your Honor," she rallied. "I don't believe that children should be indulged in such an atrocious manner. Discipline is what is needed in this day and age."

The judge nodded. "I agree."

Sebastian's attorney stood up. "Your Honor..."

"Never mind," the judge interrupted. "I've read the reports from the social workers, the psychologists and the nannies who have been hired to care for the child. Meredith Hughes, I'd like to point out that three nannies for one child should not be necessary. I'm awarding custody once again to Mr. Hughes. He seems to have the child's best interests in mind. And the child is smiling and laughing in his pictures." He glared at Meredith who was glaring back at him. "Seems that your idea of parenting is abandoning your child to the mercies of servants." And with that, he slammed the gavel down, ending the judgment.

Deni was only vaguely aware of Meredith standing up and hissing something furiously at her attorney. Most of her attention was focused on Sebastian. As soon as the gavel had slammed down on the case, Sebastian stood up and turned to look at her.

But Sebastian had kicked her out of his house. Out of his life.

So instead of waiting for him to speak to her, Deni turned and walked out, heading to her car.

"Deni!" he called, but Deni didn't stop. Pushing her way through the exit doors, she hitched her purse higher onto her shoulder and kept walking, sliding her sunglasses onto her nose as the bright sunshine hit her.

"Deni!" he called again, this time running down the stairs of the courthouse and stepping in front of her. "Didn't you hear me?"

Deni stopped and looked up at him. For a long moment, she didn't speak. But finally, she stepped around him. "I heard you, Sebastian."

"Why didn't you stop?"

She started walking towards her car again. "I heard you tell me to get out of your house, Sebastian. I heard you accuse me of giving information to your ex-wife." She hurried her steps. "I heard you accuse me of selling information to your competitors." She pulled her keys out of her purse and clicked the button that would unlock the car. Her fingers rested on the door handle. "I heard you, Sebastian. And I listened. Goodbye."

"But...why?" he asked, bewildered.

Deni knew what he was asking and blinked rapidly so he wouldn't see her tears. "Because that woman is horrible. I wasn't here for you, Sebastian. I was here for Chloe." And with that, she pulled open her car door and slipped inside. With relief, the engine turned over and she backed out of the parking spot. Driving out of the courthouse parking lot was difficult, but she made it. As soon as she could though, she pulled over and wiped angrily at the tears.

"No more!" she snapped at herself. "He doesn't deserve me!" But no matter how many time she told herself that, it didn't feel true.

She drove back to work that afternoon but she'd lost all concentration. Her relief that Chloe wouldn't be going back to Meredith's home was huge, but Sebastian...he looked haggard. Was he eating well? He clearly wasn't sleeping, she thought. And the rumors around the office were that he was snapping at everyone. The staff were afraid to go up to the executive floor, for fear of running into him and getting yelled at.

Rubbing her forehead, she tried to concentrate, but it was pointless. At five o'clock, she gave up and shut down her computer. Grabbing her purse, she walked out of her office and headed back to her apartment.

But as soon as she stepped off the elevator, she groaned. Because Carly, Jessa, and Charlotte were standing in front of her apartment door, waiting for her.

Carly was the first to notice her. "You look awful and you've been avoiding us for several weeks now." She lifted her hands, showing she held a bottle of tequila in one hand and a bottle of margarita mix in the other. "We're going to get you drunk and find out what's going on."

Deni laughed, shaking her head at her friends. "You know, I think that getting drunk is the best idea I've heard in a long time," she replied, then moved over to her door and unlocked it. The four of them crowded into her apartment and she laughed. It was big enough for her needs, but fill it with more than two people and Deni realized just how small her apartment really was.

"I'm ordering pizza," Charlotte declared, already pressing the buttons on the pizza website and adding ingredients to their order. "You've lost too much weight." She looked up at Carly and Jessa. "I told you we should have come over sooner."

Jessa was grabbing glasses from the cabinet while Carly filled the blender with ice, adding in some margarita mix and an equal amount of tequila.

"Yeah, I'm with you now," Carly replied. "But she kept e-mailing us, telling us that she was fine."

Charlotte nodded at the order. "Three extra-large pizzas with extra cheese, pepperoni, and sausage will be here in about twenty minutes." She then turned to Deni. "So what's his name and what did he do?" she asked, taking one of the drinks that Carly was pouring and handing it to Deni.

Deni smiled, but the tears still threatened. "Why do you think something is wrong?" she asked, hiding her face as much as possible by taking a long sip of her drink.

"Because you're usually an annoyingly vibrant, positive, happy person," Carly announced.

Jessa nodded. "And now you're...not."

Deni cringed. "Jeez. Thanks."

Jessa smiled gently. "You know what we mean."

Charlotte leaned forward. "Tell us what we need to know," she growled threateningly, "so we can get Oz to castrate the man."

Deni had just taken another sip of her margarita and almost choked on the drink. "Charlotte!" she gasped, laughing because she knew that the beautiful, blond therapist was just kidding.

"Yeah, I know. But it's a nice thought, isn't it?"

Deni pictured Sebastian like...that...then shuddered. "No! That sounds horrible!"

All three women looked at Deni with curiosity. "So, what's his name?" Carly asked again.

"Sebastian Hughes," she announced, then looked at the stunned expressions of her friends and nodded. "I know. I fell in love with the owner of my company. How stupid was that?" she sighed, leaning back against the cushions of her sofa and closed her eyes, balancing her margarita on her stomach.

Her friends stared, their expressions showing various stages of shock and horror.

Charlotte, who was used to being shocked because of what her patients told her during their therapy sessions, was the first to recover. "*The* Sebastian Hughes?" she choked.

Deni opened one eye. "Is there another Sebastian Hughes that works for my company?"

Carly shook her head, stunned. "Tall guy? Dark hair? Icy demeanor?"

Jessa laughed, covering her mouth with her hand quickly. "Talk about opposites attracting," she muttered.

"Really!" Charlotte agreed.

Carly shook her head. "Sebastian Hughes? You had an affair with Sebastian Hughes?" she demanded. But before Deni could answer, she continued, "I thought he married some...!"

There was a long silence as the puzzle pieces fell into place. Deni waited, watching with an almost amused expression as her friends slowly put it together.

"You're married to Sebastian?" Carly finally whispered.

Deni nodded.

"But...?" Jessa stammered.

Carly filled in the blanks. "How? Why? Why didn't you tell us?"

Deni leaned forward, taking another sip of her margarita before setting the glass onto the coffee table. It was time to tell them everything. "I suspect that you ladies all know Sebastian?"

"He's a good friend," Carly clarified. "He's part of the group of guys that plays poker every month or two."

Deni knew about the poker nights. She and her friends were teaching themselves to play poker as well, not wanting to be left out of the fun.

"Right," she sighed. "Okay, so you all know Sebastian and I..." she closed her eyes for a moment. "Let me back up a bit. You know that my mother passed away, right?"

"Yes," Carly said, her voice soft. "We remember. The funeral was..."

"Horrible," Deni filled in. "But my father...he fell apart and I didn't know. I was so overwhelmed with my own grief, working on my recovery, that I didn't realize what was going on with my dad."

Charlotte leaned forward. "You should have called me. I would have brought Bart over," referring to her emotional support dog. Bart was a big, adorably ugly bulldog that curled up with her patients when they were dealing with emotional turmoil. Somehow, Bart's heavy body and rough fur helped Charlotte's patients deal with their pain, easing it somehow.

"I appreciate the offer, but...well, before I knew what was going on, my father was in some serious debt. We had the medical expenses from the hospital and oncologist. The insurance company didn't cover all of her medical bills. They covered some, but they argued that some of her expenses weren't necessary," she explained, her voice quavering as she thought back to her beautiful mother who struggled so valiantly to live, only to pass away in the end.

"You should have come to me," Jessa soothed. "I would have gladly covered her expenses."

Deni sniffed and smiled at Jessa's generous offer. "I know," she whispered past the lump in her throat. "I know that any of you would have helped me." She blinked and sniffed. "But Sebastian offered me the money to cover my father's debt and...a bit more."

"In exchange for...?" Carly prompted.

"In exchange for marrying him so that he could regain custody of Chloe."

"So that's how he got custody of Chloe back!" Jessa exclaimed. "We were all wondering, but Sebastian's so quiet and reserved."

Deni smiled at the memory of that sweet child. "Yes. I married him and, at first, it was a perfect arrangement. I lived in Sebastian's house, continued to work, and Chloe came back to him. But she was...something was wrong. She was so quiet and still."

"I remember that," Carly agreed. "Chloe wasn't herself. But she got better."

Deni nodded. "I know. She came out of her shell and started smiling again." She took a deep breath. "And I got to know Sebastian a bit better." She thought back to that initial dinner with the two of them. "She smiled and laughed and we went camping together and then..."

Carly choked on a sip of her margarita. "Wait. Sebastian? He went camping? Like in the dirt and outside and all of that?"

Deni laughed, nodding her head. "Yep. You should have seen him making s'mores! He wasn't impressed with marshmallow stickiness all over his fingers and his daughter."

All three women laughed at the image of the always reserved, icy-cold friend of theirs with sticky marshmallow on his fingers.

"That was sort of the turning point. I couldn't watch Sebastian during that camping trip and not fall in love with him. He would do anything for his daughter, even sleep in a tent and make foods that he'd normally never touch." She looked down at her hands, then up at her friends. "We came back and...things just got better and better between us," she sighed. "I loved him." She shook her head. "But something went wrong. Somehow, his ex-wife heard that Sebastian and I didn't sleep in the same bedroom. She'd deduced that our marriage wasn't real and demanded custody of Chloe back."

"But..." Charlotte blinked, confused. "He still has Chloe."

Deni sighed, nodding. "I know. I was at the hearing." She shook her head. "I couldn't stay away." But she took a deep breath and looked back up at her friends. "He...he thinks that I'm the one who told Meredith. He also accused me of taking money from Meredith." Deni shuddered. "That woman is horrible! I wouldn't even speak to her, much less give her information that would hurt Chloe or Sebastian. And there's no way I would accept money from her."

Jessa rolled her eyes. "I could have told Sebastian that!"

Charlotte nodded. "But we had no idea," she replied, watching Deni with "the look".

Carly tilted her head. "Although, we suspected something was going on. Sebastian has been extra grumpy lately."

Deni asked the question she'd needed to know over the past two weeks. "Is...is Chloe okay? She hasn't heard about any of this mess, has she?"

Carly leaned over, putting an arm around Deni's shoulders. "Chloe is doing great," she assured Deni.

Good, she thought. That was all that mattered. "Okay, then that's done!" she announced and lifted her glass, finishing the rest of her drink. "Now that you ladies all know of my latest stupidity, let's drink and..."

The doorbell rang, indicating that their pizza had arrived.

"...And eat until we're sick!" she finished.

Charlotte laughed, standing up to answer the door. Carly stepped into

Deni's tiny kitchen and whipped up another round of margaritas, topping off drinks as Charlotte set three pizzas on the coffee table.

For the rest of the night, they drank and devoured the pizzas, laughing and having a good time. Oz arrived around midnight, looking at the four of them with an amused expression. "It's a good thing none of you are pregnant," he muttered, herding the three thoroughly buzzed ladies into his vehicle. Turning to Deni, he looked down at her with eyes that were disconcertingly observant. "Are you okay?" he asked softly.

Was she okay? Deni didn't think so. But Oz was a sweet man, and a dangerous one. If he even suspected that she was hurt, Deni didn't want to know what he might do. "I'm fine," she assured him.

Oz didn't move for a long moment, but then he leaned forward, pulling her into a gentle hug. "No, you're not. If you need help, any help at all, you come directly to me. Got it?"

She hugged him back, grateful for his brotherly assurance. "I will," she promised.

Chapter 31

Sebastian wanted to hit something.

Since that was so out of character for him, he continued walking down the hallway, irritated with life in general and everything else specifically.

As soon as he entered his office, he sensed that something was wrong. Sure enough, as soon as he opened the door, he found Oz and Jayce standing in his office.

"Go away," he snapped, walking around to sit at his desk.

Jayce and Oz moved closer, sitting down across from him. Sebastian hadn't really believed that his friends would leave, but a man could hope.

"He looks miserable," Oz commented conversationally as he lowered his tall frame into the leather chair in front of Sebastian's desk.

"Good," Jayce snapped, sitting in the other chair and glaring at Sebastian.

Dark eyebrows lifted as Sebastian surveyed his friends. "*Good?*" he scoffed coldly. "You're glad that I'm miserable?"

Jayce shrugged. "You hurt our wives' friend. It's good that you're hurting as well."

Sebastian wasn't aware of their friend. "To whom are you referring?" he snapped.

Oz's eyes narrowed. "Deni Stenson is our friend."

Sebastian's body ached at her name. He looked away, pushing out of his chair and moving to look out one of the windows. "Is she okay?" he asked softly, and dropped his head, muttered a curse. He shouldn't care! She'd betrayed him! She'd given information to Meredith!

"No. She's not okay," Jayce replied. "We didn't know about the connection with Deni and our wives, but now that we know...!"

179

Sebastian swung around, his eyes sharp. "What's wrong with her?" His eyes moved to the doorway. "Is she...?"

"Why do you care?"

Sebastian stopped, reminded once again that he shouldn't care. "She's...!" he stopped, not sure what to say.

"She's your wife?" Oz prompted blandly.

Sebastian heard the word and, once again, his heart ached. But then and there, he resolved to figure out a way to...what? Keep her? Divorce her? Leave her alone?

No, that wasn't the solution. He'd been trying that for the past several weeks. It hadn't worked!

"Just...is she okay? Is she eating enough?"

"No," Oz replied flatly. "She's lost weight and she looks miserable. What did you do to her?"

Sebastian shook his head, trying to ignore the need to order food for her. "She told Meredith about...that mess with the separate bedrooms," he finished off, sighing heavily as he rubbed the back of his neck. "And put Chloe in jeopardy."

Oz and Jayce stared at the man, then they both shook their heads. "No. It wasn't Deni Stenson," Oz replied emphatically. "And if it was, then it was an accident."

Sebastian thought for a moment, recalling the amount of money sitting untouched in that bank account. It hadn't occurred to him that she might have revealed the information to Meredith accidentally. But that would make more sense!

Standing up, his whole body lightened. "Do you think so?"

Jayce shook his head. "No. She didn't reveal anything, you ass!" he snapped. "Deni is an intelligent woman! She would know what's going on and she wouldn't have said a word!"

Sebastian slumped back down behind his desk. "Then...who told Meredith? I almost lost Chloe to my ex-wife because of what Meredith found out."

Jayce shook his head, leaning forward. "Yeah, and you kept custody of your daughter because of Deni. She showed up at that courtroom after you kicked her out of your house. She didn't need to be there. And yet, it was because of her that you had those pictures on your phone. Deni had a bunch of pictures on her phone too. And it was Deni's dad who risked being arrested to go to the judge's chambers before the hearing to show the judge pictures of Chloe."

Sebastian had agreed with all of that right up until they commented about Mark. And he didn't even question how these two men knew about the court hearing. The men seemed able to get information out of a rock! So it seemed just par for the course that they knew all about it.

At that moment, his office door whipped open and he turned, ready to snap at whoever would dare to enter his office without permission. But instead of an employee, a dark haired giant of a man, Ryker Thune, walked in with...!

"Martha?" Sebastian blinked as his housekeeper walked in next to Ryker. Then panic hit him. "Is Chloe okay?" he demanded, standing up. The woman's eyes were teary and she looked absolutely miserable.

Ryker understood where Sebastian's mind had gone and hurried to reassure him. "Chloe's fine. She's with Jenny."

Sebastian sank back into his chair, relief surging through him. "Thank goodness!" he muttered. He pulled himself together and looked at the older woman. "What are you doing here?" he asked of his housekeeper.

Ryker tossed a file folder onto Sebastian's desk.

Sebastian opened the folder and...there were several pictures of Meredith walking into a store and Sebastian recognized the name of the store. It was the place either Jenny or his housekeeper purchased most of Chloe's clothing. "What's this?" he asked, flipping through the pictures. One by one, he understood. Martha stepping into the store, then Meredith several minutes later, according to the time stamp. Then there was Meredith coming back out, and her expression was one of fury and frustration. There were several more pictures. Then one of Martha coming out, with just one package and walking in the opposite direction.

"It was me, sir," Martha admitted.

Sebastian looked up, confused. "It was you...what?"

Martha sniffed, but her shoulders pulled back. "I'm the one," she explained. "I accidentally told your ex-wife about the separate bedrooms. My only excuse was that I was irritated. Your ex-wife took over the shopping trip, making me purchase all of these horrible dresses when Chloe only wanted a simple dress. Meredith Hughes even demanded I give her your credit card! I was so angry with her, sir! But I thought I was alone as I walked out that day. Unfortunately, someone heard me mutter and...well, that's how Meredith found out about the two of you sleeping in separate rooms, sir. I've already packed up my things and I will be out of the house before you get home. But just to make sure...."

"You told Meredith that Deni and I slept in separate bedrooms?" he demanded, stopping her explanation.

The woman nodded.

"So...it *wasn't* Deni?"

Martha shook her head. "I think it was me. And I'm so sorry, sir!"

Sebastian shook his head, lifting a hand to stop her apology. "You...

you didn't mean to do it."

"No, sir! I never liked the first Ms. Hughes, sir. I'd never, ever, do anything to hurt you or Chloe."

Sebastian's heart lifted and he had an almost dizzy sense of relief. "That's fine, Martha. I appreciate you telling me."

"If I'd known that I was the one who slipped up, I would have come to you sooner, sir."

Sebastian smiled, shaking his head. "I know you would have. Thank you."

Ryker put a comforting hand on Martha's arm and led her out of the office, then quietly, but firmly, closed the door, leaning his shoulders against it. "So, now that you know it wasn't Deni, what are you going to do?"

Sebastian smiled, which was odd. "I think I'm going to go find Deni and..."

"No!" Oz snapped. "Sorry, old man, but she's our wives' friend, now ours, and you hurt her."

Sebastian chuckled. "I thought I was your friend too."

Jayce stood up, walking over to stand next to Ryker. "You are our friend. But the problem is, Deni is a good person and our wives care about her."

Oz stood as well, taking his place next to his brother and friend. "We'd protect you if there were any issues," Oz assured Sebastian. "But now we need to protect Deni."

Jayce nodded. "From you."

Sebastian leaned back against his desk, crossing his arms over his chest as he surveyed the human wall that blocked him from leaving his office. "So, what's your plan? Are you going to stay there like that forever?"

"If we need to," Oz replied.

"Even if I tell you that I plan to make it up to Deni?"

Ryker stepped forward. "How?"

Sebastian opened one of the desk drawers, lifting a small, black box and tossing it into the air, catching it on the way down. "I love her," he began. "I love her and I'd bought this over a month ago, intending to marry her, for real this time."

Ryker shook his head. "You don't know Deni very well if you think she'll just accept a diamond ring and forgive you."

"I don't care how long it takes me," he warned both of them. "I'm going to win her back. I was stupid to have believed she'd do something like that. Deni would never betray me and I was an idiot."

"Why did you believe it in the first place?" Oz demanded.

Sebastian knew that these men might be the key to winning Deni back. "Because I was in love with her. And I've learned not to trust women or love."

The three men stared, but it was Oz who broke into the tense silence with a frustrated epithet. "Damn it!" he sighed. "You said the one thing that would convince us."

Ryker chuckled. "I wasn't going to keep him from her anyway," he said, slapping Jayce and Oz on the backs."

"Why the hell not?" Jayce demanded.

Ryker was always the quiet type, but his eyes caught everything. "Because they are miserable without each other."

Oz conceded the point, but turned to face Sebastian with a grin. "He's right, it's going to be hell for you to convince Deni to forgive you."

Sebastian's smile evaporated. "And you three aren't going to do anything to help me, are you?"

Ryker laughed, but it was Jayce who answered. "We've all been in your shoes, my friend. It's our turn to sit back and watch, reveling in the fact that you're in the doghouse and not us."

Sebastian wasn't amused. "I'm relieved that my pain will entertain you."

Oz chuckled and clapped Sebastian's shoulder merrily. "More than you will ever know."

Chapter 32

Deni rolled over, feeling sleepy and...!

Her eyes popped open as the nausea from the previous night hit her. Jumping out of bed, she raced to the bathroom. Several minutes later, she leaned back against the wall of her small bathroom, her body aching as she regretted the three...no, four...uh...maybe five margaritas Carly had pressed on her.

Of course, Deni could have just set the glass down, but it had felt so good to not hurt anymore. To feel...numb. To not feel the absence of Sebastian and Chloe every waking moment of her day.

With a sigh, she pushed herself up to her feet and...yelped when she noticed her appearance in the mirror. Her lips were red, her hair going every which way, and her skin looked...a bit green.

Turning on the shower, she leaned her head against the wall, wishing that her stomach would calm down. Her head was achy too, but not as bad as it should be after last night's indulgence.

It was probably the pizza, she thought as she stepped under the warm water. "This is ridiculous," she muttered, grabbing the soap. Fifteen minutes later, she felt better, but still achy. "Time to stop looking like a ghost," she told her reflection. Bending down, she grabbed the hair dryer from under the sink and...

"Oh no!" she gasped, spotting the box of tampons in the corner of the cabinet.

The hair dryer slipped out of her numb fingers. A moment later, she rushed to her bedside, picking up her cell phone and flipped to the calendar, then through the months. Not last month. Not the one before but...

"Oh no!" she moaned, collapsing onto the bed as she realized why she'd thrown up this morning. It hadn't been the margaritas. At least, not entirely.

She was pregnant! If her calendar was correct, two months along!

The doorbell rang at that moment and she glanced out the bedroom door. For a long moment, she considered ignoring the bell. But it might be Carly or one of the others and...well, right now, she could use a friend.

Grabbing her robe, she pulled it on and tossed the wet towel into her laundry hamper, walking to the door. Pulling open the door, she opened her mouth, ready to offer a greeting when the tall, dark haired man turned.

"Sebastian!" she gasped, stepping backwards, her hand automatically coming up to grip the neck of her robe. "What are you doing here?"

"May I come in?" he asked softly.

For a moment, Deni considered slamming the door in his face. But the reality was, she was too starved for news of Chloe. And him! But mostly Chloe.

"Yes. Please." She stepped back and looked around at her apartment. It was a bit messy after last night's ladies night. Her first instinct was to clean up the small places that weren't pristine. But then she remembered how much she hated his house and the elegantly clinical atmosphere. So instead, she left everything as is. Pillows weren't straight and there were glasses in the sink, the pizza boxes were tilted at an angle in her garbage bin. And there was a bit of dust on everything because she'd been too tired and heart sore to do a thorough cleaning.

"I just got out of the shower. I'm going to get dressed," she told him and walked out of the room, closing her bedroom door firmly. She hoped that the action demonstrated that she didn't want him any longer. It was a lie, but she had to grab onto any shred of dignity she could muster under the circumstances.

Quickly, she grabbed a pair of well-worn jeans and a sweater, not caring what they looked like. Running her fingers through her hair in lieu of a comb, she grabbed a band and pulled her hair up on top of her head. For a moment, she thought about doing a better job of smoothing out her hair. But then she remembered that it was just Sebastian and she no longer was interested in being attractive to him.

Her hand came to rest on her stomach, thinking about the baby nestled inside of her. She should tell him, Deni thought. He had a right to know.

But not right now. She needed to confirm the pregnancy. Right now, it was just a possibility. She was late on her period. Very late, but...that could also be due to stress and lack of eating.

Not an issue for now, she thought. When she had confirmation, she'd tell him. She owed him that much. But nothing more.

Taking a deep breath, she pulled open the door and stepped out, finding him standing in front of her bookcase, perusing the titles.

"Interested in something?" she asked.

He picked up the picture of herself and another woman. "Is this your mother?" he asked gently.

Deni looked at the picture and a stab of longing for her mother went through her. She took the picture away and stepped back. "Yes." She lifted her chin, refusing to tell him anything more. "What do you want? Wanna throw a few more accusations at me?"

He sighed, shaking his head. "No. I..." he looked around. "I came to apologize."

That was new! "About what?" she demanded, fighting back sudden tears.

"I was wrong, Deni."

Shifting on her feet, she crossed her arms over her chest. "Yes. You were." Lifting her head, she glared up at him, refusing to think about how his eyes were the sexiest, most incredible eyes she'd ever seen. "Anything else?"

He looked uncomfortable. But she didn't care. Not even a little! He'd tossed her out of his house like yesterday's trash, not even giving her a chance to defend herself! Not that he'd have believed any of her claims of innocence. And there had been no way she could prove she hadn't done it. In this kind of issue, he just had to trust her. Believe in her.

"Please, could we start again?" he asked, his grey eyes...they were no longer icy. But right now, they were filled with an emotion Deni couldn't quite identify.

"Why?"

He blinked down at her. "Because...I...care for you," he stumbled.

Deni closed her eyes, the pain stabbing her heart unlike anything she'd ever felt before. When she opened them again, it seemed as if his look was longing. But that was impossible! Sebastian didn't long for anything or anyone! He simply went out and bought whatever it was that he wanted.

"Well, I'm so glad that you...care...for me, Sebastian. Because," she sniffed and turned away from him. "I love you. I fell hard and fast for a man who has no emotions. I love you and you *care* for me." She looked out through the glass of her tiny sliding glass doorway. "I'm so glad that you have lukewarm feelings for me, when I feel as if you cut my heart out when you kicked me out of your life. And, not just that, but I love Chloe. You bought me, brought me into your life, let me share the beauty of that child, then snatched her away from me."

She turned back to face him and was startled by the heated look in his eyes. "So..."

"If you love me, then marry me, Deni," he growled, the sound so guttural and demanding that a shiver of awe and awareness slithered up through her body.

Marry him? Seriously?! She pulled back, refusing to allow the hope to gain a footing in her mind. Turning away from him again, she shook her head. "I already did. I can't do it again, Sebastian. Being around you will only make my feelings harder to kill." She took a deep breath and looked up at him with a determined expression to her eyes. "I'm going to get over you."

"Don't!" he snapped, moving closer. He reached out to her, but his fingers closed into a fist, then spread out as if he wanted to touch her. "Don't get over me, Deni. Please! Don't give up on me! I'm a mess. I know this. Meredith really messed with my mind."

She turned and glared up at him. "You never cared for her," Deni retorted.

He ran a hand through his hair. He turned and paced the few feet her tiny apartment allowed. "I was lured in by her outer beauty, but by the time she became pregnant, I was more than ready to get away from her. So no, I never truly cared for her." He sighed, shaking his head. "Sometimes, I wonder if that's why she's so vindictive. She knew that I never fell under her spell." He stopped and looked over at Deni. "But I fell under yours."

Oh, such sweet words! For several long moments, Deni looked up at him, wanting so much to believe him. "Your words sound nice, Sebastian." She swallowed hard. "Better than nice, actually." Deni turned away. "But I won't settle for nice. Especially when I love you. Nice is so...bland."

With obvious frustration, he stared up at the ceiling, then back at her. "I don't have the words to describe how I feel for you, Deni."

She turned, crossing her arms over her chest. "Well, that's...nice," she replied sarcastically.

Sebastian knew that he was blowing this and wasn't sure how to fix it. He wanted to pull her into his arms, but she looked so...distant. So cold and unlike herself. The Deni he remembered was always smiling, always hopeful. Her eyes...they were dead now.

Since he couldn't seem to get out the right words, he just started talking. "I know that I hate walking into the house without you at night," he told her. "I know that Chloe and I don't laugh anywhere as much during dinner without you." He sighed. "I also know that I miss holding you. I'm not sleeping because you aren't in my arms. Even before that mess with the courts, I wanted you all the time. Every morning I woke up and went back to my bedroom before everyone else woke up. It was wrong, Deni. I knew it was wrong, but I didn't have the words to figure out why it was wrong. And damn it, I miss you! I feel only half alive without you! And there's no sunshine!" When her eyes widened, he nodded. "You brought the sunshine, Deni! You made the world warm, sunny, and happy! Damn, I remember the first time I saw you, you were dancing in the rain and I couldn't figure out how to get warm. Then I saw you and it was as if you brought the warmth with you as you walked into the building!" He stepped closer to her, but didn't touch her. "I'm a mess, Deni. I don't trust very well. Especially women."

"For a man who doesn't speak a whole lot, that was a mouthful."

He chuckled and moved closer. "Deni, please, don't leave me out in the cold. Teach me to trust," he said softly, reaching out to touch her, taking her hands in his. "Teach me how to..." he stopped, not exactly sure what to say, how to finish. He just stared at her for a long moment.

"What?" she prompted, enthralled by his words despite her determination to not feel anything more towards this man. Unfortunately, where Sebastian was concerned, she couldn't seem to help herself. "What do you want to learn?"

He laughed, shaking his head. "I don't need to learn to love you, Deni," he told her, moving closer. "I just realized that I already do."

Beautiful words...so beautiful that she closed her eyes, letting the happiness wash over her. But then she opened them again, looking up at him. "So, why did you kick me out of your house? Out of your life?" This time, she couldn't stop the tears from falling.

He pulled her into his arms, relieved when she allowed the caress. "Because you scare the hell out of me!" he rasped. "You're so bright and sunny and happy! And I'm...not! So I believed whatever the first excuse was that allowed me to push you away." He sighed, his arms tightening around her. "Damn, Deni. I need you! I need you to show me how the world can be. Not the way I see it," he told her. "Marry me. For real this time! We can have a huge wedding, anything you want. We can invite all of your friends and make it a massive affair. You can wear a huge, white wedding dress and I'll pay for all of it. Just...marry me and bring the sunshine back into my life!" he groaned.

Deni couldn't believe what she was hearing. Stiff, formal, icy Sebastian wanted her! He called her his sunshine! Oh, she knew that she should resist him. But how could she? How could she ignore him when he said things like that?

"I don't want a big, formal wedding, Sebastian."

"What do you want?" he asked, pulling back so that he could look down at her.

"You," she whispered. "And Chloe."

"You have me. And Chloe misses you fiercely."

She stared up into his beautiful grey eyes, debating her next request. But in the end, she knew that she had to be honest with him. "And a new house," she added, cringing as she said it.

He was startled for a moment. "A new house?"

"Yes," she replied, looking wary now. "I hate your house, Sebastian. It's cold and soulless. And it's so massive and formal!"

He blinked. Then he threw back his head, laughing with delight. "A new house it is! You can choose any house you want, as long as you and Chloe are in it."

"And maybe, a few more children?" she asked, her heart pounding as she waited for his response.

He hesitated, and shook his head, even shuddering slightly. She felt his fingers clench and unclench around her waist, not sure what was going through his mind.

"That's going to take a bit more time, Deni," he warned. "Meredith... she threatened to abort her pregnancy several times. When she got mad at me, or if I didn't come home when she called, when I didn't increase her credit limit or pay for some extravagant piece of jewelry she wanted...she'd threaten to abort our child." He sighed, wrapping her arms around her. "I lived in fear of coming home to find out that she'd killed my child in a fit of temper." He shuddered. "So, that might take a bit more time."

Deni wasn't sure what to say. But it was better to get this all out into the open. Honesty, she thought. "Well, could you give me an estimate on how long it might take you to trust that I won't have an abortion?"

Sebastian shook his head. "I don't know, Deni. I just..." he stopped, her words echoed through his head. Deni just stood there, waiting. He was an intelligent man. He stiffened, and pulled back, looking down at her. "Deni, what are you telling me?"

She shrugged, sliding her fingers up his chest. "I don't know for sure, but I think I might be pregnant," she whispered.

Sebastian stepped back and Deni's hands fell to her sides. She looked up at him, watching warily.

"How?" he rasped, running a shaking hand through his hair.

"I don't know," she replied. "And I don't know if I'm truly pregnant." That was only sort of a lie. She suspected strongly, but hadn't confirmed it yet. "But...I'm late. My cycles are irregular, but never this late."

The pacing started again. Back and forth and he glanced at her several times, working through something in his mind.

Finally, he came to stand in front of her. "Do you want more children?"

She looked into his grey eyes. If he'd asked her yesterday, she would have said no. No because she didn't want to acknowledge her feelings.

But now? Now she wanted to take him into her arms and shower him with so much love that he never doubted for a single moment that he was a wonderful, exceptionally amazing man. "Yes," she finally answered. "I want children, with you, very badly."

"And an abortion?"

She felt as if he'd just slapped her. "If you don't want this child," she whispered harshly, her hand coming up to cover her stomach defensively, "then that's fine. I'll have this baby on my own. I'm *not* aborting our child."

He stared at her for a long moment. Then the air seemed to gush from his lungs and he pulled her into his arms. "Thank god!" he groaned, and he held her tightly and Deni lost the battle against her tears.

"I love you, Sebastian!" she told him with heartfelt honesty.

"I...love you too." He stumbled over the words, but Deni thought they were more poignant for that stumbling.

Epilogue

"What do you think?" Sebastian said, holding Chloe in his arms as they both stared down at the two basinets.

"They are boys," she whispered, obviously unimpressed.

Her father chuckled.

"Yes, they are boys. Twins."

"I wanted a *sister*," she pointed out, emphasizing the last word.

Sebastian hugged her slightly. "I already have one perfect daughter that I love very much," he explained. "I think that God decided that we needed boys instead of another girl."

Chloe was soothed by her father's words, but still...she looked skeptically down at the babies that were sleeping at the moment. "What do they do?"

He laughed and sat down on the edge of the hospital bed where Deni was sipping herbal tea and watching them. "Well, eventually, they'll get bigger and the three of you can play together."

She sighed, still not convinced. Leaning her head against his shoulder, she reached out to poke one of the tiny infants. "I'm not going to have to leave again, am I?" she whispered, her chin trembling as she contemplated the addition of brothers into her world.

Sebastian turned to glance at Deni over his shoulder. Looking down at his beautiful daughter, he shook his head. "Never, honey!" he told her forcefully. "You never have to leave! Having brothers only means that we'll have a bigger family. And we're going to need your help with them."

Chloe looked at him, her eyes sparkling with the unshed tears. "Help? How can I help?"

He held her close, wishing that he could somehow wipe away the time his precious daughter had spent in Meredith's house. But he couldn't.

All he could do was fill every day of her life with love and security. With Deni's help, he was doing that.

"Well, these two little guys don't know how to make s'mores," he explained. Immediately, Chloe's eyes widened with excitement. "And they don't know how to put up a tent or go hiking. You and I go hiking together a lot these days and I was hoping that you might help teach them how to walk and to laugh, just like you do all the time."

She nodded her head. "I could do that!" she brightened. "I'm really good at making s'mores!"

He laughed. "I know. Deni taught you how to find the right coals in the fire and you are an expert now. So now, we're all going to have to teach them to make s'mores too. What do you think?"

She bounced eagerly, nodding while her blond curls danced. "I can do that! I promise!"

"Good! I know that you'll be the best big sister any brother could hope for!"

Excerpt from "That Night with the Sheik"
Release Date: November 15, 2019

(Author's Note: There's a prologue to this story that gives a bit of a back story to Chloe and Girad's romance, but I went ahead and chose this excerpt for you lovely ladies. I hope you enjoy this snippet!)

Chloe stood behind Avi, staring into her eyes in the mirror. It was a week before her wedding and Avi was absolutely miserable as they did a final fitting for her wedding dress. "You're going to be okay," Chloe whispered comfortingly, putting her hands on Avi's shoulders gently. "I've met Sheik Lugar. He seems very nice."

Avi shivered, lowering her eyes. "I hate him, Chloe," she whispered. "He doesn't understand me. He thinks Otis is ridiculous," she spat, referring to the ugly, abused donkey that Avi had rescued several months ago. The donkey wouldn't let anyone touch him but Avi and a few of the stable hands. As soon as Avi came down to the stables, Otis brayed and raced through the other horses in the pasture, determined to get to Avi first. Otis adored Avi and she loved him right back. But then, Avi loved all of her rescued animals, right down to the latest batch of kittens that she'd snuck into the stables just yesterday.

"He might not understand you now, but be patient," Chloe advised, then closed her eyes, shaking her head. "That's such a stupid thing to say!" She moved around to face her friend. "I'm American, so I'm struggling here. I don't think that any woman should *have* to be patient and wait for her husband to learn to understand her! But this isn't my country and I don't understand why you would agree to marry a man that you don't even like, let alone love."

Avi burst out laughing, which turned into tears as she threw herself into Chloe's arms.

"I know!" she sobbed into Chloe's shoulder. "I know and I agree! But I don't know what to do!"

"Avi!" a deep voice came from the doorway. Chloe and Avi both spun around, finding her brother standing in the doorway, looking furious. His sharp, dark eyes moved from his sister to Chloe, obviously disapproving of the tears before announcing, "Your finance has arrived, Avi. He's asking for you."

Avi stiffened, her chin tilting defiantly. "Ah, well, then I must go to him shouldn't I? I've been summoned, just like a dog!"

"Avi!" he snapped, his dark eyebrows lowering with anger.

She didn't reply, but only glared back at him. But Girad was the stronger willed and won the contest. With a sniff, Avi turned and headed back into her dressing room to take off the delicate wedding dress.

Chloe continued to stare at Girad. Other than television or news articles, she hadn't seen him in over ten years. He seemed bigger now, his shoulders wider; Chloe suspected that there were significantly more muscles on his tall frame. Unfortunately, he still had the same effect on her, which she resented.

His dark eyes softened as he approached.

Chloe realized that his anger had vanished, a teasing glint had replaced it. "I see that you've grown into the beauty your youth foretold, Chloe," he murmured, standing close.

Chloe glared up at him, startled to find that she wasn't as immune to him as she'd hoped. After ten years, she still trembled when he was close.

Of course, ten years ago, she'd trembled when he was far, so maybe this was progress!

He nodded toward the room his sister had just disappeared into. "You don't approve of Avi getting married, do you?"

Chloe gritted her teeth, determined to keep her opinion to herself. She shouldn't say anything. It was none of her business.

Except...darn it, Avi was her best friend! And this man was forcing Avi into a loveless marriage!

Facing him head on, she straightened her shoulders and glared back at him. "No. I don't approve."

He stepped closer still as she struggled to not fidget under his intense gaze. "You just don't understand our culture."

She gritted her teeth, refusing to be charmed by him! "Maybe not, but I understand Avi. And she's miserable!"

He smiled slightly. "She'll get over it. More quickly than you might realize."

Chloe desperately wanted to slap him! He was so smug. So confident! He had no idea how terribly sad and confused Avi was.

"So tell, me, oh wise one: how did this fantastic, soon-to-be love match come along?" she demanded as she stepped back, needing more space.

"Would you be as angry if I told you that Sheik Lugar made an offer of a hundred goats and I accepted?"

"It might make more sense," she retorted.

He laughed, and leaned back against his sister's desk. "So, tell me why you're so against this marriage."

Girad was more entranced than he wanted to be. Chloe was a golden goddess. Her almost-white hair shimmered in the sunshine and her pale skin was almost translucent. Except when she blushed, he remembered. Damn, he wanted to see her do that again. Her cheeks glowed pink and her lips softened. It was...amazing. Sexy!

"A man and a woman should marry for love. Not for political gain," she explained and he swallowed a chuckle at her sarcasm.

"In *your* world," he countered. "In my world, families marry for political purposes all the time. For expediency among other reasons."

"So, this is a political marriage? What benefit does Cardaire gain from a marriage with Shardir?" she demanded. "Your country is strong enough. There are already robust economic ties between your countries. There is no war, not even tensions where a marriage might ease the hostilities. So...what's the gain?"

"Perhaps stronger ties. Stronger economic agreements." He stood up and walked towards her. "And maybe, the potential for love and a strong family." He lifted Chloe's hand, wrapping his fingers around the delicate bones of her wrist. Looking down, he contemplated the texture of her skin and the contrast of his tanned hand against her pale one. "Or maybe, I just think that Avi needs a man like Lugar. I think that he could be a good influence on her." His fingers tightened on her wrist, not closing tightly, but loosely holding her in his grip. She felt good, he thought. Despite her angry tone, Chloe Hughes was surprisingly delicate and feminine.

She pulled her hand away, that delightful pink staining her pale cheeks. But she rallied quickly. "So, you're saying that Avi needs a strong man to temper her radical and feminine impulses?"

He laughed, shaking his head. "You said that. Not me."

Girad thought that Chloe Hughes was a breath of fresh air. Only his sister dared to challenge him in this way. He reclaimed her wrist, toying with it gently. "Yes, but you think it, don't you?"

"I think that Avi is a strong-willed woman. And yes, Luger might be able to temper some of her wilder inclinations. Lord knows I never figured out how."

She jerked her wrist, but he didn't let go. He liked the fire in Chloe's eyes. And he liked that she was fighting for Avi even better. His sister didn't have enough advocates in her life. And Chloe was determined and strong enough for several! She was a tigress! Would she be this passionate in bed?

Girad wanted to find out. Just thinking about all of that fire and passion directed towards him made his body tighten with excitement and need. Damn, she was beautiful! Those soft, rosy lips, which were spewing fire and anger right now, would be incredible when he finally kissed her.

Idly, he wondered if he'd agreed to Lugar's marriage offer simply because he knew that Avi would ask Chloe to be her maid of honor, so she'd have come back to the palace for the wedding.

But no...there was so much more to Lugar's offer. It was important that the two marry. Imperative, actually.

Seeing Chloe in his home once again was simply an added bonus.

"Avi doesn't need her impulses tempered!" Chloe declared. "She's passionate about her causes, which is not a bad thing!"

He laughed. "Have you been down to the stables lately?"

Her grey eyes sparkled. "No, but Avi has told me about Otis."

Girad growled at the reminder of that beast. "I hate that donkey!" he sighed. He stood up, tucking her hand into his arm. "The stupid animal thinks he's a stallion and keeps nipping at my mares."

Her sudden, soft laughter caught him off-guard and he paused in the middle of the hallway, staring down at her.

Those grey eyes...they were actually laughing at him? Immediately, he thought about kissing her. Would she be this defiant after a kiss? Or would she melt into him, releasing that fire and anger while returning his kiss?

She didn't look intimidated by his look of disdain at her laughter.

"Aww, poor babies. Are they suffering from an alpha male's ornery temperament?" she mocked. Those taunting eyes turned serious. "I know the feeling."

He lifted a dark eyebrow in warning. But wasn't surprised when the feisty blond beauty ignored it.

"I'm sure that your prized, million-dollar mares can handle one small, formerly-abused donkey. And if they can't, then move Otis into another pasture."

He sighed. "Tomorrow morning, I'm taking you down to the stables. You are in for a surprise," he shook his head. "But for now, it is time that you dressed for dinner. It's formal tonight. We're having guests and dancing." He stopped in front of the door to her suite. "Will you save me a dance?"

She pulled back, blinking up at him with surprise in her eyes and her full, soft lips parted ever so slightly. Damn, she was beautiful!

"I don't think so," she told him. "I think I'm on the side of your mares and want to avoid annoying alpha males." And with that, she slipped into her suite to the echo of his startled laughter.

(Continue reading for another Elizabeth Lennox excerpt!)
Other Books in The Diamond Club Series:
Resisting the Sheik's Commands

The Sheik's Arrangement
The Sheik's Vengeance
The Sheik's Gentle Triumph
Love and Secrets
His Baby Bargain
Forbidden Lover
That Night with the Sheik
Inconveniently Tempted
Her Secret, His Heir

Excerpt from "Over Heated"
Release Date: October 25, 2019

August sunshine and black wool were *not* a good combination!

Roxanne sat on the bench, trying to absorb everything that had happened over the past week. For a long moment, she wondered if she were living in an alternate universe. Or was she being punked? Was there a hidden camera somewhere? Unfortunately, she was too stunned to even look for cameras.

The papers in her hands were...outrageous! The requirements...impossible!

Her mother...was gone. After years of verbal and emotional abuse, Myrtle Halley was gone.

Roxanne's fingers curled, crushing the edges of the papers as she sifted through the emotions rushing through her. Her mother's funeral had been last week, but today...today had been the meeting with her mother's lawyer. Roxanne hadn't known that her mother had ever needed a lawyer! In fact, Roxanne hadn't known that a lawyer even existed in this small town! Carlton, Colorado had one grocery store, one bar, one hair salon, one...of everything. Apparently, there was also one lawyer.

But...growing up, there'd never been a whole lot of money so...it hadn't occurred to Roxanne that her mother would need a lawyer.

Correction. There hadn't been a lot of money *for Roxanne*. Apparently, Myrtle Halley had saved up a great deal of money! Over half a million dollars in a savings account, plus the woman's home was completely paid off.

And a cat.

Nope, Roxanne definitely couldn't forget about the cat!

Everything had been left to the cat! All the money, even the house, had been left to care for the cat!

Roxanne had learned never to expect much from her mother other than criticism. Nothing Roxanne had done...not the straight As in high school and college, the great job in the hospital surgical department, nothing had been good enough for even a kind word. If she got straight As, Roxanne's mother would snipe that Roxanne hadn't taken hard enough classes. If she took the advanced placement classes, Myrtle would ridicule Roxanne for trying to be "uppity". When Roxanne had landed a coveted job at the hospital an hour away in Denver, Myrtle had complained that Roxanne was abandoning her for a better life. But every time Roxanne had come home, Myrtle had snapped at Roxanne not to expect a meal, or sympathy for traveling an hour just to "sit around waiting for idle chit chat".

Nothing Roxanne did was ever good enough for her mother and it had always been a mystery as to why her mother was so....angry.

And now, there was no way to discover answers to her mother's angry personality, because she was gone.

Roxanne lifted her face up to the sunshine, sorting through her emotions. Was she sad? Surprisingly yes. A little. And that felt...wrong somehow. Why was she sad about a woman who had made her life miserable? Roxanne told herself that she should be relieved. Or angry because of what she'd just learned! Sadness had no place in her life right now!

But in reality, Roxanne was sad. And angry because she was sad. It felt as if there was a gaping hole in her chest...because a woman who had never had a kind word for her daughter had left this earth and...

Nothing made sense! She shouldn't be sad! Yet, her eyes burned and her heart ached.

Her eyes dropped to the papers that outlined her mother's last will and testament.

Yeah, Roxanne was angry. Furious, actually. And the anger felt better than the sadness! Anger was easier to deal with, she thought and pushed the sadness away.

Myrtle had continuously informed Roxanne that she was a hussy. That she was a slut, even though Roxanne rarely dated. Not in high school, because there was no way she'd ever bring a boy home for fear that he might meet the horrid woman. And not in college, because Roxanne had maintained a full class load, plus she'd worked two jobs in order to pay her tuition and the rent on her tiny dump of an apartment, not to mention paying for her books and food.

And now, Roxanne was supposed to sell her mother's house and use all of the woman's savings so that she could care for the woman's cat? Oh, and let's not forget that Roxanne was supposed to care for all of those ridiculous, cheap glass figurines! There weren't just a few of the stupid things. Her mother had been an obsessive collector of glass animals and clowns and...whatever! There were hundreds of them all over her mother's house! What in the world was Roxanne supposed to do with them? Her mother had dusted those stupid things every week, taking most of Saturday morning to ensure that they "sparkled" in the sunshine!

There was no way that Roxanne was going to take care of those damn figurines! And the cat? It was evil! Totally evil! The cat hissed at her every time she walked into the house. Her mother used to laugh at the cat when Roxanne jumped back, then pet the satanic feline as if he'd done something miraculous!

Now Roxanne had to swallow the news that the horrible cat had inherited everything! Roxanne had been listed as the executor of the will and caretaker of the cat. Sheesh!

What kind of lawyer would write up a will like that?

Roxanne had thousands of dollars in student debt she still owed, a car that ran only when it felt like it, a tiny apartment that was barely large enough for herself, and now she had to bring in an almost feral cat and thousands of pieces of glass...junk?

"I need a drink!"

Roxanne rarely drank alcohol, but after her meeting with the town's one lawyer, she felt as if she'd earned a strong drink. Looking around, she spotted the bar across the street. Never mind that it was a biker bar with about twenty motorcycles parked in front, all with varying degrees of chrome and steel shining in the hot afternoon sunshine. It was a bar. She needed a drink. Enough said. She barely glanced at the tattoo sign. It was the alcohol that she needed, not a tattoo.

Stepping through the heavy doors, Roxanne stopped and looked around, blinking her eyes to adjust to the dimmer light. It wasn't nearly as gross as she had anticipated. But there was nothing elegant about it either. Wood walls. Wood floors stained by decades of use and spilled beer. Pool tables in the back and a wooden bar with neon lights advertising various brands of beers glowing on the wall behind it. Off to one side, there was a door that she assumed led to the tattoo parlor, but she focused on the bar.

Walking over, she carefully perched on a wooden stool.

"What can I get you?" a bartender with the most incredible white mustache asked her, leaning against the bar with what she suspected was amusement.

Roxane looked around, completely aware that she looked out of place and not caring. Her black suit and sensible black shoes were boring. Professional, but boring. She was prim and tedious while the others in the room competed with each other for the most amount of leather on their bodies. Roxanne wasn't even sure if her shoes were leather! For the amount she'd paid for these stupid, ugly shoes, they were probably pleather. Great. She was outclassed by a biker gang.

"A beer," she replied. When the bartender opened his mouth to ask what kind, Roxanne only pointed to the man a few stools away. "Whatever that is, it will work for me."

The bartender glanced over at the other man, nodded and grabbed a chilled beer mug. Less than thirty seconds later, a beer with a foam top was placed in front of her.

Roxanne stared at the beer for a long moment, then glanced at the papers next to her. "A freaking cat!" she snapped, then lifted the beer and, despite the vile taste, downed half of it.

The deep laughter behind her warned Roxanne that her day was about to get even worse. She recognized that voice, but she wasn't going to turn around. Not this time. She wasn't going to do it! Besides, there was no way that he was here! Not in Carlton, Colorado! The town was too small to contain the man she hoped and prayed was not behind her.

"That was mighty impressive!" the laughing voice commented.

Resigned, Roxanne turned her head and, sure enough, the man she hated more than anyone else in the world was sliding onto the bar stood next to her.

"Please," she whispered, burying her face in her hands, "let this nightmare end!"

His husky laugh told her that God had not granted her wish. "What brings the prim and ever-so-proper Roxy to the wrong side of the tracks?"

Oh, how she hated that nickname! Every horrible thing Roxanne's mother had said about being a hussy, about being evil and slutty...they all flooded to mind when Doctor Abe McCullough said her name like that.

"What on earth are you doing here?" she demanded, not bothering to look at him. She couldn't. Not tonight. She'd look at him tomorrow. Or more specifically, she'd look at his perfectly knotted tie and his impressively pressed, tailored shirt. The man was tall and handsome, with a hard, square jaw and a five o'clock shadow that started appearing around ten o'clock in the morning. And eyes! Goodness, his eyes made all the ladies swoon! Dark, sexy eyes with just a hint of gold towards the iris! He literally oozed charm, was a brilliant trauma surgeon, and had all the nurses cooing over him, bringing him his favorite exotic scented coffee from a specialty store – they all knew what he preferred. Cookies were brought in as a way to impress the hunky doctor with their home-making skills. Too often, one or more of the nurses just happened to have an "extra" sandwich, which they offered to him so that he wouldn't starve. Right! It was disgusting!

"It won't work," he commented.

Roxanne sighed, keeping her eyes resolutely on her beer. "I'm not going to ask," she whispered to herself. "I'm *not* going to ask!" There was silence for a long moment. She squeezed her eyes tightly shut to try to block out the temptation. But she couldn't stand it. "*What* isn't going to work?"

"The mug. You can't kill it with your bare hands."

Roxanne opened her eyes and stared down at the beer mug. Sure enough, she'd tightened her grip on the mug until her knuckles were white.

She released the beer and flexed her fingers. "Doctor..." she turned, ready to blast him in an effort to make him leave her alone. But the sight of the man sitting next to her stopped whatever words she might have uttered.

Doctor Abe McCullough, sexy man-extraordinaire and the heartthrob of every female within a fifty mile radius of their fair city...had tattoos! Not just one, either. Nope. First of all, instead of the ironed and starched dress shirts he normally wore, today he had on a soft faded blue tee shirt that was tight around his arms and chest. Loose around his waist but...dear heaven! Where had he been hiding all of those muscles?! The man was ripped! Holy cow!

Her eyes moved over his broad shoulders, down over bulging biceps and lower, noticing the taut muscles barely hidden by the soft cotton. When her gaze moved back up, they took in the dark swirls and lines along one arm. She wasn't sure what the design represented and she didn't care! Muscles and tattoos and...oh my!

Holy cow!

She'd already said that, Roxanne thought. Maybe several times. But the muscles rippling along his arms and shoulders and...good grief, everywhere...deserved a few more "Holy Cows!" He was quite literally buff, ripped...whatever was the current vernacular for a man with that many muscles.

"You're ogling," he commented archly.

Yeah, but...holy cow!

"Do you bench press a bus every morning?" she exclaimed, her eyes once again moving to his arm. Just one arm. One large tattoo that darkened the tanned skin on his shoulder, bicep, and forearm. There was a bit of red mixed in with a few lines and she wasn't aware of her tongue darting out to wet her lips. Because...good grief! The supremely confident Doctor Abe was hotter than she'd expected!

Okay, so if she hadn't been avoiding him for the past month since he'd come on board, she'd probably have seen him in his scrubs and seen that long, sexy tattoo and all those amazing, shocking muscles. But since she scheduled the surgical rooms, she knew when he would be around. Roxanne made sure that she was in her office or, even better, out of the office, when he was scheduled for surgery.

"Do I get to return the ogling?" he asked, leaning forward as if they were sharing a joke.

Roxanne jerked backwards, unaware of her mouth hanging open as she gazed into those fascinating eyes of his. How had she missed those gold flecks? "Seriously, I know how many hours you work," she snapped. "When do you find the time to work out?"

He shrugged and her eyes were pulled back down to that tattoo covered arm. Yum! Roxanne had never thought to be attracted to a man with a tattoo. But then, she'd never seen Doctor Abe like this before! He was hotness on a whole new level!

Doctor Abe simply shrugged. "Some doctors drink after a difficult surgery. Others have sex." He grinned and her attention was pulled to his lips. "I train."

Despite her vow to be distant, she couldn't hide her curiosity. "Train? How?"

"Martial arts. Boxing. Karate. Krav Maga. Anything that focuses my mind on something other than the surgery I just left behind."

"Ah," she replied, impressed and...amazed. "And are you good?"

His smile widened. "Yes. I'm very good."

Were they still talking about the training? Somehow, she didn't think so.

Turning away, Roxanne snorted quietly and picked up her beer. The papers beside her elbow reminded her of her morning and she sighed. "Go away. I'm getting drunk."

He lifted a hand and the bartender brought him a Corona in the bottle. "I didn't think you were the type to drink."

She took a long sip of the beer, smothering her cringe of revulsion as she carefully set the mug back onto the polished bar. "Why would you think that?"

"Because you're too uptight," he took a long swallow of his beer.

"I am *not* uptight!" she snapped.

"Sure you are," he teased. "You run our surgical unit as if you were invading a foreign country." He winked at her. "Fortunately, you're good, so most of us don't mind."

Roxanne took another sip of her beer, debating if she should focus on the "invasion" aspect of his comment, or the fact that he'd complimented her. Since she wasn't used to compliments, she focused on the negative. "I just want things to run smoothly. The surgical teams need everything to be just right."

"I'm not criticizing, Roxy," he argued, waving to the bartender to bring him another beer. "In fact, it's one of the best surgical units I've ever worked in."

Roxanne heard his words, but it took several moments to absorb and understand what he'd just said. When she grasped the meaning of his words, Roxanne's head lifted slowly and she stared at him, stunned. She realized that her mouth was hanging open when he put a finger under her chin and closed her mouth.

Jerking back because her chin felt as if it were on fire, she kept her gaze on her beer, toying with the glass. The stupid legal documents rustled when she bumped them and she did a mental shake, lifted her beer and downed the rest of it. When she set the glass down, she cringed again at the horrible taste, closed her eyes, and tried to relax.

"How about a glass of wine instead of another beer?"

Roxanne's eyes narrowed at the amusement she perceived in his voice. "Are you laughing at me?" she demanded.

He lifted his hands into the air, palms out. "I would never laugh at you, Roxy!"

She glared at him, but with his hands lifted like that, his tattoo distracted her. "You're a doctor. Why do you have a tattoo?"

He laughed softly, and sipped his beer. Roxy couldn't stop admiring his muscles. Huge muscles!

"Is there a rule against doctors having tattoos?"

Rules! Her lips pressed together at the word. "I'm sick of rules," she muttered furiously.

"Ah! Now we're getting to the crux of the issue."

She huffed a bit, shifting on the wooden stool. "I don't have any issues."

"Sure you do," he laughed. "Lots of issues. We all do."

"I don't!" But she did! Including cat issues. Mother issues. Abandonment issues since her father had walked out of her life before she'd learned to crawl. Her mother claimed that he hadn't wanted the trouble a baby would bring.

"What's *really* wrong?" he probed.

Roxanne turned, surprised by the gentle, compassionate tone. Usually, he seemed to thrive on pushing her buttons. He flirted, he teased, he asked to change the surgical schedule, and he asked for specific nurses…okay, that was fine, because the surgical staff loved working with him. He was a genius in surgery and everyone wanted to learn from him.

"You always wear a long shirt under your scrubs," she blurted, glancing meaningfully at the tattoo running from his shoulder to his forearm. "Is that because you're trying to hide that?"

His eyes narrowed for a split second, then he seemed to relax once more. "Maybe a bit. But it's more because we have to keep the room cold. I get hot at times, but normally, it's a chilly room and I don't like being cold."

Roxanne made a noncommittal noise and turned away, not wanting to think about him being hot. He was. But she didn't need to think about it. Bad idea, thinking about him being hot. Or heated. Or...whatever! Bad!

"Joe, can you get the lady a glass of wine?" Abe called.

The bartender nodded once and started to reach for something, but Roxanne wasn't regressing. "I don't want wine," she decided. "How about a whiskey?"

The bartender hesitated, then glanced at Abe.

Roxanne gasped, horrified. "Seriously? You're looking to *him* for permission to pour *me* a whiskey?"

Roxanne stood up, prepared to leave and get drunk somewhere else! "Fine!"

Abe laughed and grabbed her arm, pulling her back into her seat. "Slow down, Roxy. He wasn't asking permission to pour you a drink, honey. He was looking to me to see if I was going to give you a ride home. Joe doesn't allow anyone to drink and drive."

"Oh," she replied, her anger deflating as fast as it had exploded. "Well....that's good then. I mean...," she sighed, rubbing her forehead as she looked at Joe. "Please, could I have a whiskey? I will call a cab tonight. I just..." she glanced down at the papers, then away again.

"What's in the papers that's so upsetting?" he asked gently.

Roxanne eyed the papers as if they were a snake. "Nothing important." There was silence for a moment. "Do you like cats?" she asked.

Abe eyed the woman that had fascinated him since he'd hired on with the hospital a month ago. The strawberry blond hair and golden eyes, pale, almost white, skin plus that wide, sexy mouth were a combination that was enough to light any man's imagination. Add in her saucy comebacks, her take-no-prisoners way of getting things done, and her long, long legs...he'd been a goner since the first time she'd turned her back on him.

Ironic that the other female staff in the hospital were annoying in their attempts to ask him out and yet, the one person he would actually consider violating his rule about dating in the workplace for rejected even his friendship overtures.

"Cats?"

She smiled as Joe put the small glass of whiskey in front of her. "Yes. Cats. Do you like them?"

Actually, he was more of a dog person. "Since I'm at the hospital about eighty hours a week, sometimes in surgery for twenty-four hours straight, I don't think it would be fair to own any pets."

She sighed, nodding her head. "Understandable." Then she glanced at the documents again.

"Why? Do you have a cat?" he asked, prompting her for information.

She cringed. "No way! No pets here!"

He laughed. "Not an animal person?"

Roxy took a brave sip of her whiskey, cringed slightly, then shook her head. "I love animals. And I love cats and dogs equally. I'd love to have a whole bunch of pets and kids and…" she looked at him self-consciously, then at his tattoo again and clammed up, turning back to the bar. "Well, I don't have any."

"But you *want* a cat?"

Roxy laughed and Abe's stomach tightened with the sound. Her laugh was deep and rich, filled with humor! Damn, she should laugh more often. Roxy was always so serious at work. Although he understood. She had a great deal of responsibility at her job and any mistake would cause the surgeons and nurses to rant furiously at her. But still…that laugh was practically lethal!

"Actually, I just inherited a cat." She tilted her head slightly and Abe looked at her neck. He wondered what would happen if he kissed her neck. That skin was so pale, so delicate, he'd bet that it was extremely sensitive. Again, his body tightened at his wayward thoughts.

"How did you inherit a cat?"

She sighed, looking up at the ceiling as she blinked rapidly. His gut tightened when he realized that she was trying to keep herself from tearing up. "My mother died recently."

That piece of information startled him and he eyed her thoughtfully, thinking back through the last few days. She'd never missed a day of work, and yet, her mother had just passed away? What the hell?!

"Roxy?" he prompted.

She laughed, a stilted sound that was more of a hiccup and his heart lurched. She picked up the napkin and angrily wiped away an errant tear. "My mother's will," she explained, tapping the papers on the bar. "She left her house and all of her money to her cat. I got her collection of glass figurines with the stipulation that I have to dust them every week."

There was a long silence as Abe absorbed that information. Her mother had died and left…glass ornaments to her daughter and everything else to…a cat?!

That was ludicrous! "You're kidding, right?"

"It's pathetic, isn't it?" She sighed and took another sip of her whiskey. "My mother never approved of anything I did, so it shouldn't be a shock that she didn't leave anything to me. But," she sniffed, "well, it would be one thing if she hadn't had anything to give away. But she had a bloody fortune! Over half a million dollars, plus a house that was fully paid off...everything, all of her money as well as the proceeds from the sale of her house, is going to the cat." That's when Roxy turned to look at him, obviously forgetting that she hated Abe. "That cat is horrible! I mean, he's vicious, evil, and aggressive at every opportunity! He hates everyone but my mother."

Abe chuckled. "That bad, huh?"

Roxy took another sip of her whiskey, only wrinkling her nose a little this time. The flavor was beginning to grow on her. "Worse. He's evil." She rubbed her forehead. "And now, I've inherited a very wealthy cat." She took another sip. "And a bunch of cheap, tacky glass figurines." She turned to face him and Abe had to concentrate when her knees brushed against his inner thigh. He knew that he was man-spreading, but it was just easier to watch her in profile this way. Well, easier until she turned to face him. Now her legs were between his and...damn, she looked hot!

"Every week in high school, my mother ordered me to dust all of those damn bits of glass. It took hours! I had to lift every one of them up, dust it with a feather duster, then wipe off the shelf underneath. One at a time. She didn't trust me to take all of them off, dust the stupid shelf, then put the stuff back on it. Nope! One at a time!"

"Sounds tedious." She was on a roll now and it was interesting to watch her let loose. Roxy was always serious, always in control at the hospital. She was alert and aware of everything, more than ready to take on whatever challenge came her way. Obviously, the whiskey and the beer were helping her ease up.

"And another thing!" she snapped, holding the glass and pointing at him with the same hand. "She has money! A lot of it! Why couldn't she have helped me get through college? Not that anyone is entitled to a college degree. I understand that. But a few bucks for books or something when she was sitting on all of that money would have been greatly appreciated!" She took another sip and Abe debated cutting her off versus letting her vent.

"Of course, it's her money and she should do what she wants with it. But how about a vacation? She didn't take vacations because only *hussies* take vacations! Or lazy people who have no self-discipline," she said, obviously mimicking her mother's voice. "And college? She taunted me with college all through high school, telling me I was too stupid to get in. Then she ridiculed me for getting into college with a full scholarship! She said I didn't deserve it and that I was going to fail out in the first semester. When I got straight As that semester, she sniffed and surmised that I probably cheated!"

The woman sounded like a first class bitch, Abe thought, but kept his mouth shut. He understood that Roxy had been holding back on this for a while.

"I dress like a prude, you know!" she told him, leaning forward as if telling him a secret.

He was fully aware of her prim outfits. They were part of her allure, in his mind. She might dress like a librarian, but with her round hips and full breasts, there was no way she could hide behind the stiff fabrics. Roxy was hot! Not skinny or fat, just rounded and soft in all the right places. His hands ached to touch her, to feel what was hidden underneath those horrible outfits. He took another slug of his beer, but shook his head when the bartender silently asked if he wanted another. A moment later, ice water appeared at his elbow.

"Why did she make you dress like this?" he asked, referring to the ugly, wool dress. Why the hell was she wearing black wool in August anyway?

"She said that only insecure hussies wear revealing clothes. 'Hussy' was her favorite term." She sighed. "Once I came downstairs in a short sleeved shirt with long pants for a school picnic in July. She ordered me right back upstairs to change, then she took the shirt and shredded it." She smiled slightly, but Abe suspected that what was to come next wouldn't be very funny. "She even poured lighter fluid onto the shirt and lit it on fire, telling me that I was going to burn in hell if I exposed skin like that."

She sounded like a lunatic! "So, now that she's gone, are you going to continue to follow her guidance?" He thought about Roxy in clothes that fit her, something that might flatter her soft, sexy figure and his mind blanked for several moments. She was beautiful and...damn if she wore nicer clothes, he might just lose his mind.

Roxanne considered his question for a moment. "I don't know," she replied. "I'd really love to go out and get a new wardrobe, things that she'd hate. Unfortunately," she sighed, her shoulders slumping even more, "it's difficult to get her voice out of my head."

Abe knew that she'd had enough to drink. "Why don't we go play some pool and you can tell me more about this cat that has inherited so much money?"

Roxy glanced at the pool tables, then at her drink. "I need to pay for my drinks," she muttered, pulling back on his grip as she reached for her wallet.

"Don't worry about it. The bartender put your drinks on my tab. I've got it covered."

"I can't let you pay for me, Doctor McCullough!" she asserted with stiff dignity that was a bit lost since she was digging into her ugly purse.

"Sure you can. Just think of it as your first defiance against your mother's..." He almost said "abuse" but pulled back at the last second, "...strict rules. I think it's time that you broke every one of her rules and got your life back."

She stumbled a bit when she slid off of the bar stool, but Abe didn't mind at all. It gave him the opportunity to wrap his arm around her waist, holding her against him. As he led her to the pool tables, he was amazed at how good she actually felt. But he kept his hand on her waist, refusing to violate her trust. She didn't need a guy to cop a cheap feel tonight. Roxy needed someone to help her get through the next twenty-four hours and maybe a shoulder to cry on.

Abe thought that he was just the man for the job!

Printed in Great
Britain
by Amazon